FATE PLAYS FAVORITES . . .

"We have company! Watch it!" Camellion warned Tensor and Weems.

He opened fire with both Black Widows, just as Roy Gomoll and Otis Anderson cut loose with slugs, Gomoll using a Heckler and Koch P9S auto, Anderson a Colt Detective Special.

Eugene John Itaska, the third gunsel, had a Colt Trooper .357 Magnum in his right hand, but he was behind the other two apes and was still trying to get into action.

Death plays favorites and so does Fate. When Camellion fired, he had automatically ducked to the right, this action saving his life. Gomoll's FMJ bullet burned through the air and came dangerously close to his left hip. Anderson's .38 hollow point came even closer. It burned through the material of his charcoal gray coat and ripped across his rib cage, so close to his skin that it left a faint burn mark on his blue-gray shirt.

Camellion didn't miss. The powerful bullet from the left Black Widow's number .308 brass cartridge case ripped through Gomoll's coat and crashed into his stomach, the tremendous shock almost doubled the dying man over before the impact pitched him backward and started him on the journey that all men must make alone.

THE DEATH MERCHANT SERIES:

#58 in the incredible adventures of the

DEATH MERCHANT

THE SILICON VALLEY CONNECTION

by Joseph Rosenberger

PINNACLE BOOKS NEW YORK

DEATH MERCHANT #58
THE SILICON VALLEY CONNECTION

An original Pinnacle Books edition, published for the first time anywhere.

First printing, March 1984

ISBN: 0-523-42002-1

Can. ISBN: 0-523-43144-9

Cover illustration by Dean Cate

Printed in the United States of America

PINNACLE BOOKS, INC.
1430 Broadway
New York, New York 10018

9   8   7   6   5   4   3   2   1

Four things have changed the 20th Century: the automobile, Adolf Hitler, television, and the microprocessor—a "computer on a chip."

Not that it matters. The fifth will be a shifting of the poles in 1999. The human race—what's left of it—can then start over.

Richard J. Camellion
Votaw, Texas

SPECIAL ADVISER
Colonel George Ellis
of
Le Mercenaire

This book is dedicated to
John P. Bahr
&
David C. DeVore
And to George and Dorothy
Of Aurora, Illinois

CHAPTER ONE

In Richard Camellion's opinion the only difference between Hell and Los Angeles was that one met a better class of people in Hell—and Hell was a lot safer. In Hell one didn't have to slink around at three o'clock in the morning, the way the Death Merchant was now doing, especially in dangerous places like the Los Angeles-Long Beach Port which, with the West Basin, formed one of the largest harbor complexes in the world.

Smelling oil, rust, smog and water, Camellion was keenly aware of the risk that he and Max were taking. In order to keep Dr. Revlon in sight after he had parked his Nissan Sentra, Max had been forced to pull the Ford Bronco II up close to a warehouse. Camellion had then gotten out and had begun following Norman Revlon on foot.

In this section of the harbor the police were as thick as Cholos[1] in East Los Angeles. Suppose the harbor police spotted Camellion and demanded that he identify himself and state the nature of his business? Or hauled Max out of the Bronco and demanded the same of him? Not any problem. While Camellion could prove he was "Jason Sanford," such identification would not tell the police why he was here. It was different with Max. His "blue card" gave his real name—Maximilian Weems—and identified him as an employee of the Central Intelligence Agency. But precious time would be lost while the police checked, and, possibly, word would leak out that the CIA was snooping around the docks.

Revlon had parked his car close to a wharf, leaving the vehicle right out in the open and not even bothering to lock

[1]The various Hispanic youth gangs that roam through the bario.

1

the doors, further evidence that whatever Dr. Revlon was up to, it was extremely important.

Keeping to the side of the darkened warehouse, the Death Merchant crept forward, his eyes on the tall figure of Dr. Revlon who was walking rapidly several hundred feet ahead on the dock and carrying a brown alligator attache case. Camellion waited—*Revlon's taking the same chance I'm taking, risking that he, too, might be stopped by the harbor police. Under the circumstances, he has to be up to something illegal.* . . .

All the while watching Dr. Revlon, Camellion unsnapped the strap of the shoulder holster under his left armpit, freeing the Safari Arms .45 Black Widow[2] for instant action. Other than the Black Widow autopistol, he was also armed with a .45 stainless steel Sokolovsky autoloader carried in a belt slide holster on his right side.

He paused by the corner of the warehouse and saw that Dr. Revlon had turned on the dock and was walking up the short, enclosed gangplank of a sleek yacht. Another man was waiting at the top of the gangplank. The two spoke briefly, then went through a bulkhead in the main deck housing, on the port side of the vessel.

From his vantage point by the corner of the warehouse, Camellion studied the long craft that was every bit of 75 feet long. A two-masted Viking, the Craft was technically a 73' trawler, diesel powered and in the million dollar class. No stranger to such luxurious vessels, Camellion knew that the owner's stateroom would be on the second deck, toward the stern. Going toward the bow, there would be port and starboard staterooms, just to the rear of the twin diesels—*probably 320 HP GM 8V-71 jobs*. The crew's lounge and quarters would be toward the bow.

The question was—*Has Revlon gone below deck or is he somewhere in the above deck housing to the rear of the bridge? Let's go find out* . . .

---

[2] The "Black Widow" is mechanically identical to the Safari Arms "Enforcer." The difference is appearance. The frame of the Black widow is more lightweight; it's fashioned out of a special aluminum alloy and has been nickel-plated by Armaloy.

Camellion left the corner of the warehouse and started toward the dock. This section was not well-lighted, the sodium-vapor lights, on tall steel columns, being seventy feet apart. Farther to the east there was quite a bit of activity. Lift trucks were moving back and forth and stevedores were unloading a freighter. But in the immediate vicinity, no one was in sight. There was only the semi-darkness and the gentle summer breeze.

A straight line is often the path of least resistance. It was now. The Death Merchant headed straight for the yacht where night lights were burning all around on the bridge, in the stateroom in the midship housing, and below the main deck, in the midship region and toward the stern.

Camellion came to the bottom of the gangplank and noticed that the name of the vessel was the "Gold Rose." He scanned the deck. The way was clear. Calmly, as he started up the gangplank, it occurred to him that he wouldn't be sticking his neck in this particular noose if it weren't for the Soviet KGB's desire to steal the revolutionary GA-1 microprocessor recently invented by Kordic Micro-Electric Corporation whose headquarters were in California's famed Silicon Valley.

Those damned Russians! The Soviet Union had mounted a major espionage offensive in the United States, unprecedented and growing. It's highest priority was the uncovering of secrets of American military technology, followed by anything they could get their hands on—civilian technology advances, business data, and American economic and political developments.

It was no accident that the Soviet Union had sixty-five "diplomats" in its San Francisco consulate. Silicon Valley[3] was only an hour's drive away. The coordinating hub of the Soviet network was of course the Soviet Embassy in Washington, D.C. The KGB and GRU officers in D.C. worked closely with the 180 Russian employees at the United Nations who were working as spies under diplomatic cover.

The Russian agents were brazen in their efforts, especially

[3] "Silicon Valley" is in the Santa Clara Valley south of San Francisco. It developed around Palo Alto and spread some 20 miles to San Jose. The Silicon Valley phenomenon embraces 13 cities in this corridor, whose combined populations total more than 1.2 million.

in trying to tap the rich intelligence field that Congress represented. They even went so far as to stroll into Congressional offices and openly ask questions, or else assiduously attempt to cultivate relationships with various Congressional experts in an effort to obtain intelligence data through casual conversation.

Because of the openness of American society and American greed, the KGB and the GRU were often very successful. For example, there was William Holden Bell, an electronics engineer/radar expert who sold top radar secrets to the KGB; and Joseph G. Helmich, Jr., an Army officer, who sold the data on the United States' best military cryptological machine. Or Christopher John Boyce, a worker in a company that produced ultra-secret spy satellites for the CIA. Boyce had sold any number of top secrets to the KGB before he was caught, convicted and sent to prison.

The main target of Soviet intelligence was the hundreds of electronic firms located in the Silicon Valley. The CIA had learned that toward this end the Soviets had allocated extra manpower and had formed a special apparatus, a special intelligence-gathering network that extended from the Soviet consulate in San Francisco to Los Angeles and Denver, Colorado.

At first, the Federal Bureau of Investigation had been on the case. The Bureau first learned of the special KGB "Otdel"[4] by listening in on "bugs" placed in the office of the House of Pandemonium, a sleazy nightclub owned by "Dandy" Phil Butler, the leader of Satan's Gentlemen, a motorcycle gang whose members were so vicious they made the Hell's Angels look like timid Boy Scouts.

The FBI was astonished by what it put together from conversations heard over the hidden transmitters: that Satan's Gentlemen were working for the Soviet KGB and that the immediate target was Kordic Micro-Electric Corporation and its brand new GA-1 microprocessor.

The FBI had infiltrated Satan's Gentlemen. When they vanished the Bureau called in the CIA. Wanting a quick end of the special Soviet network, the Company turned to the Death Merchant and his efficient but usually illegal methods.

---

[4]Means "special cell" or special organization

4

*   *   *

Moving up the gangplank, Camellion felt that with any luck he might be able to catch Doctor Revlon in the act of turning over the secret of the GA-1 to a Soviet intelligence agent. *But is Revlon the inside man at Kordic?* The Death Merchant didn't think so. He didn't know why. It was only a hunch.

Reaching the deck, Camellion stepped off the gangplank, paused, drew the Black Widow .45, and looked up and down the length of the Gold Rose. The deck was deserted. He next turned his attention to the bulkhead only a short distance in front of him, the same door through which Dr. Revlon and the other man had gone. Beyond the bulkhead and its door was the main lounge of the top deck. It wasn't likely that Dr. Revlon was in the lounge. Camellion could see through the portholes that only small night lights were burning. In contrast, there were bright lights behind the curtained portholes of the second deck.

The Death Merchant carefully opened the door of the bulkhead and stepped inside the half-dark lounge. Just as he had expected, it was empty. The forward door, to the control compartment or bridge deck, was closed.

Toward the center stern of the lounge was the opening of the stairway that led below to the second deck, a polished brass railing framed the square aperture and bright light filtered upward from below. The Death Merchant stopped and shifted his mind into second gear, mentally picturing the interior of the second deck. The stairway would end in a tiny passageway. At the stern end of the midget T-sized hallway would be the door to the owner's stateroom. Going fore toward the bow the hall would move between the port and the starboard staterooms and, at the other end, the galley or the crew's lounge.

He listened. There wasn't anything but the low sound of a bilge pump and the faint humming of one of the diesel generators. Quickly, he crossed the lounge, stepped into the stair well and started down the stairs, the leather soles of his suede casuals silent on the rubber matting of each step.

Very quickly he came to the bottom, stopped, listened and looked around. Three ceiling lights were burning in the fore section of the small hall, on either side of which was a stateroom door. Another door was at the bow end of the hall. Five feet to Camellion's right, toward the stern, was the door to the main or owner's stateroom.

He crept to the door, put his ear against the wood and heard voices, but the words were too faint for him to understand.

Camellion didn't have any trouble making sense of the next words he heard. They were loud, clear and ominous and came from the hallway toward the bow.

"DON'T MOVE OR I'LL FIRE!"

"I won't miss either!" another voice said sadistically, this one from above Camellion, from the top of the stairs. "Don't turn around. Put your gun on the floor and your hands on the back of your neck—now!"

I could get one, but not two! No dice! No way! Feeling trapped, which he was, the Death Merchant leaned down, placed the Black Widow on the floor, then stood and placed his hands on the back of his neck. For the moment, there wasn't anything he could do.

The man at the top of the stairs hurried down and stood in front of Camellion, keeping the barrel of his Czech M-61 Skorpion SMG pointed at Camellion's stomach. Dressed in a green turtleneck sweater, green slacks and wearing a black cowboy hat, the joker had a big ugly face and was built like a brick shipyard. Camellion figured that if his brains matched his brawn, he'd be a second Einstein. The man, however, was a pro. He didn't attempt to pick up the Black Widow; instead, he waited until the other man, who had been waiting in a port side stateroom, had walked up behind Camellion, shoved the muzzle of the Smith & Wesson .44 Magnum revolver into the small of the Death Merchant's back and snarled, "Move an inch and I'll split your backbone with a slug."

Only then did "Cowboy Hat" stoop and, carefully watching a stonefaced Richard Camellion, pick up the Black Widow pistol and jam the weapon into his belt. He then turned and knocked loudly on the door of the ship owner's stateroom. A key turned in the lock. The door swung open. Framed in the doorway was a man whom Camellion recognized from photographs he had studied, 8″ × 10″ glossies of Satan's Gentlemen. The piece of trash that walked like a human being was William "Big Willie" Wartz, a forty two-year-old thug who was one of the original members of the motorcycle gang that Philip Butler had organized in 1971. Muscular, of medium height and with a chin like the cowcatcher of a steam locomotive, Big Willie had the reputation of being a sadist and Camellion knew his methods of interrogation would not be gentle.

Bit Willie's cruel brown eyes raked Camellion up and down. "Get your ass in here, you stupid son of a bitch. You're going to tell me why you and that other guy were trailing Revlon. You're going to tell me damned fast."

"You heard the man. Move, stupid!" ordered Edgar Biskupski and, for emphasis, again jammed the muzzle of the .44 mag into Camellion's back.

With a feeling that he had indeed been stupid—*Damn it! Revlon spotted me and Max and these creeps were waiting for me!*—Camellion moved slowly into the stern stateroom, his eyes quickly analyzing the area. On the port side was a hanging locker, a bureau and a fold-out-from-the-wall table, the latter between the bureau and the port side of a queen-size bed whose head was at the rounded stern. To starboard, was a short sofa, another bureau, and a sink.

In front of the bed, at its foot, a card table had been set up. Dr. Norman Revlon was seated at the table, his back toward the foot of the bed. Next to him on the floor, to his left, was his attache case.

A slim man in his late forties, the computer expert looked guilty as he glanced at the Death Merchant. He got to his feet and remarked nervously to Big Willie Wartz, "I have to go to the toilet. If you'll tell me—"

"Sit down! You ain't going nowhere," snapped Big Willie. "For all we know, you and this bird and the other guy are in this together."

"But I assure you—"

"Shut your face and sit down!" growled Big Willie, then grinned while Revlon sat down as if he had been hit on the head with a trip-hammer. Standing in front of the card table and six feet in front of Camellion, Big Willie then turned his full attention to the Death Merchant who was doing some lightning fast calculations, all of them based on previous experience with extreme violence and the various intricacies of Thanatology.

Big Willie was packing an AMT Combat .45 autoloader in a left-sided quick-draw shoulder holster. Cowboy Hat had sauntered to Camellion's right and was holding the Skorpion submachine gun loosely in his right hand, the little SMG dangling at his right side, his relaxed movements indicating he wasn't on guard. Evidently he and Big Willie felt secure. After all Eddie Biskupski was still behind the Death Merchant, holding the muzzle of the .44 magnum revolver against Camellion's back and his hands were still clamped to the back of his neck. Even if Camellion's intended moves didn't work, he was positive he wouldn't be any worse off—*These lice aren't about to let me leave this tub alive. They can't.*

Big Willie thrust out his mammoth jaw at the Death Merchant. "Now, sucker, we'll get down to cases," he said quickly, his every word a warning. He didn't know it, but it was the last sentence of his life.

Camellion did what he had to do, moving with such incredible speed that his hands and arms were only half a blink of a blur. He twisted his body to the right, striking his right elbow against Eddie Biskupski's right wrist, the sudden movement pushing the barrel of the magnum away from his back.[5]

Pivoting to his right, Camellion expertly placed his left wrist against Biskupski's right wrist and grabbed the barrel of the magnum with his right hand, palm up. Moving so fast that only he was aware of what was happening, Camellion applied pressure to Biskupski's right hand and trigger finger by pushing the barrel toward Biskupski's upper right arm, this quick, sudden motion freeing the .44 magnum from the hood's grasp and breaking the man's index finger. Biskupski yelled in pain and fear, intuition telling him he was doomed. He was. The Death Merchant now had the S&W revolver in his right hand,

[5]This is one of three genuine ways to disarm a man who has a pistol in your back. In one method the opponent must have the weapon in his right hand. The same with the second method. With the third, the pistol and/or weapon can be in either hand. None of these methods should be tried unless one is an expert.

and had the Cosmic Lord of Death on his side. Still moving with inconceivable speed, he slammed Biskupski in the left side of the neck with the barrel of the weapon and, at the same time, stuck out his left foot and hooked his instep behind Biskupski's right ankle, tripping the half conscious hood as he started to go down, making him fall to the Death Merchant's left—*stupid am I!*

Camellion was counting on two factors to achieve success: his own speed and Dr. Revlon's not having a weapon. He spun to his left just in time to wreck the plan of Jerry Joe Spain—Cowboy Hat—who, recovering from his surprise, was swinging up the deadly little Skorpion SMG, an expression of mingled fear and desperation on his face.

Well, dumb butt! You could be worse. You could be twins! Camellion raised the .44 magnum, snap aimed and pulled the wide trigger, the dynamite roar of the big revolver filling the stateroom with a tornado of noise. Spain was dead before the sound could even reach his ears, the big flatnosed bullet striking him in the forehead just above the bridge of the nose, the terrible force splitting open his skull the way a hammer would squash an orange. His head split open, blood and brain particles streaming down his face, Spain dropped the SMG, staggered back in a cute little one-two step and started to drop just as Camellion spun around, threw himself to his left, swung the Smith & Wesson revolver toward Big Willie and squeezed the trigger a split second after a frantic Big Willie fired his .45 AMT autoloader. Bit Willie's bullet burned air only a few inches to Camellion's right, the slug striking the metal hanging locker on the port side.

The Death Merchant didn't miss. His .44 projectile stabbed Big Willie in the left center of his chest, cut a bloody tunnel all the way through his body, shot out his back and, narrowly missing Dr. Revlon, struck a book on the book shelf above the head of the queen size bed. Dying, his big mouth open, Big Willie blinked, half turned, dropped and crashed to the rug on his face.

The Death Merchant, already convinced he was going to have an extra-bad day, knew he was worse off than a legless man at the butt kicking contest. The shots, sounding as loud as sticks of dynamite exploding, would surely bring the police to investigate. But before the fuzz arrived, what about other

9

crewmen on the boat? Camellion had to assume, for his own protection, that more men were on board. Worse, he didn't have time to question Dr. Revlon—*And I can't take him with me either!*

Dr. Revlon, who had fallen from his chair and was crouched at the foot of the bed, squawked like a terrified chicken when he saw the Death Merchant swing the .44 magnum in his direction. He raised his hands in front of his face, so paralyzed with fear that he could only blubber and choke on his own tongue. He was wasting his time. In Camellion's own private system of ethics, a traitor was at the bottom of the scum barrel, even lower than rapists, child molesters and people who mistreated animals, especially pigs.

The .44 mag revolver roared, the big bullet banging Revlon high in the chest and tearing a hole in him the size of a man's fist. The man sagged, his face frozen in time and in death, with a look of disbelief and horror.

The telephone on the starboard wall rang. *Men on the bridge or in some other part of the vessel? It's certainly not the good tooth fairy—and not the kind of fairies they have in 'Frisco either!*

Camellion tossed the S&W .44 mag revolver on the bed. He wasn't concerned about leaving fingerprints. He couldn't. His hands, up to his wrists, were coated with a liquid plastic/rubberized substance that, while permitting the skin to "breathe," concealed all finger and palm prints.

He rushed over to the dead J.J. Spain, pulled the Safari Arms Black Widow from the belt of the corpse, picked up the Czech Skorpion SMG, turned and hurried over to the card table. He placed the Widow and the small submachine gun on the table, picked up the attache case, opened it and dumped its contents on the bed. He noticed that the papers appeared to be diagrams and engineering schematics of computers and certain kinds of microprocessors. He couldn't be sure; he was not an engineer.

Glancing fearfully at the open door, Camellion hurried to port and removed a brass "Fastnet" oil lamp from the wall. The cabin was lighted by ordinary electricity, from bulbs recessed in the ceiling. The port and the starboard oil lamps were for show and to lend atmosphere; however, they were not ornaments but genuine lamps that worked.

The Death Merchant, shaking the lamp, returned to the bed. *Good!* The lamp was full of oil. Quickly he removed the glass chimney, turned the lamp upside down and unscrewed the large bottom cap. Then he poured the oil in the lamp over the papers and charts on the bed, tossed aside the lamp, took a book of paper matches from his coat pocket, struck one and tossed it in the middle of the pile. With a *whoooshhh* the papers and the black velour covering on the bed ignited.

Camellion swung from the bed and soon had the Black Widow in his left hand and the M-61 Skorpion SMG in his right hand. The sub-gun had its stock retracted and he was able to hold the chatter-box pistol-style—not the best way in the world, since the SMG was over-balanced, but he could still fire it with accuracy. First checking to see how the firing cycle was set—it was on three-round burst—he then went to the port side of the doorway and listened. By now, other men on the yacht could have had time to reach the cabin, but only if they had tossed away all precaution and had come charging below pell-mell. Only rank beginners would have used such stupid tactics.

So. . . . They must be waiting! Camellion told himself. He had already reasoned that his position was extremely dangerous since he was still below and had to reach the upper deck. There were only two ways to go: either the way he had come down or to follow the short hall to the bow and use the steps that led to the bridge. Either way he still had to go up a short flight of steps.

It might as well be the way I came down!

He looked around the molded frame of the doorway. No one was in the hall. The three doors were closed. Smelling smoke and the burning bedspread, he moved from the stateroom at the stern and started up the steps, ready with both the Skorpion and the Black Widow.

There were three ways they could hit him: from the port, from the starboard bulkheads in the upper deck lounge, or from the door between the lounge and the bridge deck. The gunmen aboard the Gold Rose were experienced—and shots had already boomed out into the quiet early morning. Being

11

pros, they wouldn't want to be caught waiting on deck by police who might arrive at any moment; they would want the ambush to be inside the vessel—which means they should have an ambush set up from the door between the lounge and the Bridge.

When Camellion's head was only a foot below the square opening, he paused and shoved the Black Widow into his belt. Sure, it was a risk but so was crossing the street at high noon or walking down any street at midnight.

He took a deep breath and, keeping hunched down, went up a few more steps. He switched off the safety of the Skorpion SMG, reared up, faced the bow and fired on pure intuition, on his remembrance of the position of the door, his bursts of 7.65 millimeter projectiles slicing into the sides of the doorway between the lounge and the Bridge. Other slugs zipped through the open space and wrecked a Seth-Thomas quartz time and tide clock, a SI-Tex navigation receiver and a 640 radio direction finder.

Other than the trash that Camellion had whacked out in the stern's stateroom, there were three other men on the yacht. One was a regular member of the four man crew. The other two pieces of dog dung had come aboard with Big Willie and were members of Satan's Gentlemen.

Spitting out a stream of curses, Charles ''Chuckie'' Sizewell pulled a sliver of wood—slug-chopped from the doorway—from his right cheek and glanced at Benjamin ''Buster'' Lorocco and Paul Berbasshoout, the latter of whom was the only man on board who was a member of the crew.

Buster Larocco, a ferret-faced freak whose main ambition in life was to own a whore house with 22 rooms, clutched a Mini-Uzi submachine gun and whispered nervously, ''What does that son of a bitch have—a crystal ball? How the hell did he know we was here?''

''Because he's damned good! He's a professional, you idiot!'' Sizewell said between clenched teeth. ''God damn it! Who cares. We've got to get him before he get's off. Buster, you and. . . .''

''You guys are nuts!'' burst out Paul Berbasshoout, his

voice frantic. "Doncha smell that smoke. That son of a bitch has set the boat on fire. We gotta get off this tub."

"We'll get off as soon as we kill that son of a bitch," spit out Sizewell, standing up straight and scratching the side of his beefy neck with the muzzle of the eight-inch barrel of a .357 Colt Python revolver. "We'll have him within the next few minutes or he'll be off the boat and on the dock. Bus, we'll go out the starboard door; he'll be on the starboard side. He's too damn slick to head right for the port door and the gangplank—and put away that damned tommy job. Stick it in a locker. If the cops get here and see it, we'll have some explaining to do to them and mostly to the Feds. We ain't got no license for an automatic weapon. The fuckin' ATF[6] would be all over us."

"Screw the ATF!" argued Larocco. His pinched face underwent a series of contortions. "If we blow sky high with this damned boat, who gives a damn about Uncle Sugar's boys?"

"You want to go back and tell that to Phil?" snarled Sizewell who was a hulk of a slob, big in chest and big in belly, with gimlet eyes and very bushy brows, both of which gave him a sinister appearance. "You go back and tell him we run out and he'll pull your eyeballs out of their sockets and step on them—and mine too! Now do what I tell you. Paul you go up the port side—move!"

The Death Merchant raced up the remainder of the steps and dropped the Skorpion. It had only had a 20-round magazine and he had used all the ammo in firing at the doorway. Without bothering to glance in the direction of the bow, he raced across the half-dark lounge, opened the starboard door, stepped out onto the deck, closed the door and glanced toward the bow. He pulled the .45 Sokolovsky pistol, thumbed off the safety, turned, and headed for the stern. He had thought of crossing the rear of the deckhouse and going directly to the gangplank. But he didn't dare. It would be too easy for anyone on the bridge to fire down on him, especially

[6]Bureau of Alcohol, Tobacco and Firearms, a Federal agency.

13

after he had reached the dock where there wouldn't be any cover for 125 feet in all directions.

By now thick black smoke was pouring from the top of the stairwell in the main deck lounge and through two ventilators in the stern. Camellion could see flames flickering on the water, to the stern of the vessel and on the starboard side, the dancing glow emanating through the portholes of the second deck. Those that weren't open had already lost their glass to the heat of flames that were growing larger every second.

After Camellion reached the rear of the storage locker, he discovered that he wouldn't be able to remain there for any length of time—a few minutes at the most. The heat from the second deck stern stateroom was too great. Very soon the fire would be eating through the walls.

Camellion looked around the left side of the rope storage locker and, much to his surprise, saw a man running up the port side to the stern. He was surprised because the man didn't have a weapon in his hands. Camellion watched and waited.

Paul Berbasshoout ran down the gangplank and sprinted for the dock. Reaching the dock, he kept right on going, heading east. The hell with it. To Berbasshoout, a dead hero was only a dead man, nothing more.

The Death Merchant smiled. The rats were deserting the burning ship.

But is he the only one? Camellion looked around the right side of the locker and scanned the edge of the starboard side of the deckhouse. All clear. He studied the portholes in the rear of the deckhouse. They were closed. *OK—make tracks!*

He moved from the back of the stern's locker and, every nerve and muscle alerted for instant action, headed for the gangplank. He was halfway to his goal when Chuckie Sizewell and Buster Larocco stepped from the corner of the deckhouse on the starboard side. Seeing him, they did a double-take and raised their weapons, Sizewell jerking up his big Colt Python, Larocco trying for a kill-shot with his MAB P-15 autopistol. Both hoods fired a hair-thin slice of a second apart. Camellion detected them and dove to the deck, bringing up his own kill-pieces.

Sizewell's flat-nosed .357 projectile came within a foot of

14

Camellion's head, streaking by his right temple and speeding off into eternity. That micro-moment difference in the firing time of the two gunmen was the disproportionate balance between life and death for Richard Camellion. If he had not been taking a nosedive to the deck, Camellion would have bought it. Larocco's 9×19-millimeter slug would have caught him only a few inches below the hollow of the throat. As it turned out the bullet burned air a quarter of an inch above his head, coming so close that it cut through his short brown hair.

Camellion triggered both the Black Widow and the Sokolovsky when he was only three feet from the deck, the big weapons making a sound like midget thunderclaps. The Widow's powerful 230-grain hardball FMC bullet stabbed Sizewell in the midsection, giving him another navel two inches below the one he had been born with.

"Chuckie" might as well have been caught in the middle of an explosion. The blob of metal cut through his body, broke his spine, severed the cord and killed him instantly, while the impact of the slug knocked him back to the railing. The corpse kept right on going. Over the railing it went. A splash in the water and the dead man was gone.

The .45 200-grain Lawman projectile from the Sokolovsky auto-pistol crashed into Larocco's chest, going in at a steep angle and stabbing into the sternum. Zip! Deflected by the bone, the slug changed course and stopped in the heart. Shock reflex made Larocco's finger tighten again on the trigger and the French autoloader spit out another 9mm slug, but by then he was falling backward and his arm was raised. The slug went up toward the stars, going 13 feet over Camellion. Larocco crumpled and hit the deck.

I'm still in trouble! Getting to his feet—his left forearm, with which he had broken his fall, ached—Camellion heard the high screaming of rubber on concrete as the drivers of the two cars slammed on the brakes. The police had arrived on the deck.

Camellion quickly switched on the safeties of the two pistols, holstered the weapons and turned toward the dock.

Mercy, mercy! Mother Mercy! How do I manage to get myself into these messes? I must not be living right!

To make sure some trigger-happy hotdog cop didn't blow

15

him away, he raised his arms high above his head as he moved to the gangplank, noticing that the fire below was not eating its way up through the stern deck. The two police cars had parked close to the dock, only fifty feet from the Gold Rose, their blue and red top lights revolving and flashing, the two vehicles facing the doomed yacht. The four cops had gotten out of the patrol cruisers and had drawn their weapons, one of the bluecoats levelling down on Camellion with his service revolver, both hands wrapped around the butt of the .38.

"Keep your hands up and get down here, fella," he yelled at the Death Merchant.

Camellion hurried down the gangplank, his hands reaching for the moon. The only thing that really troubled him was the possibility of media publicity. The disbelieving cops would haul him in and he would give the Watch Commander a certain number. The disbelieving Watch Commander would call a certain number and a CIA Case Officer would come after Camellion while another Case Officer made a call to the Chief of Police. Camellion would be released and the arresting officers told to forget all about it. But would they? The catch was that a lot of cops were slipped a little $$$ now and then by police reporters to reveal anything unusual. All Camellion and his Blood-Bone Unit needed was for the *L.A. Times* or *Herald-Examiner* to hint of a CIA operation in the area.

Halfway down the gangplank, Camellion shouted at the cops, "I'm a Federal officer." *At least I'm working for the Feds!* "I'll explain later, but first we've got to move back. The boat is going to explode."

Not one of the policeman had a chance to reply. Suddenly, each man jerked and shuddered violently, and there were several loud *ping pings* from the two police cruisers. In an instant, the four dying men had fallen and were lying still and crumpled on the dock.

Double fudge! I told Max to wait and to retreat if things got rough for me. Damn him to Section B of Hades!

Camellion didn't have to think twice to know what had happened. Maximilian Weems had left the Bronco and had opened fire with the "silenced" Ingram M-10 submachine gun.

Reaching the dock, Camellion glanced in dismay at the four dead cops and sprinted toward the northwest corner of the long warehouse, deducing that Max had fired from there. He saw a firetruck coming up fast from the east, its blinking red lights revolving, siren screaming.

"Over here!" yelled Max Weems. "I'm over here."

In the glare of the fire on the boat and the leaping shadows, Camellion reached the corner of the warehouse and saw that Max had driven the Bronco to within ten feet of the corner of the long building and was shoving a full magazine into the MAC-10 chatterbox, an extra-long magazine containing 50 9mm armor piercing supersonic cartridges.[7]

For a second, all Camellion could do was glare at the tall, goodlooking CIA street operative. He intensely disliked uncalculated risks and blowing up the four cops had been exactly that.

"You pop-eyed pinhead with pox!" Camellion said hoarsely. "Look what you've done!"

"Stop wagging your tongue," responded Weems, unconcerned. "I saved you from having the fuzz put shiny bracelets around your wrists, didn't I? Watch our rear while I stop the firetruck. All I have to do is wreck the engine."

Way ahead of Weems in the Big Think Department, Camellion had already pulled the Black Widow and the Sokolovsky. He began moving toward Bronco, knowing that he and Max were a long fat way from "home." If they didn't get the hell away from the area before the police arrived in force—*We'll have had it—period!*

BBBERRRROOOOOMMMMMM! The Gold Rose blew itself apart with a giant flash of red and orange fire, the blast sending twisted parts and pieces of wreckage into the water and onto the dock, some of it slamming into the windshield of one of the police cruisers, breaking it. More twisted and burning wreckage splattered on the dock, some of it striking the corpses of the four policemen.

---

[7]Developed by American Ballistics Co. for one principle purpose: to have the most effective stopping power and incapacitating performance of any ammunition commercially manufactured.

The explosion forced the driver of the fire truck to slow the big vehicle. As yet, he and the other firemen didn't know that the four cops had been killed. At the time of the slaughter, the fireman had been too far away, and they hadn't heard the Ingram firing or the MAC-10's being silenced.

The fire truck was only 180 feet away from the two police cars when the driver and the other man in the cab saw the four bodies, both thinking that the four policemen had been either killed or stunned by the explosion. A moment later, Max triggered the MAC-10, sending a stream of 9mm armor piercing S-S projectiles through the grill in the front of the fire truck. All the driver and his partner heard were a dozen very loud ringing sounds as the slugs stabbed into the engine block. Instantly there were strident knocking sounds as the first two cylinders and their pistons fell apart while piston rods kept right on trying to move. Oil began to flow and the engine quit before the astonished driver could shift gears or turn off the ignition. The vehicle began to lose speed. The driver started to apply the brakes.

Trouble came from the west in the form of two more police cars that were speeding toward the area as Weems was returning to the Ford Bronco. The Death Merchant, raising his two autoloaders, was wishing he were back in Texas. With four cops already maggot bait in the market place, neither Camellion nor Weems had much of a choice. The approaching police had to be whacked out.

The two police cars were still a fifth of a block away when Camellion said to Weems, "I'll take out the first one. When it swerves out of the way, you smear the second."

"You had better open fire at—say twenty, twenty-one meters," Weems advised. He was now crouched down beside Camellion in front of the Bronco. "Waiting until they got closer would be too risky."

"Right. I estimate that seventy feet will be the right distance."

The police cars roared in to their own destruction. Timing the hit almost to the split second, the Death Merchant reared up and did what few men could do: he double body-pointed[8]

---

[8]Basically, this is firing by pure instinct.

with the Black Widow and the Sokolovsky, firing both big autoloaders simultaneously. He kept pulling the trigger of the Sokolovsky.

The .45 projectile from the Black Widow hit the left front tire of the first police cruiser at the same time that the first slug from the Sokolovsky struck the driver in his lower teeth. The bullet tore out his tongue, zipped through the back of his neck, continued on its way and struck the rear window, cracking it. The bullet, its power spent, dropped into the rear seat. With its left front tire flat, the police car started to swerve to the left as two .45 slugs from the Black Widow popped through the windshield. One missed the driver's partner. The second bullet caught him high in the right side of the chest, just below the clavicle.

The second police cruiser was thirty feet behind the first one which was headed toward the glass front of Grindenberg's Marine Supply Equipment Company. The driver of the second car, realizing they were in an ambush, began to brake his vehicle. Too late!

Camellion again fired the Sokolovsky autopistol, its roar blending with the *phyyyts* of the silenced MAC-10. At the same instant that the left front tire went *BANG!* from Camellion's .45 slug and the first police car crashed into the right-side plate glass window of Grindenberg's, 14 nine-millimeter S-S projectiles dissolved the car's windshield and cut into the driver and the cop sitting next to him, the vicious blast almost decapitating the two men. With blood spurting from the two corpses, the vehicle tore to the left to join the first police car that had been turned into a morgue.

"Now, that's what I call true grit!" chuckled Max, lowering his Ingram SMG.

Camellion, shoving a fresh clip into the Black Widow, glanced curiously at Weems. "Uh-huh. What do you mean?"

"I mean us. It takes true grit to smoke two cops."

"Possum poop. It requires only necessity. Let's go, or it will be us who gets burned next."

A few minutes more and Camellion and Weems were in the Bronco and Max had turned the vehicle around and was driving it west, both men hoping that they wouldn't meet more police. They didn't. Weems had turned north when they heard sirens far to the east.

"We'll be long gone on Del Mar by the time they figure out what's happened," Weems said happily. "Oh well, it's too bad about those cops we had to ace out."

"It's not really all that terrible," Camellion said. "The tragedy of life is not death. We all die. It's what dies inside a man while he lives."

"Sure, if you say so," Max said cheerfully.

CHAPTER TWO

Major Rostislav Krylivsky liked the two room suite on the 9th floor of the Hotel Woodward in mid-town Manhattan. There was a large bedroom with double beds, a walnut dresser and a chest of drawers, replicas of furniture of the Victorian era. The bath was between the bedroom and the sitting room which was large and comfortable, even if Krylivsky did dislike the pink flowered wallpaper. There was an upholstered couch, wing back chair, dropleaf coffee table and Queen Anne chair. The imitation fireplace was a nice touch, giving the room a lived-in look. But the small modern bar, with all its chrome, looked out of place, as though it were from the future.

Better yet, Krylivsky was positive the suite was "clean." Two members of the Soviet Commission of Agriculture at the United Nations had rented the suite only two days ago and one of them had remained in the suite at all times. There wasn't any way the CIA or the FBI, or any other American agency could have placed hidden transmitters in the rooms.

Krylivsky settled down comfortably on the couch and adjusted his rimless glasses. "To think that we almost had the plans for that special microprocessor and then lost them," he said in Russian. "I don't suppose you have anymore information about what happened on the Gold Rose?"

He and Julia Uzhgorod looked toward Colonel Pyter Gorsetev, who, down on his knees in the northeast corner of the sitting room, was making sure that the portable "white sound"[1] generator was functioning and broadcasting to the 18 tiny speakers he had scattered throughout the two rooms, the

---

[1] Random noise. Also called "shot" and "thermal" noise.

bath, and the large closet in the bedroom. As head of *Narodnoye opolcheniye*[2], the *Osoby otdel*[3] or special KGB network that was concentrating on the Silicon Valley, Gorsetev was an extremely cautious man who never left anything to chance.

Satisfied that the white sound generator was working at full capacity, Gorsetev stood up, turned around and glanced at Major Krylivsky. Only three years from forty, Pyter Alexander Gorsetev was a striking man with the cunning of a Rasputin. He had pearl-gray eyes, a fine head of coffee-colored hair, and spoke English better than the average American. An expert in American culture and customs, he loved baseball, wore expertly fitted suits and neither smoked nor drank alcohol, with the exception of light table wines.

"No one alive was left on the vessel to make a report," he said to Major Krylivsky, walking to the wing back chair and sitting down, careful of the creases in the trousers of his cream-colored suit. "Major Romashin first knew that something was wrong when Philip Butler sent word to one of Romashin's agents that the yacht had been destroyed. Butler reported that his five men who had gone to the yacht had not returned. He was becoming more and more worried when he heard on the early morning television news that the Gold Rose had exploded."

"This Philip Butler. . . . Is he not the leader of the disreputable motorcycle organiztion that is working with our Special Department?"

Gorsetev nodded. Krylivsky continued. "What puzzles us in the Washington, D.C. *Residentsii* is why the CIA agents who invaded the yacht killed eight Los Angeles policemen. We must assume it was the CIA who killed Butler's people and Dr. Revlon."

Colonel Gorsetev again nodded. "The only other information I have is that only two men handled the wet affairs on board the vessel—actually one man. I suppose you saw in the papers that the police found six corpses presumed to be on the ship. One was Doctor Revlon."

[2]Means "Home guard."
[3]Actually means "Special Department."

Krylivsky's eyes raised slightly. Julia Uzhgorod, sitting in the Queen Anne chair, frowned.

"The Washington and the New York papers didn't say anything about two men," Krylivsky said slowly, automatically reaching for a pack of Players cigarettes which were in his shirt pocket underneath his coat.

"Neither did the Los Angeles newspapers," explained Gorsetev. "They only reported that the murders were committed by persons unknown. We obtained our information through informants in the L.A.P.D. that. . . ."

"L.A.P.D.?" Krylivsky stared at Gorsetev.

"The Los Angeles Police Department. Naturally the contacts did not know they were giving the information to our agents, or rather that the information would reach our people. What happened is that a watchman on the fourth floor of a warehouse saw two police cars stop on the dock. A single man came off the boat and surrendered to four policemen. It was then that the long man's partner opened fire with what had to be a machine pistol fitted with a firing suppressor. I say that because the watchman told the police hd did not hear any weapons firing. The police withheld this information from the press. The watchman then hurried down to the first floor and saw the two men kill four more policemen who had come to the scene."

Julia Uzhgorod inhaled audibly with surprise. "This watchman! He did nothing. He did not fire his own weapon at the two men?"

Gorsetev smiled, revealing even, white teeth. "He didn't have a weapon. Not all watchmen carry sidearms in this crazy, gun-happy nation. He did tell the police that he could see only dimly the two men who did the firing. He didn't get a good look at their faces. They were in semi-darkness and he was at an angle that did not afford him a clear view of the men. The sum and substance of it all is that the enemy suspected Dr. Revlon and had to be watching both the front and the back entrances of his apartment building, otherwise they couldn't have trailed him to the dock."

"What matters is that the operation failed," Krylivsky said bitterly. He tapped ash from his cigarette into a large white ashtray in the center of the dropleaf coffee table. "Months of work and careful planning—all for nothing."

Colonel Gorsetev switched from Russian to English. "Yes, it is a definite setback," he said calmly, thinking that the plan had been almost foolproof. Illegals,[4] a man and a woman couple, had rented an apartment in the Coral Gables, the apartment building where Dr. Revlon and his wife, Esther, lived. Frank and Mabel Sims, the illegals, has spent long months cultivating Norman and Esther Revlon, and their work paid off. Just as Gorsetev had predicted, greed—the Achilles Heel of all Americans—had been the fatal weakness of Dr. Revlon and his wife. Revlon had finally agreed to turn over the plans of the GA-1 microprocessor for a cool one million dollars in cash. The only thing that Norman and Esther Revlon had not been told was that when he returned from the boat to his apartment with the money, he and his wife would be killed.

Only Esther Revlon had been eliminated. As soon as Yuri Kunavin had learned from Philip Butler that the Gold Rose had been destroyed, Kunavin had immediately contacted "Mr. and Mrs. Frank Sims," the two illegals, by phone and instructed them in code to silence Esther Revlon. The Sims had killed her with a *vergift*[5] tube that sprayed prussic acid.

It was Major Krylivsky who broke the short silence. "I don't suppose there's any danger of the police suspecting that Mrs. Revlon was murdered? The Americans are very good with forensics."

Gorsetev made a motion with his left hand. "None whatsoever. Hydrocyanic, once inhaled, quickly induces death by contracting the blood vessels. Soon after death, the blood vessels relax so that it appears that the target died of cardiac arrest. Esther Revlon was fifty years old, just the right age for a heart attack, and that's what the newspapers called her death—'a heart attack, probably induced by the sudden death of her husband.'"

Julia Uzhgorod abruptly changed the subject. "Comrade

---

[4] Russian nationals who have entered the U.S. illegally and are living like Americans, with all sorts of background papers to prove their American citizenship.
[5] Means "poison" in Russian.

Krylivsky and I were almost certainly followed from Washington by the CIA," she said in a low voice. "It was to be expected. Naturally the CIA will think we are—I believe the American vulgarism is 'shacking up.' "

She got up, walked to one of the northside windows and looked out, studying the view on West 55th Street.

Gorsetev's eyes followed her. Julia Maria Uzhgorod was not a beautiful woman, yet with her slim figure, she did not appear Russian. Close to thirty, she had high strong bones, pretty eyes and dark brown hair worn in a fluffy bob. Officially, she was Major Krylivsky's private secretary. Also officially, Rostislav Krylivsky was the Attache of Commerce to the Soviet Embassy in Washington, D.C. The reality was that he was the assistant chief of the KGB *Rezidentsii* at the embassy, second only to Lieutenant General Kaarlo Aleksei Galkinn, the *khoziain*, or boss, of the entire KGB apparatus in the United States.

As a cover, General Galkinn held the lowly post of second assistant secretary of Information at the Soviet Embassy.

The wily Gorsetev knew that the *Rezidentsii* in Washington disapproved of the separate Home Guard network and his complete autonomy within that special department, and believed that the intelligence efforts against the companies located in the Silicon Valley should be directed from the KGB headquarters in the U.S., the *Rezidentsii* at the Soviet Embassy in the American capital.

Almost a year ago, Lieutenant General Galkinn had spoken to Moscow Central, stating that in his opinion two separate otdels could only lead to confusion and inefficiency. In reply, Moscow had coldly advised Galkinn that Gorsetev would remain in control of Home Guard; furthermore, Home Guard would continue to operate and function independently of the main *Rezidentsii*.

Colonel Gorsetev didn't blame Lieutenant General Galkinn and the other officers of the Washington, D.C. *Rezidentsii* for resenting him professionally. It was only natural; they were only being human. Not only had Moscow Central informed Galkinn that all authority of Home Guard would rest with Gorsetev, but also that the Washington *Residentsii* would be subject to Gorsetev's orders, provided those orders involved Silicon Valley.

With a slightly malicious joy, Gorsetev imagined how Galkinn felt being reduced to a kind of grandiose "messenger boy," nothing more than a contact between Home Guard and Moscow Central. How Galkinn must have gritted his teeth in frustration at having to send Major Krylivsky to New York City to confer with Gorsetev, who now said, "I sent for someone from the Embassy because I wanted to make an oral report and to let Moscow know that in spite of the recent failure—I refer to the disaster in Los Angeles of a few days ago—I have a new plan, one by which we will—if you'll pardon the American expression—'kill two birds with one stone.' "

Major Krylivsky's wintry expression never changed as he waited for Grosetev to continue.

"In a sense, we've been using more and more people to accomplish less and less," Gorsetev said in a musing tone. "What we will do next will be the unexpected. Comrade, you realize what American intelligence will expect us to do, now that that Doctor Revlon is dead?"

"To lie low. To do nothing for the time being?" Krylivsky said gravely, uncrossing his legs. "But they won't expect us to give up."

"That's right—and they won't expect us to kidnap Dr. Burl Olin Martin either," Gorsetev said enthusiastically.

Krylivsky's eyes narrowed.

"Dr. Martin is the inventor of the GA-1 microprocessor," explained Gorsetev, folding his arms. "By grabbing him and getting him to our country, he can not only redesign this special microprocessor but can also be made to do research for our government."

"I should think he will be well guarded," Krylivsky said, privately thinking that Colonel Gorsetev was oversimplifying the situation. Then again, who could really say that Gorsetev's scheme wouldn't work. He was an expert in industrial espionage, perhaps the best the KGB had. It was Gorsetev and his hand-picked agents who had arranged to use the International Institute for Applied Systems Analysis near Vienna, Austria, to link "talking" Soviet computers with the

U.S.-built CRAY-1 of Reading, England, a master feat that had enabled Soviet scientists to make complex calculations about the dispersal of NATO missiles. That was another reason why Moscow Center had decided to keep the Home Guard otdel separate from the network at the embassy in Washington. Gorsetev was always at his best when in total control of his own people.

"Dr. Martin was not as well protected as one might think," Grosetev said, sounding like an instructor giving a lecture in semantics. "He has only three bodyguards who accompany him to and from work, and they aren't trained. They're part of the guard force that works for Kordic Micro-Electric. You realize how ineffective they would be against our own experts."

Major Krylivsky crushed out his cigarette in the ashtray, then looked closely at Colonel Gorsetev. "We in the Washington *Rezidentsii* could never quite understand why you had our illegals recruit those low scum from that motorcycle organization. They're nothing but hooligans and gangsters. The American FBI and other police agencies are always watching them."

A master actor, Gorsetev didn't show his discomfiture, nor his dislike of Krylivsky's probing questions. That's what the man was doing—snooping, delving, obtaining all he could to take back to Galkinn. Inwardly, Gorsetev wanted to roar with laughter. Within days, he would know every single word that Major Krylivsky had reported to Lieutenant General Galkinn, and Galkinn's response. There is one thing that Galkinn would never know: he would never receive any information about the armored car. . . .

Gorsetev favored Krylivsky with one of his most reassuring smiles.

"Of course Satan's Gentlemen are under constant surveillance by the FBI, the CBI—that's the California Bureau of Investigation—the drug enforcement people and the local police. So what? Those agencies would never suspect those cutthroats of working for a foreign power. We're protected in other ways. Only Butler and his top people know they're working for another nation. They don't know it's the Soviet Union. They think we're the East Germans."

"What makes you think none of them would talk, if caught?" Krylivsky regarded Gorsetev with a strange, cold eye.

"They wouldn't because of their warped code of ethics, their ridiculous code of honor similar to the Sicilian Mafia's. It's for that reason that the police are never able to prosecute the swine for their crimes."

"Their value must be very limited," Krylivsky said.

"Wrong! Satan's Gentlemen can go where we wouldn't dare be seen. Face it, Comrade. The CIA and FBI watch every movement our people make once they leave the compound in San Francisco. But Satan's Gentlemen are a common sight on the streets of San Francisco, Los Angeles, and all through southern California." Gorsetev added in a harsher tone, "Remember, Comrade: it is my responsibility, and I have to answer only to Moscova!" A gentle reminder also to Lieutenant-General Galkinn!

Julia Uzhgorod turned from the window and looked directly at Colonel Gorsetev. "It is our understanding that there are several working models of the special microprocessor locked in the main safe in the office of Kordic Corporation," she said. "Wouldn't it be possible to open the safe with explosives? Surely some of the trash that belong to the motorcycle gang have had experience in such illegality?"

"I've considered that possibility," Gorsetev said. "It can't be done; the safe can't be blown open. For one thing, it's built like a bank vault. For another, there isn't any way to bypass the various alarm systems."

For some indefinable reason it gave him pleasure to hear Julia Uzhgorod's low voice. He reflected that there was no subtlety about her and he wondered if she and Krylivsky were sharing the same bed. Rumor had it they were. Well, she was not all that unattractive. Dressed in a pink pant suit and wearing high heels, she reminded Gorsetev of some of the call girls with whom he had done business. The black ones were especially good in bed.

Suddenly he thought of Merle "Doc" Sasser and Edward "Skinflint" Warsonfold, the two old hoods who had specialized in robbing armored cars. Several weeks ago, Dr. Revlon had revealed to Major Romashin that the special microprocessor was to be taken in an armored car to a special airplane and flown to the Pentagon. Dr. Revlon didn't know the exact date of the transfer, but he could find out. This bit of information, passed on to Grosetev, had led him to speculate about having some of the tougher element of Satan's Gentlemen hit the armored car. Accordingly, he had gone about having illegals in New York locate the old specialists. The two men had met with Colonel Gorsetev at 3:30 AM in an apartment in the Amsterdam House on Amsterdam Avenue and West 64th Street.

How difficult would it be to stop and get inside an armored car? Major Gorsetev had asked Sasser and Warsonfold.

"Son, you must be from Mars?" Sasser said with a laugh.

An old man in his seventies, Warsonfold had only shaken his head, then had said, "Well, armored cars ain't designed for winning style awards. When you say 'armored car,' you're talking about a riveted 12-gauge steel-plated body that's a fortress on wheels. All the major companies have the best cars that science can design—Brinks, Loomis, Wells Fargo, Purolator and Armored Transport. And that's where the money is. At any given time an armored car has more money in it than what you could score from fifty tellers' cages in a bank. The safety factor is that no one knows for sure how much they're carrying, whether its a grand in pennies or a million in bills."

Sasser had downed another shot of whiskey and had said, "Dog days for armored deals and their two man crews—sometimes there's three or four guys—are Fridays, Saturdays, and Sundays—in addition to the first and the fifteenth of every month. The active truck in a metro market will carry roughly 3 million to 4 million bucks on those days. That's a lot of dough."

"I'll give you an example," Ed Warsonfold had said. "Now you take Los Angeles. In L.A. alone, you have three major armored car companies and several smaller branches. You got all this to serve a 78 community area. OK. This means that on any day there are slightly more than 200 armored cars picking up and delivering cash, checks and securities. This means that on any given dog day there's about $700 million in transit."

"You got to consider the men who drive the jobs and the guys riding shotgun," Sasser had told Gorsetev. "You have to consider them because while the trucks are pretty goddamn

secure, the weakness is in the men inside. The A-C companies want iron-assed loners, bad marriage jokers and divorced
men. They want the social outsider, you know, the son of a
bitch who don't mix well. They want suckers who'll be
married to the job and the dumber the better. Shit, married
men ain't the type. They'll think about their families, about
staying alive, in case of trouble. But they don't want ex-cops.
They're bad risks. They tend to be rude and too pushy and
too damn quick to pull their piece and shoot.''

Colonel Gorsetev had listened very patiently and learned a
lot about armored cars. He learned that, in Sasser and
Warsonfold's opinion, the chassis was not designed properly
for the weight of the average armored car—''Ford and GM
are to blame,'' Sasser said. At a gross vehicle weight of
24,000 pounds, the chassis and body weigh roughly 12,000
pounds. ''This means,'' explained Sasser,'' that the gear ratio
is bad and the engines and transmissions are not the best. This
means that you get very poor power-to-weight ratios. Hell,
most trucks don't have the power to get out of their own way.
And you know what they do with a truck when it's worn
out—huh? The companies cut it up for scrap metal. It's a
matter of security. They don't want people to know there
aren't any big secrets inside. The less the public knows about
armored cars, the better.''

Most armored cars carry 55-gallon or twin 50-gallon gas
tanks beneath the floorbed so that a robber deciding to blow
his way up from a manhole would incinerate the drivers—and
the money. The tires are standard heavy-duty truck tires. It
would be useless to shoot them out because the crew could
radio for help before the truck came to a halt.

Warsonfold said, ''Another protection for both the truck
and the jokers inside is that the armored car may be under
surveillance by company investigators and security men, or
by insurance and bonding companies. So you see, when you
hit one, you're always taking a risk in that direction.''

Doc Sasser had told Gorsetev about the inside of the truck.
A steel door with a bulletproof window lay between the
driver's cab and the main shell, or rear, of the truck. All
companies stressed a policy that the compartment door had to
be closed at all times; however, this rule was loosely followed.

Often the door was left open for conversation and air circulation. The main function of the door was not to protect the driver but to safeguard the bags of money that rode with the driver.

"You see, it's standard procedure," explained Sasser, "for armored car companies to place bags of money on the jumpseat in the cab next to the driver, while bags of coins are placed in the rear. If the guard is held up while entering or leaving the truck, the bulk of the currency is safe with the driver behind the locked compartment door."

As for weapons, there was an assortment—from .30-30 lever action Winchesters and Marlins to Mossberg pump-action riot guns with 18½ inch barrels. A lot of guards also carry shotguns loaded with sabot, which are small missile-rockets that can tear through an automobile or a brick wall. For ordinary sidearms, most of the men carry .38 revolvers.

Colonel Gorsetev had finally lost his patience. "Gentlemen," he had said, "all I want to know is can the two of you successfully rob an armored car in the Los Angeles area? If so, how long would it take?"

"Six months of planning," Edward Warsonfold had said promptly. "At least six months."

"We'd need a minimum of four men to help us," Doc Sasser had said. "They would have to be experts and we would have to choose them. When we do a job on an armored car, we do it our way."

Six months of planning! That ended Colonel Gorsetev plans regarding the armored car that would carry the microprocessor to an aircraft.

Two days later, Doc Sasser and Skinflint Warsonfold were found dead in their respective hotels.

A medical examiner diagnosed their deaths as. . . . "heart failure."

"Comrade Gorsetev, your plan is then definite," said Major Krylivsky. "You and your people will abduct Dr. Burl Martin?"

"Yes," replied Gorsetev, watching Julia Uzhgorod sit down. "There is no other way, especially since the disaster in Los Angeles. Somehow American intelligence knows what we're

31

after, and the sooner we grab Dr. Martin, the sooner we can conclude the project with total success."

Krylivsky leaned forward and put his hands on his knees. "Once you have possession of the target, it should not be difficult to transport him to one of our submarines. Such a transfer will call for precise coordination between your network and ours in Washington. Naturally, Moscova will have to approve such a highly dangerous operation. But you know that." Off to one side of his mind, Krylivsky wondered again about Radio City Music Hall. He had always wanted to see Radio City Music Hall.

"There's still another reason I requested this meeting." Gorsetev uncrossed his legs and shifted his weight in the wing-back chair. "We can always radio the Rezidentsii at the embassy from the Consulate in San Francisco. What I want you to do is to have Comrade Galkinn contact Moscova and find out which of our submarines will be cruising within three hundred kilometers of the California coast from San Francisco to San Diego within the next six weeks."

Julia Uzhgorod remarked, "Using one of our submarines will present technological problems. The United States is constantly using tracking buoys and other equipment to spy on our underwater vessels."

"The Americans will suspect at once that we would transfer Dr. Martin to a submarine; they would be counting on such expediency," Major Krylivsky said urgently. He quickly amended his obvious disapproval with, "But as you said, it is your responsibility."

For a moment Colonel Gorsetev studied the older man whom he considered odd-looking and something of a fool. Rostislav Krylivsky was the unfortunate possessor of a long, gaunt face topped by a large bald head fringed with a ring of hair that was very black just above the ears, but gray where the hair turned to fuzz on the rounded skull. He had a large nose, a large mouth and eyes that were always suspicious. He spoke Russian with a strong Georgian accent and his stiff erect carriage gave the impression of a rugged presence.

"The United States Navy can't be everywhere at once," Gorsetev said at length. "We'll put our prize package in a cabin cruiser and move eighty kilometers or so out into the

Pacific. How long does such a transfer take? Fifteen minutes at the most, if that long." He gave a tiny laugh. "After all, I don't intend for the submarine to surface under the Golden Gate Bridge."

Major Krylivsky wasn't amused by Gorsetev's remark, and, judging from her stony expression, neither was Julia Uzhgorod.

Krylivsky said stiffly, "As soon as Comrade General Galkinn receives word from Moscova regarding the submarine, we'll contact the Consulate in San Francisco. Your people there can contact you."

"Use the special computer code, as usual—triple scrambled," Gorsetev said forcefully. Then, almost instantly he detected a change in Major Krylivsky. The man's expression became intense and hesitant, as though he were replowing a furrow in his mind.

He surprised Colonel Gorsetev by saying in a friendly voice, "Comrade, how far are we from Radio City Music Hall?"

In spite of his constant awareness of his facial expressions and his "body language", Gorsetev drew back slightly in surprise. He noticed Julia Uzhgorod smile.

"Why do you ask?"

"I have always wanted to go there."

Colonel Gorsetev thought for a moment, then said, "Radio City is on West 51st Street and Sixth Avenue. Let's see. . . . From here you go east on West 55th for a block. That will bring you to the Avenue of the Americas. Turn south on Avenue of the Americans and go four or five blocks. You'll bump right into Radio City."

A satisfied smile crossed Krylivsky's face. . . .

After Rostislav Krylivsky and Julia Uzhgorod left the suite of rooms, Colonel Gorsetev felt well satisfied with himself. In spite of the risks involved, his own cover was secure. As First Secretary to Dr. Josef Serbidov, who was head of the Soviet delegation to the United Nations Council on Oceanography, he had diplomatic immunity. The worst that could happen to him would be to be declared persona non grata and be booted out of the United States.

For now, everything was under control. In industrial operations like this one, one had to estimate progress daily and at the same time use one's instinct to calculate tomorrow's move and the reaction of the enemy.

And it was all for nothing! All useless! It was an operation that, even if successful, added up to one big fat zero. What did one microprocessor mean, or a thousand microprocessors, when the world was poised on the brink of Armageddon?

World War III was only a year or so away. The trouble was that Andropov and the other bosses in the Presidium were underestimating the Americans. My God! Some of the plans those idiots had in mind, such as the colonization of Siberia with four million Europeans after a successful invasion of Europe! Madness. Pure lunacy. And they were positive they could win because the first strike would be a massive air and missile attack on nuclear storage sites in the United States, England and other nations in Europe, such as France and Germany. There was a possibility the Kremlin was right! The Soviet Union just might win—which was why the Kremlin was counting on the Peace Movement in the West, particularly in the United States, and was itself insistently demanding disarmament. That was the prime goal of Andropov and the other war lovers—the complete paralysis of American deterent.

But such matters were of no importance, not now. The important thing at the moment was to fly to California and personally supervise the kidnaping of Dr. Martin.

There it was again, reflected Colonel Gorsetev: that subtle warning of danger. He thought of how one man had terminated everyone on board the Gold Rose. Only one man, unless the report was incorrect.

Who was that single individual?

Major Pyter Gorsetev intended to find out. . . .

CHAPTER THREE

Under different circumstances, Oran Cathhart could have enjoyed himself on this sunny afternoon. The special safe house, five miles northeast of Altadena, was only a long spit away from Angeles National Forest, and the entire area, less than 30 miles from the murderous mess that was Los Angeles, was peaceful and pleasant. Why Mount Wilson Observatory was only 12 miles from Blood Bone Unit's safe house! A nice area in which to retire. No! Not with all the earthquakes indigenous to California. Anyhow, he couldn't have afforded it; homes in the area started at $300,000. However, now was not the time to enjoy the peace and quiet. It was time to get definite answers from Richard Camellion and the three persons of his network.

Settled comfortably in the large leather armchair with the spoonfoot legs, Cathhart looked severely at the Death Merchant and said in a voice that was demanding, "See here, Camellion. The home office wants some answers. The people you terminated on the yacht are of no consequence, but the eight policemen you and Weems put to sleep are a different matter. The newspapers are still harping on their deaths. The DD/I[1] is very upset. He wants an explanation and he sent me here to get one. Why do you think I flew to Los Angeles?"

"Huh!" snickered Max Weems who was lying on his back on three modular cushions spread on the floor, his legs crossed at the knees, the back of his head resting on an attache case. "He would have been more upset if the police had arrested Camellion and the true story had leaked out. That would have given the whole damn Company a stroke!"

[1]Deputy Director of Intelligence.

"I don't see what all the fuss is about," said Joseph Tenson. "The Fox in C.A.[2] isn't complaining, and from what you've told us the boys in O.S.T.[3] aren't unhappy. All they care about is smashing the Soviet ring out here."

"I wasn't talking to you," Cathhart said acidly to Tensor, emphasizing each word. "Nor to you." He glared at Max Weems who, looking up at the ceiling, couldn't see his angry face.

Richard Camellion, moving slowly back and forth in a Victorian walnut-finished rocker, looked very seriously at Cathhart whose plane had landed at Los Angeles International Airport only four hours ago.

Camellion sighed. "Did I ever tell you about the old Indian Shaman who was named Flying Go-Cart?" he asked the CIA messenger.

Puzzled and suspecting he was being led into some kind of verbal insult, Cathhart frowned. "What the hell are you talking about?"

"Flying Go-Cart was the healer of the village. But one day a cloud passed over the village and Flying Go-Cart himself fell ill. His people prayed to the Sun Spirit. They prayed and prayed, but Flying Go-Cart only got sicker. Well, sir, out of nowhere, a small boy appeared. He took hold of the Shaman's nose and squeezed as hard as he could. The sick man then sat up, turned the boy over his knee, and spanked him soundly. Do you know the moral of the story?"

Cathhart stared in dismay at the Death Merchant. "No, but you're going to tell me!"

"It's 'Please don't squeeze the Shaman.' "

A small, sinewy individual, Cathhart went rigid with indignation and his face purpled.

"I've had quite enough of this nonsense," he said and stood up. Only with effort could he keep rage and resentment out of his voice. "I'll report that you're uncooperative and that, in my estimation, you're idiots more suited for a rubber room than running an operation of such a delicate nature."

"Sit down," Camellion said, a hint of mirth in his voice,

[2]Courtland Grojean in the Covert Action Department.
[3]Office of Science & Technology.

"and I'll tell you in detail what happened four days ago on the docks."

"It's about time!" Cathhart sat back down.

"I had no choice but to eliminate the four cops coming at us," the Death Merchant said in a serious tone. He stopped rocking. "I could have permitted the police to arrest me, but there was too much danger of a leak afterward. If even a hint of what we're doing reached the papers, the operation would have to be scratched—and the DD/I knows it."

"Eight policemen were killed," Cathhart said icily. "Four on the docks and four by the warehouse. Which four are you speaking about?"

"Oh, what's the difference?" Catherine McManus said. "What's done is done."

"The home office wants to know the truth—that's the difference," snapped Cathhart.

Camellion had no intention of telling Cathhart the truth, that he would have preferred capture to killing policemen and that it was Max Weems who had smoked the first four fuzz on the dock. But it was against his nature to toss an aide to the bureaucratic wolves.

Four, eight, or a baker's dozen! What's the difference? The Death Merchant was about to say that he had also smoked the four cops by the dock when Weems sat up on the modular cushions, looked at Cathhart and said pleasantly, "I aced out the four by the yacht. If I hadn't, they would have arrested Camellion and the headlines in the newspapers might have been far different. In short, I did what I felt had to be done."

Interjected Joe Tensor, "Besides, the papers are now working on the theory that it was IRA terrorists who killed the cops, that it all had to do with smuggling arms to the crazies in Northern Ireland. Personally, I think the 'tip' we planted with the L.A. *Times* was a stroke of genius."

"So do I," said Baxter Lincolnwell. "After all, Philip Butler owned the vessel, and Satan's Gentlemen have been investigated more than once for illegal firearms and smuggling on an international scale."

"Or could it be that some of our Irish-American Senators, who secretly agree with the aims of the IRA and even the

I.N.L.A.[4], don't care for the story we planted with the *Times*?'' a bemused Catherine McManus offered.

Cathhart swung angrily toward her. ''That's damned nonsense,'' he said. ''You're jumping to nutty conclusions that don't make any sense.''

Cathhart let his eyes roam over the young woman, taking a hard, objective look at her. In her mid-twenties, she had good features and better than average eyes, large and lustrous. Still, there was something wrong with her. Her red-brown hair was pulled back too tightly from her forehead and bound in a heavy chignon that exposed her ears too nakedly. Yet she did have good, well-rounded breasts, and she obviously wasn't wearing a bra, unless it was made of the finest of tissue paper which permitted her nipples to struggle furiously for freedom beneath her crepe de chine blouse that was tucked into a pair of pink bermuda shorts. She did have nicely tanned legs, although they were a bit heavy in the thighs. Hmmmm. . . . was she sleeping with Camellion or one of the other three? Or perhaps with all four? Well, it was no concern of his, concluded Cathhart. She could be screwing a mummy for all he cared.

For twelve years Cathhart had been an employee of the Central Intelligence Agency, and during those twelve years he had been behind a desk, a pusher of papers, a reports and coordination man. Because of the thousands of reports he had read, Cathhart was convinced that all spooks in the field were of a different breed than normal human beings—oddballs all of them. In this particular case, even the safe house this small group was using was weird, as if designed by a psychotic architect.

Originally, the house had been built by an eccentric heiress who had designed the structure herself. The main section of the house was a three-story stone tower—three rooms to a floor—with part of the north side built of wood, curved outward like half of a barrel. The windows in the tower were narrow but tall, the glass tinted blue.

The second section of the odd-looking house was a cube

---

[4] The Irish National Liberation Army. Small and very violent, the I.N.L.A. openly admits it is Marxist and out to win any way it can.

built of fieldstone, two stories tall and without a single window. It was connected to the square tower by a totally enclosed walkway two stories above the ground. Oddly enough, there wasn't any garage. There wasn't a swimming pool either. R.D.K. Romix Corporation of Tacoma, Washington, owned the house and the nine acres on which it sat. Taxes on the property were always paid promptly.

"Jumping to conclusions, am I?" retorted Catherine McManus smugly. "Then tell me why the DD/I is so concerned? Why he sent you out here when he knows full well that Camellion and Weems silenced those policemen because they were forced to?"

"You are climbing the wrong tree, Cathy," said the Death Merchant, who had gone over to the bar and was pouring himself a glass of buttermilk. "All the DD/I is doing is trying to make himself look good with the White House. He couldn't care less about the dead fuzz." Camellion's bright blue eyes burned into Oran Cathhart. "Was there anything else you wanted to know?"

Cathhart tugged at the lapels of his burgundy blazer. "No. What you and Weems said covers everything. I was sent only to find out why the eight policemen were murdered. . . . uh. . . . terminated."

"Okay. Now you know. Don't let us keep you—bye!" said Joe Tensor. He was seated at a tea table, cleaning an Ingram M-10 that had been fitted with a wooden buttstock and a 10″ barrel with upper receiver.

"It's almost six," announced McManus, getting up from the lounge chair. "I'm going over to the other section and put on some steaks. Should I put one on for you, Mr. Catthart?"

"Yeah, you're welcome here," Max Weems said with a toothy grin. "Don't mind Joe. He doesn't like anyone from the home office."

Cathhart shook his head. "I don't have the time. I still have to drive to L.A., return the car to Avis and then take a cab to the airport. I must be back at Langley by ten tomorrow morning."

Standing by one of the tower's south side windows, Camellion looked down and watched Oran Cathhart drive away in his Plymouth Reliant. It was such nonsense. The DD/I is trying to put a feather in his cap and that is needlessly complicating an operation already tangled in a web of suppositions and ridiculous American laws, such as the Freedom of Information Act[5].

Industrial espionage was big business all over the world. Trade secrets, special processes, inventions, surveys, financial data and marketing information were always for sale to the highest bidder. Most people believed that trade secrets were always protected by patents. Very often, however, trade processes aren't patentable, and proprietary information[6] never is—*Even so, this wouldn't stop the KGB. The Russians have less ethics than a cockroach.*

Even if a new process could be patented, many companies and corporations preferred to keep the new process secret rather than submit it to the close scrutiny of the government. Worse, the enforcement of patent laws tended to be very lax, the actual implementation depending on the patent owner's surveillance of the industry and his willingness to go to court and sue for infringements, all of which is costly and time-consuming. There is also the possibility that the Patent Office would deny an application. For these reasons, many corporations use their inventions and/or secret processes without bothering to protect them by patent laws. Instead, these corporations depended upon compartmentalization, plant security, the loyalty of top executives and business counterintelligence to protect their vital secrets. All companies, in every phase of industry, had secrets that were vulnerable to industrial spies.[7]

The ingredient that ruined the security stew was that such corporate safeguards were more often than not shockingly lax, particularly so when the transmission of computer data was involved. They were so ridiculously slack that numerous corporations routinely bounced information from satellites rather

---

[5]We can thank the American Civil Liberties Union—the ACLU—which worked day and night to get the Freedom of Information Act passed. It is the ACLU that always fights in court for the hardcore criminal, but never utters one word about the victim.

[6]Information pertaining to patents, trademarks, formulae, etc.

[7]The chemicals, drug, computer and electronics fields are the hardest hit.

than sending it over telephone lines. Satellite transmissions were far easier to intercept than data sent via telephone.

Just thinking about it made Richard Camellion sick to his stomach. Even the Bank of America was guilty of a lack of security. Every day the Bank of America transferred about $20 billion without making use of either scrambling or encryption techniques for protection—*DAMN!*

Paradoxically, the most popular form of industrial spying was legal and involved companies that made extensive use of the Freedom of Information Act, with almost 90 percent of the requests coming from business. For the Soviet Union—and the Japanese, too—the Freedom of Information Act was a firm ally, although there were other methods by which foreign powers could gain access to secrets of American companies. Damaging information could leak out from any part of a company, from the execetive suite to the mail room. The motive was usually money; often it was pure revenge. There was another way, one that was common: Many high-tech companies stole secrets without even going to the trouble of hiring away another corporation's employees. They simply resorted to the prospect of a high-paying job to pump information from eager applicants during interviews. This technique was widespread among the 1,300 or so firms packed in the 250 square mile Silicon Valley. *But this is minor compared to how the KGB and other foreign intelligence agencies operate,* Camellion thought bitterly.

In many ways it was a losing battle—*And all because of loose American laws. Our Society is too open.*

The Soviet Union not only utilized industrial espionage, it depended on outright theft to obtain American secrets. Another method was for the Russians to buy devices and information secondhand from nations that were allied with the U.S. or from neutral nations that obtained secrets from U.S. firms.

Oran Cathhart's Plymouth reached the road, turned and soon was out of sight. . . .

A few hours later, after the Death Merchant and the four other members of his Blood Bone Unit had eaten an early dinner and the group was clearing the table, Cathy McManus remarked, "You know, guys, I'm not surprised that the DD/I sent a messenger to get a special report. What's the new

DD/I's name—Kornmooth? I only wish I had told Cathhart that I haven't the faintest idea why this new gismo. . . ."

"A M-I-C-R-O-P-R-O-C-E-S-S-O-R," Max Weems said with a laugh. "It's an itty-bitty microprocessor."

Carefully, Cathy brushed scraps from a paper plate into the garbage disposal in the sink. "All right. So it's a microprocessor. I was going to say that I don't know why this particular microprocessor is so important." She glanced at Camellion who was putting silverware into the rack of the dishwasher. "To be honest about it, I don't even know what a chip is!"

"I know what a chip is, but I don't think I could explain it as well as Baxter," replied Camellion. "He's the engineer and expert in computers."

A fresh cup of coffee in his hand, Baxter Lincolnwell sat down on the solid Oregon pine reproduction of a Shaker Bench and sniffed. "Well, you have to start with one of earth's most abundant elements after oxygen—silicon!" he said in his nasal voice. "Silicon is refined from quartz rocks. It is then sliced into wafers. After many more processes—all kinds of purifications and coatings—the silicon is ready to be used. Transistors are placed on the chip and the chip is diced from the wafer and bonded with conventional wires."

"That's about as clear as India ink!" Cathy said, turning on the dishwasher.

"Or another way to put it," went on Lincolnwell, "is that a chip is a very tiny piece of silicon that's been turned into a complete semiconductor device. Or we could explain it by saying it's an integrated circuit. Understand?"

Cathy finished lighting a cigarette. "Oh sure," she joked. Then, more seriously, "But do these chips, or integrated circuits, make up a microprocessor?"

The Death Merchant, thinking of the day's radio schedule, smiled to himself. An average person would have answered Cathy's question with a simple "Yes" or "No." Not Lincolnwell, who always took the long way around.

The possessor of the Ph.D. in electrical engineering, the 45-year-old Lincolnwell was a contract agent who often worked for the Company's O.S.T. section and D.O.O.[8] division.

---

[8]Domestic Operations Division, also known as the "OO" Office.

Gray-haired and aristocratic in appearance, he was one of the best computer and microelement experts in the United States. A victim of constant sinusitis, he was forever sniffing, hawking or blowing his nose into a tissue.

"Well," began Lincolnwell, "when you think of a microprocessor, the best way is to think of a gridiron of a small city as seen from a plane five thousand feet up. Now condense it all—I'm talking about the microprocessor now—to a size that it could be carried off by an ant. You see, a microprocessor is actually a computer on a chip."

He sniffed again, then explained that a typical "computer on a chip" contained on an average of 30,000 transistors and was sealed in a ceramic case. Electricity flowed in and out through wires of gold or aluminum, while a "window" allowed ultraviolet light to flood in and erase information from the chip's programmable EPRO or memory bank.

The RAM (Random-Access-Memory) was also a vital part. The RAM was a memory in which any piece of information could be independently stored or retrieved, but its contents were held only temporarily.

EPROM contains the basic program instructions for performing any given task, such as running a watch or a microwave oven. More workaday, the RAM "stores interim operational data, with the storage capacities of chip memories being measured in K's, each K representing 1,024 units of information. Near each memory section, an 'addressing' unit selects and transmits instructions which are dispatched as high and low voltage signals, traveling at near the speed of light. These are represented in the binary system, in which only two numbers, 0 and 1, convey information, in much the same way as Morse code is transmitted in a telegraph system."

Lincolnwell took a sip of coffee, then continued, "With things moving so quickly in a microprocessor, signals could easily be lost or scrambled. To avoid confusion, signals are steered into the instruction unit which interprets the entire program and breaks it down into extremely detailed steps for execution by the ALU, or the arithmetic-logic-unit. The ALU can add, multiply by successive addition, subtract and divide by successive subtraction. Oh, it's a marvelous operation.

43

Hundreds of thousands of calculations per second are possible with these simple methods.''

"But the Kordic's GA-1 microprocessor is different," said the Death Merchant who had dropped onto one of the chairs by the table. "As I understand it, the GA-1 is different not only in composition but in its basic functions.''

"You're half right," replied Lincolnwell. "The GA part comes from gallium arsenide. The 'one' because the GA-microprocessor is the first of its kind[9]. It's a combination of the elements gallium and arsenic, and—"

"What's so damned special about such a chip?'' asked Joe Tensor who had just lighted one of his La Corona Whiffs, a small cigar slightly larger than a cigarette.

An expression of dismay crossed Lincolnwell's pale face. "What's so special is that a microprocessor made of gallium arsenide[10] is faster electronically and needs less power to operate than circuits made of silicon. The speed of GA makes it ideal for use in communications where high circuit speed and low power consumption are key requirements—and I do mean speed.''

"Some day the machines will be telling us what to do!'' mused Cathy McManus.

As though he hadn't heard her, Lincolnwell continued, "Logic devices built with GA's could record speeds in the gigahertz, or billionths-of-cycles-per-second speed range. Most silicon circuits are in the megahertz, or millionth-of-cycles-per-second speed range. And remember, this is only the beginning. Think of how scientists will improve on the GA-1 in the coming years.''

No one made any comments. In a voice that shook slightly with emotion, with feeling engendered by his knowledge of the gallium arsenide microprocessor, Lincolnwell said that the GA-1 was only a quarter of an inch square; *yet it contained 182,000 circuits and could multiply five nine-digit numbers in 9.2 billionths of a second.*

[9]This is not fiction. The gallium-arsenide chip is at present the subject of a lot of attention by such companies as Motorola, Hughes and Bell Laboratories.

[10]Gallium makes up about .01 percent of aluminum ore, which is mined in several places in the United States. Arsenic is found in many copper ores. Neithr element is as plentiful as silicon.

"It's lightning logic and then some," Baxtor said excitedly. "The GA-1 can make calculations, keep numerous data in storage and hold instructions that help it to operate. Not only that, it even has the ability to sense a change in its environment and then signal changes of its own."

"Perfect for missiles," Max Weems said thoughtfully. "Sensing that its target is moving, a missile equipped with GA circuits could, for example, direct an instant change of direction."

"Exactly," Lincolnwell agreed. "In fact, there are so many applications for the GA that it's difficult at the present time to assess just how big the market potential is."

Damn the Los Angeles smog! The Death Merchant cleared his throat. "The GA could also be used for a 'superbrain' computer. This explains why the Japanese have made efforts to acquire technical knowledge of the GA. Their MITI[11] is backing a ten year research project to build the so-called Fifth Generation Computer, a machine that would have man-level intelligence. Another Japanese group, NIT[12] is trying to build a similar device."

"At least the Japs are limiting themselves to straight industrial spying," Joe Tensor said. "We can forget about them since the five GA's and the plans are locked in Kordic's main safe. On the other hand, who knows who's honest at Kordic. After all, Doctor Revlon sold out to the Other Side."

"What's this superbrain computer?" Cathy McManus looked from the Death Merchant to Lincolnwell, the latter of whom was scratching his left cheek.

Lincolnwell sniffed loudly. "A superbrain computer means a machine that is able to learn on its own. You can put a lot of knowledge inside a computer and instruct it to make judgements based on what it knows; and you can also give the computer access to knowledge stored in other places. But then we must get the computer to organize that knowledge for its own use. That's the big rub with this generation's computers. You have to give them an order at every step of the way and the orders have to be very simple, with the programs being

[11]The Japanese Ministry of International Trade and Industry.
[12]Nippon Telegraph and Telephone.

45

written to suit the machines. What the Japanese hope to do is work the other way around, or devise a new mathematics for computing, then design a machine to fit the new math. Instead of making a machine that takes only one step at a time, they're trying to build a system that will allow parallel processing. This would permit the computer to break the problem into parts—like human beings do—and work on several or more parts at one time.''

The Death Merchant tightened the belt of his safari suit jacket. ''Nothing exists but atoms and empty space, but I'll put my money on the Japanese. If a thinking computer can be built—and it can—they'll do it.''

''It all revolves around 'core memory','' Lincolnwell said. ''Anytime you have a breakthrough, it's always hardware that holds the vital key. To build a thinking computer, the planners must first have chips ten times as powerful as the most advanced models now in existence. The GA-1 fills the bill. But it can't do everything. For example, the Japanese will have to develop a core memory of up to one trillion bits of information that would be accessible within seconds. Why, it will take three or four years just to develop the special tools!''

''We're all whistling Dixie in the dark,'' sighed Weems. ''With the way things are in American society, the Ruskies and the Japanese will learn the secret of the GA microprocessor sooner or later, probably sooner.''

''I'll buy that,'' said Joe Tensor, putting out his little Whiff by dunking it into a cup of coffee, a habit that irked Cathy McManus. This time, however, she didn't ask him if he had been ''raised in a barn.'' ''Look at that Russian made subtracking buoy our Navy found last year. Its printed circuits were pin-for-pin identical with those produced by Texas Instruments.''

''There's no way Texas Instruments sold the circuit boards to the Russians,'' spoke McManus.

''Of course not,'' Tensor said. ''The ivans got the circuit boards from either an ally or a neutral. Hell, we all know what the trouble is. It's that damned Export Administration Act. The whole damned bill should be junked.''

Taking out a handkerchief, Lincolnwell said, ''I seem to recall the Soviet Union tried to buy sophisticated U.S. equipment that tests the strength of concrete. I believe it was during the winter of 1983. The Russians maintained they wanted to use the equipment to check bridges and apartment houses. The Pentagon blocked the sale on the grounds that the Soviets were more likely to use the equipment to test the hardness of their ICBM silos.''

"The problem is to find a way of insuring national security with minimal damage to the American business community," Camellion said. "It's easier said than done. The way it's set up now, the Commerce Department reviews between 80,000 and 90,000 export applications a year. Maybe between eight to ten thousand of these applications involve national-security considerations. Out of these, the Commerce Department asks the Pentagon to look over two or three thousand. What the Pentagon wants is complete veto power over Commerce, that is, complete control over any export from the U.S. that could conceivably endanger U.S. security. So far, the Pentagon hasn't gotten to even first base. It's all politics. American businessmen would rather make a bunk and risk a thermonuclear war than do what is logical. But none of that helps us with this particular mission.''

Joe Tensor sat up straight, glanced at Lincolnwell who was loudly blowing his nose and said matter of factly to Camellion, "It would be a lot easier if all we had to do was stop the KGB. We could do that by wrecking Satan's Gentlemen. All we'd have to do is cancel Dandy Phil Butler's ticket. He's always at his House of Pandemonium. Five pounds of C-4 or RDX would scatter him all the way to the moon!''

Cathy McManus shook her head.

Lincolnwell glanced in disdain at Tensor, anger and astonishment in his eyes. "It would kill Butler all right, and only God knows how many hundreds of innocent people!" he said irritably. "Is that your answer to everything—killing people?''

Tensor shrugged. "I believe in the direct approach. If I want to go to New York, I'll get in a plane and fly. I won't hitchhike by way of Florida.''

"Terminating Butler wouldn't help at all," spoke up Max Weems. "One of his lieutenants would simply take over.''

Amused at Lincolnwell's display of temperament, Weems winked at the Death Merchant who was smiling and thinking that it was for a very good reason that Tensor was known in certain circles as "The Strange One." A career employee in the Company, currently attached to the "OO Office," he was of medium height, almost muscular and appeared awkward, which he wasn't. He had large brown eyes, cinnamon hair combed straight back, and skin of a mahogany hue, the complexion of a man who had lived much of his life in sunshine.

His value to the world of intelligence was three-fold: he was a communications and proprietary information expert; even more so he was a stone killer, on a par with Lester Vernon Cole[13] and Hannibal Llewellyn (H.L.) Kartz[14]—a "blow up machine" who would just as soon ace out a human being as step on a bedbug.

Why Tensor was so strange was that he was an authority on ancient history. He could talk for hours about the Hittites, the Assyrians or the Semitic people of Akkad. Or Egypt. Or the Roman Empire. Or the Mayans or the Incas. He had even written articles for scholarly journals on the probability of the existence of Atlantis[15], the mythical continent that supposedly sank beneath the waves eleven thousand years ago.

At devising weird methods of killing, "The Strange One" was almost the equal of Richard Camellion, who now said soberly, "Max is right. Putting Butler to sleep forever wouldn't stop the KGB in their efforts, nor would it give us any hint of who else might be a traitor in Kordic Micro-Electric Corporation. As things stand now, we're in cold country without any underwear—dead end!"

Catherine McManus stirred sugar in her cup of tea. "Well, we trapped Doctor Revlon," she said to Camellion. "That should give us a few gold stars in our record book, and Company people are watching Jasper Kordic and the nine other executives who have intimate knowledge of the GA-1. And their telephones are tapped. I don't see what else we can do."

"We can stop putting the wagon way out in front of the

[13]See Death Merchant No. 47, *The Night of the Peacock*.
[14]See Death Merchant No. 54 *Apocalypse, U.S.A.!*
[15]See Death Merchant No. 67, *The Atlantean Horror*.

nag, for one thing," Max Weems said. "Let's look at facts. We're only presuming that someone else at Kordic is willing to sell the secret of the GA to the Ruskies. We don't know that anyone else there is a possible traitor. Revlon could have been the only bad apple. Another fact is that only two people know the full process of the GA deal. Jasper Kordic and Burl Martin. Martin is really the key; he designed the GA."

"In that case, what the devil did Revlon have in his attache case?" Tensor cut in sharply. His eyes pounced on the Death Merchant. "I don't see why you couldn't have brought his attache case off the damned boat. At least we could have learned what he was going to sell to the Volga Boatman boys!"

"You know why," Camellion said mildly. "I assumed the police would arrive before I could get off the vessel. I was right. Now wouldn't that have been lovely to have been caught with an attache case full of stolen plans? That would only have been more juicy news for some blabber-mouth of a bluecoat to leak to the press."

"I think you goofed, Camellion," Lincolnwell said wryly. "You should have realized that Max would charge in like a hero in some Grade-B movie—and he did!"

"The trouble with eggheads is that they are always unrealistic in practical matters." Weems turned and sneered at Lincolnwell. "I did what I felt was necessary, and I'd do it again. I have yet to hear of local police arresting a Company man and keeping it a secret."

Tensor fixed his attention on Camellion. "When you emptied Revlon's case onto the bed, you did see some of the papers, and they were schematics, weren't they?"

"They were—for all the good it does," replied the Death Merchant. "I wouldn't know the workouts of the DA-1 from the plans of a 'chip' with a byte[16] that runs your digital watch." His eyes narrowed and he became more serious. "If Doctor Revlon's attache case did contain the plans of the GA-1, we will do well to ask ourselves how he obtained them. There are only three sets of plans, and they're locked in the main vault of Kordic corporation."

---

[16] A computer term. A byte is a group of eight bits used to decode a single letter, number, or symbol.

"Maybe Revlon somehow found a way to photograph the plans?" suggested McManus.

"Let's assume he did," Camellion said. "But that would mean he then turned around and redrew them from the photographs. That wouldn't make sense. All he would've had to do was turn over the photographs to Satan's Gentlemen; and what came out of that attache case wasn't photographs but drawings."

"So we have a mystery, huh?" said Weems.

"Negative," said Camellion. "It means that whatever Revlon was going to sell to the KGB wasn't the plans for the GA-1. At least in theory."

"I don't suppose we can pick up on anything from the murder of Esther Revlon?" commented Baxter Lincolnwell.

"Murder?" Weems said with a little mocking laugh. "According to the coroner's report she died of a 'heart attack'!"

"Yeah, and another strange coincidence is that no one can locate the Sims, the good 'friends' of Dr. and Mrs. Revlon." An ironic smile crept across Max Weems' good looking face. "It's almost as strange as Esther Revlon having a heart attack the same day that Camellion knocked off her husband."

"It only goes to prove how well organized the KGB is," warned the Death Merchant. He put his hands on top of his head, locking his fingers together. "Yuri Andropov had many years to turn the KGB into an efficient intelligence and espionage organization, and he did a very good job. The fact that the KGB had 'illegals' living in the same apartment building as the Revlons proves how well established the ring is in the Silicon Valley."

Automatically, Cathy McManus dunked her tea bag in and out of her cup. "All this is well and good, but none of it explains our next move." She looked across at the Death Merchant. "We don't dare make a move directly against any of the Russian nationals at the Soviet Consulate in San Francisco. Our orders are firm on that. Even the Fox[17] insisted on our leaving them strictly alone."

"The hell with Washington," growled Weems. "They're all a bunch of hypocrites. Look at the bullshit D.C. puts out

---

[17]Courtland Grojean.

about all that damned Mex pouring across the border. We're able to station hundreds of thousands of troops all over the world but can only afford a couple of thousand border patrolmen to stop millions of ignorant trash pouring across our southern borders. Rome went down the drain when it became a socialist state. The U.S. is taking the same stupid route.''

Lincolnwell glanced at Weems, then turned to Camellion. "What about Doctor Martin? Only three Kordic guards are protecting him."

"It's a joke," Tensor said in a rough tone. "The three jokers from Kordic Protection and Security escort Martin to and from his home, and Company men trail all four."

"What's the difference?" said McManus. "The KGB isn't going to bother Martin. They don't want to stink any more than we do."

"But what about when the microprocessor is moved in the armored car?" asked Weems. "One thing about it: hitting an armored car in this day and age isn't easy, not on a crowded highway."

"I still think our next move should be against Dandy Phil Butler," Tensor said quickly and emphatically, fingering his thin mustache. "He's the one non-Russian slob who could tell us the full setup, up to a point, anyhow. Once we had him, we could certainly make the son of a bitch tell everything he knew."

"That's a high voltage turn-on," Weems said. "Hell, he's more guarded than the President, and his boys are probably better at their job than the Secret Service guys who protect Reagan. Another thing, any involving fireworks would bring the police swooping down. That mess at the docks was enough."

"If we're going in that direction, let's keep in mind that there are probably two or three FBI agents watching Butler's night club," McManus said. She suddenly looked as though she were remembering something extremely important. "By the way, did any of you learn how the FBI managed to plant a bug in Butler's office in the House of Pandemonium?"

"Negative," said the Death Merchant. "The Feds told—"

"The FBI always operates as though it were the only agency in the United States," snorted Weems in disgust.

"The FBI told the Company that the information was

51

highly secret," Camellion said. "Mr. G. told me it's all irrelevant, including how Butler and his boys discovered the hidden transmitter. Mr. G. said the information wasn't even LIMDIS[18] with the FBI. The whole nine yards is WNINTEL-NODIS[19], not only with the FBI but with the Company. It doesn't make any real difference, not to us."

"Maybe so, but it still makes you feel left out," Sensor said defiantly, "as though they didn't trust us—both the Feds and the Pickle Factory[20]. And if we knew, it could help us decide what to do next. As it is, we're smack in the middle of nowhere and without a compass."

"No, we are not," Camellion said firmly.

"And why not?" demanded Sensor.

"Because we're going to black bag Dandy Phil," Camellion told the group. "There isn't any directive that said we can't grab him."

"Oh boy," sighed Weems. "Pulling that off will be worse than trying to sell gold bricks in the poverty pocket of a disaster area!"

"Well now, ain't you a caution?" joked Camellion, affecting his best Southern accent. "Grabbin' Butler is the last thing he and the KGB would expect."

"You know, we don't have to put the snatch on him at the House of Pandemonium," said Tensor. "We couldn't anyhow; that would be impossible. We'd better plan the operation around his apartment."

"Oh sure, it's a snap," McManus said placidly. She moved the tip of her tongue slowly over her lower lip, and looked seriously at Camellion. "But you had better use that phony Southern accent to get an army from hominy grits country. Butler is always well guarded."

"We're going to walk right in and walk right out with Butler," Camellion said casually. "There won't be one shot fired."

The other four only stared at the Death Merchant.

[18]Means "limited distribution."
[19]Means that surreptitious means were used to obtain the information and that the information is not for distribution.
[20]Another term for the CIA.

CHAPTER FOUR

A city of hills (43 to be exact, with the one called Twin Peaks being the highest at 900 feet above sea level), San Francisco is 350 miles northwest of Los Angeles and is situated on a stubby peninsula bounded by the Pacific Ocean, San Francisco Bay and the two mile gap of the Golden Gate, where the waters meet.

For various reasons, San Francisco is not like most cities. First of all, it's a provincial place and cannot claim any kind of leadership in anything[1], unless one wants to consider that it has the Bank of America, the largest bank in the world. Or that it possesses Candlestick Park, the windiest baseball stadium in the United States.

Music and theatre are alive in San Francisco, but they are not in the major leagues. Its newspapers are not the best, depending too much on local gossip. In spite of these mediocrities, the city is small enough (its population is less than three-quarters of a million) to function as a true community, all of which is rare in a nation where the concept of the urban neighborhood is nothing more than a myth. This is not the case in San Francisco where urban, and diverse, neighborhoods are the real thing—all of it helped by the hills that divide townscapes and give the inhabitants a sense of "locality."

Market Street, the "main drag," emerges from a busy downtown and, running straight and wide, is a vital artery of commerce. To the right of this long street is the nearest 'Frisco ever gets to being what could be described as an

---

[1] Unofficially it is said that San Francisco has the highest number of male and female homosexuals of any city in the U.S.

53

ordinary city. To the left of Market are the various districts—Nob Hill, Telegraph Hill, Chinatown, North Beach, the Haight district and Fisherman's Wharf.

'Frisco also has its tough section, which is located in the Tenderloin district. Eddy Street is a tangle of wire, signs and outmoded architectural ornaments festooning buildings that contain cheap bars, massage parlors, flop houses, porno shops, movie houses that feature sex films and small hotels that make 99 percent of their profits from prostitutes who need the beds for johns.

The largest entertainment center on Eddy Street was Dandy Phil Butler's House of Pandemonium[2], an enormous one-story brick building on the corner of Eddy and Morrison Streets. Surprisingly the food at the infamous night club was good and the prices reasonable. The place was not a clip joint, nor were girls "in the life"[3] allowed to hustle johns on the premises. But it wasn't the food that attracted tourists and native San Franciscians to the House of Pandemonium. It was the live sex shows on the center stage that featured nude men and women who performed acts of deviation that would have made Havelock Ellis and Dr. Kinsey's mouthes fell open to their knees. Once a week, on Wednesday, there was mud wrestling between naked woman—shapely young women, none under 18 nor over 25.

When the sex shows or the nude wrestling weren't in progress, naked young women (not quite as nude as the day they were born, since they wore high-heeled shoes) gyrated—it was called "dancing"—on nine small, raised circular platforms, all to screaming noise that passed for music.

There was a second story to the building. It was built over the last 63 feet of the rear of the structure and contained Philip Butler's office and six other rooms. Three of the rooms formed the apartment of Huel Moffet, the manager of the night club; the other three rooms were used for general purposes, mostly as meeting rooms for section leaders of Satan's Gentlemen.

The second floor was reached by means of a wide staircase

[2]In mythology, Pandemonium is the capital of Hell.
[3]A term used by prostitutes and pimps, meaning a girl who sells her body for $$$$.

in a hall off the kitchen. There were two sets of stairs on the second floor. One began at the end of the hall in front of Phil Butler's office and terminated in a tiny area in front of a firedoor that opened to the outside. The firedoor was always locked. The top of the second passage started behind a bookcase in Butler's office, led downward, and ended in a six-vehicle garage attached to the rear of the building.

Captain Yuri Kunavin had used the secret stairway to get to Butler's office. As the special assistant to Major Leonid Romashin, the chief of the KGB Otdel at the Soviet Consulate in San Francisco, Kunavin was worried. Using the name of Kurt Gerlich, Kunavin didn't like the way the conference was going. Butler had a mind of his own and the offer of $300,000 in cash didn't seem to impress him.

A tall, blond man, with a perpetual look of distaste on his thickset face, Kunavin wondered if Butler really believed Kunavin was an East German. He tried again to reassure the leader of Satan's Gentlemen.

"In my opinion, three hundred thousand American dollars is a nice sum for kidnaping a man," he said in a businesslike voice. "It isn't as though we were asking you to hit the armored car. As I told you, that project has been canceled as being entirely too dangerous. As you already know, Dr. Martin is guarded by only three plant guards from Kordic Micro-Electric Corporation. However, we must assume that CIA men are following him and the three guards. But for gentlemen of your expertise in these matters, such a project should not offer any insurmountable obstacles. I'm sure you and your men could work out the problems."

Seated behind his desk and dressed in a blue seersucker suit (with white shirt and maroon tie), Butler eyed Kunavin coldly. He had never liked the man whom he suspected of being Russian, and he disliked in particular any person who minimized danger as part of a soft-sell.

"It's easy for you to talk," Butler said in a low, but well-modulated voice. "The worst that can happen to you is that Uncle Sugar will boot you out of the country. Me and my boys can end up in a Federal Penitentiary. Look what happened in Los Angeles! That was another one of your schemes that fell apart. Fortunately, the Gold Rose was heavily insured."

Crossing his legs, Yuri Kunavin tried to appear relaxed in the low-backed Captain's chair. "The episode in Los Angeles was unfortunate," he said gravely. "But don't forget: Dr. Revlon was sent to Los Angeles as a test, to see how closely he was being watched. The plans he carried of those VLSI[4] circuits were not all that important. Eventually, we'll obtain them by other means."

"We found out, didn't we?" Butler said with mock sweetness. He fingered a silver letter opener. "Not only was the CIA, or the FBI, watching Coral Gables, but they managed to trail him all the way north to Los Angeles. When you stop to think of all the traffic and the distance between here and Los Angeles, I'd say it was impossible. But the CIA or the FBI did it. They tailed Dr. Revlon right to the dock, right to the Gold Rose!"

"Nonsense," Kunavin said heatedly, losing patience. *Ya doomayoo chto eto gloopo doveriatsa etoy amerikanskoy motorzykletnoy noy svolotchi; oni khoozhe zhivotnykh!*[5] "The enemy could have used what they refer to as a 'bumper beeper.' It was no doubt one they put into the gas tank and used petrol for fuel." He couldn't resist adding, "We too have sophisticated instruments. It was our detection device that found the enemy transmitter in this very office. It was disguised as a ballpoint pen in one of your lower desk drawers. Your own detection instrument couldn't even find it; ours did. I trust you're still using the 'sweep' device we gave you?"

"Twice a day," Butler said sullenly.

Kunavin tried to sound more cheerful. "As for what happened at the dock in Los Angeles, we gave you an extra two hundred thousand American dollars. That amount, plus your insurance, will give you a profit."

Butler's expression became hard and calculating. "Money can't replace the men who were killed, and Bill Wartz was a damn good friend of mine."

"I'm sorry about the death of your friend," Kunavin said

---

[4]*Very Large Scale Integration*. Integrated circuits containing on the order of 20,000 logic gates, or more than 64,000 bits of memory.

[5]"I think we're foolish to trust American motorcycle trash; why, they're lower than animals!"

with mock sympathy. "But all men must die, and talking about it won't bring him back to life. What we must concern ourselves with now is Doctor Martin. Don't you agree?"

Butler's face remained impassive. The only kind of "agreement" in his sharp mind was that the overall project was not proceeding with the smoothness that he had anticipated. When Butler had organized Satan's Gentlemen in 1971 he had done the unexpected and it had worked. Instead of toughness, bizarre clothing and verbal filth, Butler and his group had used politeness, cleanliness, and exemplary speech that was worthy of imitation. Citizens were treated with the same respect a Boy Scout would give to a granny or a blind man. There was never any roughhousing or profanity in restaurants and roadside cafes. The rules of the road were scrupulously observed. Members didn't resemble slobs from a slime pit. There weren't any steel helmets, dangling swastikas, painted skulls or other weird ornamentations. Satan's Gentlemen didn't wear a single emblem on their uniforms of red pants, red shirt, black boots and black leather jackets.

There was another firm rule: each member had to study karate on a professional basis, i.e. take lessons from a qualified black belt instructor.

Another deviation from the average motorcycle gang was that the Gentlemen didn't have women ride with them. There weren't any "old ladies" on the buddy seats.

By 1973, Satan's Gentlemen had grown to 562 members. During August of the same year, Butler and his gentlemanly mob had their first serious confrontation with the notorious Hell's Angels. The Angels were promptly demolished, for brawn and brute strength is never a match for people trained in the martial arts. The Gentlemen than proceeded to smash the Hondas, Suzukis, Kawasakis and other machines of the Angels.

That first clash between the Gentlemen and the Angels was only the beginning. Almost always the Angels lost . . . weeks in the hospital their only reward. The Hell's Angels really started to get the message when four of their number were found with railroad spikes driven literally through the top of their skulls.

57

In only one week, four "old ladies" of the Angels were blinded by acid thrown into their faces.

The headquarters of the Angels in Los Angeles was burned.

In January of 1975, two Angels were found in the Puente Hills, east of Los Angeles. They had been tied to trees, doused with gasoline and turned into human torches.

In April of 1976, the head of Dirty Sam Mongus, one of the top men in the Angels, was found in a hatbox on a bench in San Francisco's Golden Gate Recreation Area. During the same month, two other Angels were found in 'Frisco's Buena Vista Park. They had been castrated and their eyeballs removed.

The police, who knew the Gentlemen for what they really were, were helpless. There wasn't any evidence that would stand up in court.

The public—always selfish because it has to be—couldn't have cared less. Hell's Angels were a disgrace to the human race—and weren't Satan's Gentlemen always polite and helpful? A motorist could always count on them for assistance. Owners of amusement establishments and restaurants, etc., were actually glad to see a mob of them arrive, not only because they kept order and were mannerly but because they were liberal spenders and generous tippers. And who donated free food to the poor and the needy? Satan's Gentlemen, that's who.

By 1978 Hell's Angels were as rare in the San Francisco area as boa constrictors at the North Pole. Even in Los Angeles and its suburbs the Angels traveled only in large numbers. Los Angeles was their home turf, but even in that sprawling mess they avoided the deadly Satan's Gentlemen.

By 1981 Satan's Gentlemen had grown to 2,014 in California and had chapters in Arizona, Nevada, Colorado and, strangely enough, Maine. By this time, too, they were also heavily into drugs, prostitution, "chop shops"[6], gambling and other illegal activities.

In 1982, Phil Butler and his aides began another operation: the stealing of silicon semiconductors and chips from the various firms in Silicon Valley. They often stole from one

[6]Where cars are "chopped" apart and the parts resold. As common as smog in any large area.

company and fenced the merchandise to another firm, or else sold the gold from the devices.

The KGB had learned about the activities of the Gentlemen in Silicon Valley when they sold a truckload of masks[7] and transistors to Willis Colturvane, the owner of Big Green Mountain Outdoor Supply Company, Inc., who had sold them to the Russians.

Thinking about the previous years and the fantastic success he had had with Satan's Gentlemen, Butler knew he would be finished if he made a single mistake, a single wrong decision at this stage of the game. Business was bad enough. Already the State and Federal drug agencies were making operations so risky that he had been forced to cancel six shipments of cocaine. Even small air fields in Arizona were watched constantly. It was this stoppage of drugs that cut sharply into profits. At $2,600 per ounce of coke—damn it—hundreds of thousands of dollars per month were being lost from Silicon Valley alone[8]. The IRS was constantly snooping and so was the CBI[9]. Because of the thefts from firms in Silicon Valley, the goddamn FBI was investigating the Gentlemen. Even worse, because of these East Germans—*or could the sons of bitches be Russian agents? Who gives a damn!*—the CIA was in the act.

Butler did give the East Germans a lot of credit. They couldn't steal the precious microprocessor they were after, so they were going to kidnap the inventor of the device. Pretty slick. Except that they wanted Satan's Gentlemen to do the job.

"Mr. Butler, I said we should concern ourselves with Dr. Burl Martin," Yuri Kunavin said firmly.

Butler put down the letter opener. "We take all the risks and you and your people reap all the rewards."

"You're forgetting the $300,000," Kunavin said with apprehension, "and all of it tax-free. It would seem to me that—"

---

[7]A glass photographic plate that contains the circuit pattern used in the silicon-chip fabrication process.

[8]Authorities estimate that high-paid executives in Silicon Valley consume a ton of coke a year. As far as the big shots in SV are concerned, marijuana is for the common "street people."

[9]The California Bureau of Investigation.

"It seems to me that one million in cash would be a better figure," Butler said unctuously, enjoying the look of dismay on Kunavin's face. "Another thing. This time I want to deal with your boss. This time he can personally deliver the money."

Trained as he was, Kunavin couldn't quite hide his astonishment.

"One million dollars!" he gasped. "That's ridiculous!"

"Not for the risk involved," insisted Butler, "not when the enemy is the Central Intelligence Agency. The price is one million. Take it or leave it. And that's only on condition that my Board of Imps agree to the project."

"I'll have to discuss the matter with my superiors," Kunavin said warily. "I don't have the authority to make such a decision."

"Do that," Butler said venomously, staring hard at the uncomfortable KGB officer. "But you can tell them that the million is not open to negotiation, and it must be delivered by your boss. He's to plan the job with me."

"Why?" Kunavin was all caution and curiosity. "Why is that stipulation so important?"

"I want them in this with me," Butler said, almost glowering. "Let them take some of the risks for a change, even if all that can happen to them is getting kicked out of the country."

Kunavin stood up. "I'll convey your conditions to my superiors," he said stiffly, straightening his jacket. "It might be several days before I can give you an answer."

"Good enough. Now get the hell out of here, and I'll discuss the deal with some of my boys . . ."

Without as much as a "Good Evening," Yuri Kunavin headed for the tall, wide bookcase on the east side of the room. In a few moments he was gone and the bookcase silently swang back into position.

Butler leaned back in his swivel chair and, thinking about the kidnap job, let his eyes roam over his office. The chandelier in the center of the room was shaped like the wheel of a ship and made of polished mahogany. From the wheel hung three frosted glass lanterns.

On one wall was a solid brass striking clock; next to it was a solid brass barometer. On shelves, here and there on the walls, were large models of clipper ships—the Cutty Sark, the Thermopylae, and the Golden Hind.

On a table was a scaled-down polished copper diver's helmet. On one corner of Butler's desk was a 15″ long model of the tugboat Despatch. On the other front corner was a model of the whale ship, the Charles W. Morgan.

Butler loved his office; he didn't intend to lose it. He reached for the intercom next to the Charles W. Morgan and pressed one of the buttons that would ring the phone at Section One downstairs. Presently, a voice came from the speaker:

"Yeah, this is Maple."

"Cal, find Oscar and Vic and come up here," Butler said. "Make it fast; it's important."

"Right."

Butler pressed the button that would ring the phone in the office of Huel Moffet.

"What's up, Phil?" said Moffet.

"I'll tell you when you get here," Butler said. He switched off the intercom, leaned back in the swivel chair and toyed with the idea of blaming the kidnaping of Burl Martin on Hell's Angels. No, it wouldn't work. Trying to put the blame on the Angels might make the whole damn deal backfire. The Angels were so disorganized that even a rookie cop would see through the frame, and that frame would lead straight to the Gentlemen. Better to play it straight. Kidnap Martin and then break off all contact with the East Germans.

That was Butler's biggest worry. Could he break away from the East Germans? Would they agree to it? Or pretend to agree—

And then get even?

CHAPTER FIVE

If behind every successful man stands a surprised mother-in-law, then behind every successful intelligence operation stands long hours of meticulous planning, the measuring of life's odds and . . . pure luck. Having planned for every possibility in detail, the Death Merchant reviewed the general overall plan as Max Weems expertly turned the Mercury Cougar off Geary Expressway on to Fillmore Street. Thus far, the schedule was perfect; they should arrive at the House of Pandemonium no later than 21.00 hours—nine o'clock P.M.

The watch was effective. Company men, watching both the front and the rear of the nightclub, were reporting every ten minutes by radio to Stringbean-10Y, and Stringbean-10Y was relaying the reports to Camellion and Weems and Tensor in the Mercury and to Cathy McManus and the two other CIA men in the box-van that, with the extra-large rear compartment, was trailing a mile behind the Mercury with Camellion and his two companions.

From the rear seat of the souped-up vehicle—*I hope we don't have to destroy it!*—Camellion reflectively watched the lights of other vehicles sweep past the Mercury. The night was hot and a summer storm was threatening, distant thunder growling every now and then from the west.

"Max, give me the estimated distance," Camellion said.

Weems halted for a red light. "I'd say about half an hour by the time we get to the club, park and get inside," he said. He added laconically, "I still say this nutty scheme isn't going to work. Suppose Butler wants to phone his attorney before we haul his ass out of there?"

"Let him," said Joseph Tensor who, in the front seat, was

62

watching oncoming traffic. "His mouthpiece will rush downtown to the Federal Building, only we won't be there."

"The only thing we have to worry about is the flak we'll get from the home office, when the FBI in D.C. raises a protest over the impersonations. Grojean and the others at C.S. will get a kick out of it. They have always considered the F.B.I. too arrogant in matters of national security."

"Yeah, I like the FBI jerks about as much as I love this damned city," Tensor said, sounding as if he were tasting something bitter. "This damned town is so full of perverts that they even have a 'Hooker's Ball' in October of each year—all for whores and homos. I think it was started by some fruitcake group called COYOTE. I'd machine-gun every one of them!"

Weems gave a tiny, amused laugh. "I don't mind prostitutes. I've known quite a few in my time. I don't mind queers either—male or female—as long as they're in the middle of the Pacific Ocean."

The A-7 surveillance receiver, on the seat next to Camellion, buzzed. The Death Merchant flipped the ON switch, turned on the SR-22 attached to the receiver, picked up the mike on its coiled cord and said, "Yes, this is Samson."

"This is Delilah," the voice came from the small speaker in the A-7. "The target is still there. His car is still parked in the rear parking lot of Hell. Any instructions? Over."

"Negative. Send the next report on schedule." Camellion switched off the A-7 and the SR-22. Sophisticated equipment could pick up broadcasts beamed to the A-7 receiver, since it covered a range of 5MHz to 1.5GHz, but not with a Transvertex SR-22 cipher box attached to the set that was doing the sending and the set that was picking up the message.

The Transvertex SR-22 was a cipher box whose speech signal was digitalized and enciphered by adding a pseudorandom pulse series, usually known as a superimposition series. The same superimposition series was added for deciphering, after which the signal was converted back into normal speech. The superimposition series was controlled by the actual key setting that could be altered only by the operator and was therefore known only to him. Designed for use in radio and radio link communications, the SR-22 was invaluable in VHF and higher frequency ranges. It could also be used on local telephone lines (up to 72km) by means of the SRL-12 adaptor.

The Death Merchant looked at his Heuer wristwatch. "Max, we had better slow down, or go around the block and let Cathy and her two guys pass us. We want her and Frank inside at a table or booth before we go in. We can't park in one of the lots and remain inside the car. We'd draw attention from the guards posted to watch customers' cars."

"I can't slow down too much," Weems said. "How about pulling in to some fast-food joint and having a sandwich?"

"You mean a glass of water," laughed Tensor. "That's all we'd have time for."

"I've a better idea," suggested Camellion. "Once you reach Market, turn off on some side street, park, and we'll pretend we have engine trouble."

"And if cruising cops stop and want to be helpful?" asked Tensor. "But then again, we are FBI agents with credentials to prove it."

Camellion turned on the A-7 and the SR-22 and contacted Anthony Larocca, one of the Company's "on-contract" agents riding in the box-van.

"We're going to park for about ten minutes," Camellion told the security specialist. "That will give your group time to pass us, get to the club and get inside. If anything goes wrong, at the sound of the first shot, make sure Cathy lets go with the stuff in her shoulder bag. Over."

"Riiiight. I know! We should try to park in the front parking lot," replied Larocca in a very deep voice. Over."

"You got it. It's a lot easier to get onto Eddy than make a get on Morrison. Out."

Weems had soon turned onto Market Street and the Mercury headed northeast toward the Tenderloin district. They were passing City Hall and the Civic Center when Weems muttered, "Seventh Street is just ahead. I'll make a left on Seventh and park."

There wasn't any difficulty after Weems pulled onto Seventh, got out, raised the hood, then lighted a Players cigarette and glanced at his wristwatch. There weren't any helpful police. Not a single motorist stopped to offer assistance, and for good reason: the Mercury was parked too near the Tenderloin.

Several minutes after Weems had parked, seven tough-looking blacks came ambling down the street. They slowed when they saw the Mercury. They quickened their pace when Weems pulled a Heckler and Koch 9mm P9S autopistol, scratched the side of his cheek with the muzzle and grinned a direct warning. The black toughs got the message—don't mess around with these honkies and their wheels.

A short time later, the Mercury was back on Market Street and moving slowly through the Tenderloin district, the only area where San Francisco fell short of its normal high standards of visual appeal. The spirit that made the city sing was lacking in the Tenderloin. There was, however, a kind of robust life that animated the sleazy streets in the district, but that vitality—in the porn shops, the nude encounter parlors, the cheap bars, the peep shows and the cockroach haven hotels—seemed to be directed more toward hope than anything else. The real sadness about the Tenderloin was that a large percentage of its regulars would never have a job; they would never earn anything at all. They were people who, having failed at everything, had come to San Francisco with nothing but hope. Many of them were elderly and malnourished. Most lived in single rooms or filthy flophouses which should have been closed. They were permitted to remain open because City Hall wanted to contain the misery. After all, if things got too bad and life became totally hopeless, there was always the Golden Gate Bridge from which one could take a dive and end it all.[1]

Everywhere there were neon lights and signs of all colors, shapes and sizes, and people of all colors, shapes and sizes—and ages. The prostitutes were there, walking their beats, their cheeks too crudely crimsoned, their eyes too hard for their ages, all of them moving as though they were puppets; yet they were no worse than their higher-priced sisters, the

[1]Once on an average of every 11 days someone kills himself in the Tenderloin. Most don't even leave a note, for there is no one who cares.

65

two-hundred-dollars-a-night girls who worked through bell-hops at the swank hotels. No worse morally. But the doxies of the Tenderloin were 100 percent more likely to roll a john (johns who also had a 100 percent greater chance of picking up VD from one of the sluts).

At length, a frustrated Max Weems turned the blue Mercury into the huge front parking lot of the House of Pandemonium.

"Shit, I don't see the van," Tensor said levelly. "The van had to get here ahead of us."

"No wonder you don't see it," Weems remarked. "The front parking section is full. I don't get it. Tuesday is supposed to be a poor night for this joint."

"It's not all that important," interjected the Death Merchant, who had just finished talking to Stringbean-10Y and was already feeling that he was about to move blindfolded through a nest of man-eaters. "If we can't have the imported stuff, we'll settle for the domestic variety. So we park in the rear lot."

"We have no choice," Weems said. "See what I see?"

The Death Merchant saw. A big man, with a large mustache and a shaven head, and wearing red jeans and a red shirt, was waving Weems forward with a large five-cell flashlight, directing Weems to go to the right, around the building, and to the parking lot in the rear.

"I'd love to put a hollowpoint into the gut of that slob," mumbled Tensor as Weems swung the Mercury to the right.

Weems made amused sounds. "I thought poison was your bag, Joe."

"It is, but only on special jobs," Tensor said. "That's why I came to 'Frisco several years ago. I put one guy to sleep with Nitrobenzene. It's an inhalation and ingestion poison. A hundred mgs—about two drops—is fatal to the target in a matter of minutes. I terminated the other mark with home-made phosgene. Both projects went off as slick as a frog's wet butt."

"You just might get the chance to ace out that big lummox back there," Weems said, turning the wheel. "Nothing has gone right. Can either of you guys imagine why the Pickle

66

Factory station in L.A. didn't have smoke or stink bombs? I admit there aren't many calls for such items. Luckily for us, Camellion back there is a do-it-yourself chemist.''

"There's the van," Camellion said, relief in his voice. "At least it's in a good position to pull out onto Morrison. If it comes to that.''

Tensor and Weems saw that the box-van was parked next to a large space over which hung a sign that read RESERVED FOR SATAN'S GENTLEMEN. POSITIVELY NO PARKING IN THIS AREA. Fourteen motorcycles were in the reserved space.

The van had aluminum-framed portholes—two on each side—and had to be the most fantastically decorated vehicle in all of San Francisco—at least the murals on each side were. They were unbelievable. Frank Flavelton, the other on-contract man with Cathy, had once been a commercial artist and had created an air-brush masterpiece. He had illustrated crashing waves, waterfalls, a lighthouse, planets, a moonscape, an out-of-this-world sunset and a corpse with an enormous penis. From the gigantic ding-dong protruded an American flag. Flavelton had executed the entire job with a special paint that could easily be washed off with the water from an ordinary garden hose.

"There's space on the other side of the reserved area, to our left," Camellion said. "Use it."

Slowing the vehicle, Weems objected. "What the hell! That will put us almost in the corner. Why not some of the empty spaces toward the center?"

"We could be hemmed in by other cars too easily in the center," Camellion explained. "But we could ram through the board fence if it came to that. Park there."

Muttering under his breath, Max turned the wheel and drove the Mercury to the left, finally parking it between a white Saab and a cream and brown Dodge Mini-Ram Wagon. Automatically the three men checked their weapons in the shoulder holsters under their specially tailored suit coats.

Until J. Edgar Hoover had died, agents of the Federal Bureau of Investigation had worn what had amounted to a uniform—conservative dark suits, white shirts, dark ties, dark

67

shoes, dark hats. Positively no sport clothes. After J. Edgar had gone to his reward, regulations had relaxed and agents of the Bureau could wear anything they wanted, as long as they didn't look like Godzilla.

For this kind of operation, however, the Death Merchant preferred suits. He was dressed in a lightweight charcoal gray suit, Weems in a navy chalk stripe, and Tensor in a three-button poplin deal. Shoes and hats to match.

The Death Merchant, who had placed the A-7 and the SR-22 on the floor in front of the rear seat, made final contact with the van. He leaned low as he spoke into the mike and turned down the volume of the transceiver.

"Give me a full report," he said to Frank Flavelton who had remained behind in the van, not only to watch the vehicle and its contents but to monitor Cathy McManus and Tony Larocca, both of whom were wired with tiny TS transmitters taped to their chests, Cathy's between her breasts.

"All went as scheduled," Flavelton said. "Cathy and Tony went inside exactly six minutes ago. If anything goes wrong, we've enough stuff in here to confuse the whole goddamn police force and then some."

"Make sure you keep the portholes blacked out," Camellion said. "We're going in now to get Butler. Watch yourself—over."

"You're the ones who had better take care. You have to go inside and get the son of a bitch. Anything else?"

"Nothing," Camellion said and switched off the A-7 and the SR-22. He then reached under the rear seat, toward the center, and switched on the special double-time-relay detonator connected to the half-pound block of RDX.

Weems turned around in the seat and smiled at Camellion, "I trust you haven't forgotten the warrant?"

The rear parking lot was as brilliantly lighted as the front area, and the Death Merchant and his two companions soon saw the steel door at the bottom of the stairs to the second floor, it was to the left of a long garage built onto the rear of the main building. The three double doors of the garage were closed.

"We could save time by knocking on the steel door," Sensor said lightly. "That would make the hoods in the rear lot suspicious. So far I've spotted five of them."

Weems and Camellion were aware that Sensor was joking, but neither thought his remark the least bit humorous. In theory, the arrest of Philip Butler should go off as planned. He was too professional to resist arrest, preferring to make a fool of the law by using the best criminal lawyer available; in Butler's case the attorney was Neil S. Ware, of the law firm of Ware, Davis, Hogwirth and Blomburg.

No . . . there shouldn't be a problem. . . .

But there was always that first time. . . .

There was always Factor-X. . . .

"Sure, Joe. We could walk right up to that steel door," said Weems in a lazy manner. "But whoever heard of Feds going to the rear door?"

"Dandy Phil's an honest man," mocked the Death Merchant. "He wants the cars of his customers protected. In this area, cars would be stripped to their frames within minutes if guards weren't roaming about on the parking lots."

Tensor said, "What I find so paradoxical is that this disaster area is only a short distance from Nob Hill. Of course, the Hill's no longer the truly ritzy section of this town. Most of the swells now live in Pacific Heights."

The Death Merchant wasn't concerned with the proximity of the Tenderloin to Nob Hill. His full attention was on the House of Pandemonium. A sickness to any normal eye, the building was painted a fire engine red, the flat roof of overlapping tile a flat but vivid black. In front was the wide entrance, which appeared to be an open mouth of the devil, but was actually the double doors opening in a face hideously and vividly painted on the building. There were no windows.

All young and shapely, the waitresses were clad in scanty red halters and very brief bikinis. Each wore a pair of felt horns attached to the top of her head by means of an elastic band that fitted behind the ears and rested snugly under the chin.

After Catherine McManus and Tony Larocca had paid the $10.00 cover charge at the door, a near-naked waitress escorted them to a north side table some distance from the center stage where three heterosexual couples were engaged in sexual acts. A black couple and a white couple were performing sexual intercourse, each using a different position while an oriental couple was performing an oral act, the woman fellating the man.

Cathy and Tony pretended to be half-drunk. Adding to the role they were playing was the way they were dressed. Cathy wore a silver pant suit that had a large hole cut in the abdominal region revealing her navel. If the hole had been a few inches wider, some of her pubic hairs would have been revealed. High-heeled gold boots completed her outfit—and a large silver shoulder bag.

Larocca, a short, well-muscled man with twice as much black curly hair as he needed, had never felt more foolish in his 31 years. He was decked out in blue and black checkboard pants, a pink shirt with flared sleeves and gray Western boots with pointy toes. He also carried a small gray shoulder bag that he swung around on its strap and placed in his lap after whispering "Two Bloody Marys" to the bored waitress— whispered because, in spite of the several hundred suckers present in the enormous room, one could have heard a feather fall on the floor. There wasn't any music, nor were the patrons engaging in conversation or drunken banter; instead, they were goggle-eying the three naked couples on stage with their mouths half open (some of the men were even fondling the breasts of their dates who didn't seem to mind). Cathy and Tony, both embarrassed, avoided each others' eyes.

The only sounds consisted of heavy breathing and the click of cameras, another reason why the House Of Pandemonium was so popular: cameras were permitted. People could take all the photographs they wanted of the various sex acts— "It's good for the jackoff trade," Butler was fond of saying.

Cathy, having placed her large shoulder bag under the table, wondered if Richard Camellion's chemistry was accurate. But, she hoped the stink bombs and the smoke bombs wouldn't be needed. She was positive of one thing: the

70

House of Pandemonium was the most fantastic place she had ever seen in her life. She had to admire the decor: The glass walls had been painted with enormous flames (with a devil and a pitchfork here and there). Flashing lights behind the glass made the flames appear to be real, to be leaping and moving.

"The others should be here in a short time," Cathy whispered to Larocca, who nodded slowly, his left hand unzipping half of the shoulder bag in his lap. The bag contained two Smith & Wesson M-469 nine-millimeter autopistols, four spare magazines for each weapon, and a remote control device.

A hard-faced man stepped forward as the Death Merchant, Weems and Tensor entered the House of Pandemonium.

"Good evening gentlemen," the man said in a too-friendly tone with a too-friendly smile. "There is a cover charge of five dollars per person. You pay the young lady behind the cash register."

"We're Federal agents," Camellion said in a no-nonsense voice. He reached inside his coat and pulled out a leather identification case. He flipped open the case and thrust it under the face of the man who stopped smiling and stared at the gold badge on which was printed *Federal Bureau of Investigation*. On the other side of the ID case, under the plastic, was the Death Merchant's photograph and other vitals, such as height, weight, etc. At least the photograph in the case matched the face Camellion was wearing, just as the photographs in the IDS of Weems and Tensor matched the results of the makeup job Camellion had performed on them.

Camellion—"Henry L. Ward"—pulled back the case. "Where can we find Mr. Butler?" he asked the man. "We know he's on the premises."

"Mr. Butler is in his office," the man said calmly, without the least trace of nervousness. "You go straight and—"

"We know where it is," Camellion said, business-like.

Grim-faced, he turned away and headed for the main section of the night club, Weems and Tensor behind him. The hood who had greeted them gave them a long look, then hurried to a house phone on the wall.

Barely noticing the three couples engaged in sex on the stage, Camellion, Tensor and Weems threaded their way purposefully through tables and headed toward the north/south hallway between the kitchen and the dressing rooms of the waitresses, the "actors" who performed on the stage and the go-go dancers who wriggled and shook their milk bars at moronic customers.

Having crossed the large area, Camellion, Weems and Tensor entered the hall and instantly found their way blocked by two creeps built like miniature Mack trucks.

"You guys are mixed up," Otis Anderson said easily. He put his hands on his hips and eyed Camellion up and down. "The restrooms are on the other side, to your left."

Roy Gomoll, the other Satan's Gentleman, who had a face like a concrete mixer, moved in closer, ready for trouble.

"We're agents of the FBI," Camellion said, staring coldly at Anderson who now looked surprised and a bit confused. Again Camellion produced his badge case, opened it and showed it to Anderson who took a long look at the photograph, then fixed his eyes for several moments on Camellion.

Tensor added, "We're here to see your boss. If you try to stop us, you might get off with a five year sentence."

"You Feds never stop tryin', do you?" sneered Anderson, backing off. "Hell, no, we ain't goin' to try and stop you. You guys ain't got nothin' on Phil."

"Yeah, be our guests," Gomoll said sullenly and waved his right hand toward the stairs. "If you want to make fools of yourselves that's OK with us. Phil's in his office at the end of the hall."

"Have a drink of rat poison on us," Camellion said pleasantly. Turning, he started toward the steps down the hall. Weems, glaring at both hoods, followed. Then came Tensor, but not before he had patted an angry Roy Gomoll on the cheek and said, "I'm looking forward to the time when we get you to the Federal Building downtown."

Halfway up the stairs, Weems whispered to Camellion and

Tensor, "We can count on Butler's knowing we're coming. The crud at the door had to have tipped him."

"Yeah, we can count on it," Tensor said.

The Death Merchant knew there were seven rooms on the second floor. He had seen the blueprints of the building the CIA had obtained from the Permits & Building Construction Department of the City of San Francisco; and he knew from the CIA and the FBI that Butler's office was at the end of the hall shaped like the letter L. It was the last room at the top of the L. What he didn't know was the layout of the other six rooms.

The top of the stairs was at the bottom of the L, in the section of hall situated in an east/west direction. North of the bottom of the horizontal section of the L were four rooms, three of which were the apartment of Huel Moffet, with the living room being Moffet's office. This office also contained a four foot wide space that was hidden behind the east wall. That space contained files relating to various illegal activities.

The fourth room was a one-room apartment used now and then for a Satan's Gentleman being sought by the police.

All four of these rooms were on the east side of the hall that was the long perpendicular section of the L. This lengthy section was laid out from south to north. On the west side of the hall were three rooms. The first room, to the south, was a meeting room; so was the room north of it. The third and last room, at the top of the L, was Dandy Phil Butler's office.

All the rooms were empty except the one-room apartment, Butler's office, and the center room west of the hall, the meeting room south of Dandy Phil's office.

Galen Evinhouse, wanted by the Phoenix police for assault with intent to murder, was in the one-room apartment, drinking vodka, watching television and cursing his bad luck.

In contrast, Jasper "Little Man" Powell, one of Butler's bodyguards, could hardly believe his good fortune. For two months he had been doing his best to get to the precious treasure under Susan Davalle's bikini, but she had refused until tonight.

Naked and doing what comes naturally, Little Man and China Sue (she was called "China Sue" because of the oriental cast to her large brown eyes) were on one of the tables, he pumping away furiously, she squirming beneath him and crying our hoarsely, "Harder, honey. Do me harder!"

Little Man was having second thoughts, wondering what he had gotten himself into. He had not earned his nickname because he was small in stature but because he had a high-pitched voice which did not fit his 200 pound frame; and while he wasn't a King Kong in the sexual apparatus department, he wasn't a Wee Willie Winkle either. Yet all he had heard for the past few minutes from China Sue was "Harder! Harder!"

Never missing a stroke, Little Man gasped, "If I do it any harder, we'll break this damned table and probably go through the floor!"

Richard Camellion only had to tap once on Dandy Phil's door. Immediately the door was opened by Victor Denser, a tall, slender man with cat-yellow eyes and a perpetual sneer on his slash of a mouth. He didn't say "Come in." He didn't have to. "Henry L. Ward" strode into the office. Weems and Tensor took a position on either side of him as Denser closed the door, then sat back down in the captain's chair to the right of the door.

In an instant, Camellion and the two other "FBI agents" had sized up the layout in the office. Two men were relaxed on a couch to the left, a couch shaped somewhat like a bunk aboard ship. One joker had an enormous mustache like the horns of a water buffalo; the other creep was broad, with hair like Brillo, and sleepy brown eyes.

Two other goons were seated to the right. One was the tall gunman who had opened the office door. The other hood, also sprawled out in a captain's chair close to the north wall, was so thickset he bordered on being fat. Cruel-looking, his eyes were frosty next to his suntanned skin.

The Death Merchant took out his ID case, flipped it open and shoved it toward an amused Dandy Phil who was hunched forward, his arms on his desk.

"You are Philip Harley Butler," Camellion stated, then pulled back the ID case from Butler who had hardly glanced at the genuine Bureau badge. (Camellion also noticed something about the model of the Charles W. Morgan on the corner of Butler's desk—*The mizzen skysail has not been strung properly!*)

Dandy Phil grinned crookedly. "Cut the bullshit. You know damn well I'm Butler. Now what the hell do you want? I'm busy, and you guys are stinking up my office."

"Mr. Butler, we have a warrant for your arrest," Camellion said mechanically. "You have the right to remain silent. However, should you choose to speak, anything you say may be used against you in a court of law. If you do not have an attorney, the court will appoint one for you. Do you understand what I have said, Mr. Butler?"

Butler's eyes widened in surprise. The four other mobsters in the room stiffened. A warrant for Dandy Phil's arrest! This was a turn of events that was totally unexpected.

"You had damn well better believe I choose to speak!" snarled Butler, who jumped to his feet and glared at the Death Merchant. "What the hell am I charged with?"

"The charge is being an accessory to the theft of semiconductors from the Dermotox Corporation of Santa Clara, California," Camellion said matter-of-factly.

"It's a goddamned frame!" raged Butler. "I've never heard of the—let me see that damned warrant. I have a right to read it! It's the law."

"Of course," Camellion said politely and handed the warrant to Butler who began to read it. Everything was in order—so it appeared. The warrant was dated for that very day and was signed by U.S. Commissioner John Evan Banes of San Francisco. What stung Butler and instilled fear in him were the words: *Philip Harley Butler Vs The People of the United States.*

A clever man who never overlooked anything, if he could help it, Butler began to open the warrant, which was actually one large sheet of thick paper folded in the proper places.

The Death Merchant knew that all was not going as planned—and Weems and Tensor shifted uneasily—when Butler, having unfolded the Warrant, held it up to the light of the three frosted glass lanterns hanging from the shipwheel chandelier.

Camellion knew what Butler was doing; so did Weems and Tensor.

Who would have thought the mobster was that cautious, but he was. He was looking for the *United States Department of Justice* watermark.

There isn't any watermark! Camellion thought with regret. There hadn't been time to obtain genuine Government paper.

Or maybe Butler is merely the curious type! I hope!

"Mr. Butler, you are under arrest. You will have to come with us to the Federal Building," Camellion said. On full alert now, he watched Butler and, from the corners of his eyes, the other four hoods.

"I'm allowed one phone call," Butler said half-angrily, starting to refold the warrant along its proper creases. "That's the law. I want to phone my attorney right now."

"Go ahead," Camellion said. "Here or at the Federal Building, it doesn't make any difference. Of course, you will be permitted to post bail."

Butler returned the warrant to Camellion and sat down in his swivel chair. He was reaching for the cordless Muraphone on his desk when he suddenly threw himself to the left and yelled, "GET THEM! THEY'RE NOT FBI! THEY'RE IMPOSTERS!"

The Death Merchant could almost hear Max Weems' thoughts screaming at him.

When this is over, if Max says "I told you so!" I'll kill him!

CHAPTER SIX

That certain kind of time (or rather the lack of it) that favors one opponent over another is often the difference between Life and Death. It's called lag-time, and in this instance it was on the side of Richard Camellion and his two men. To begin with, they had been expecting trouble. They had prepared for it even more when they saw Dandy Phil inspecting the forged arrest warrant.

Butler's four men were not as lucky. Dandy Phil's unexpected warning had taken them totally by surprise. It was during this microfraction of a moment that the Death Merchant and his two little helpers made their move, all three knowing that the operation had failed.

While Dandy Phil, down on his knees behind the desk, tried to open the middle drawer and pull out a 9mm Model-92SB autopistol and his four goons frantically searched for their own weapons, Camellion jerked backward, his right hand streaking for the Safari Arms Black Widow in its left shoulder holster. With almost equal speed, Max Weems and Joe Tensor reached for their own lifesavers nestled in leather.

It would have taken a high-speed camera to record the incredible swiftness with which the Death Merchant had the Black Widow in his hand, was tumbling off the safety and swinging the big nickel-plated weapon toward the desk. He had guessed that when Dandy Phil had dropped, he would reach for a piece, and he had guessed right.

Crouched low, Phil had pulled open the drawer a foot and was about to reach inside for the Beretta when Camellion's Black Widow roared, the crushing explosion of the cartridge crashing against the walls. The Death Merchant had snap-aimed at the center edge of the rear of the desk and the hardball bullet had gone where it was supposed to. It struck the edge of the glass-topped desk, tore downward at a steep angle, blew apart a roll of Scotch tape in the center drawer and narrowly missed the right side of Dandy Phil's left hand. The projectile zipped between his arm and the left side of his body, went through the rug and buried itself in the floor. Dandy Phil was too battle-wise to make a second attempt. He dropped flat and waited to see what would happen. He soon found out.

No one outside the room had heard the shot. The office was soundproof. Anyone standing in the hall could have heard a muffled boom from the Black Widow. But no one had been in the hall.

Joe Tensor, jerking out one of his snubnosed .44 AST Ruger revolvers with his right hand, was the first to reach the office door and jerk it open at about the same time that Calvin Maple—the hood with the sleepy eyes—had managed to pull his Smith & Wesson M-38 "Bodyguard" revolver from his right rear pocket and was bringing it up.

Across the room, Huel Moffet, the fat slob who had been in the captain's chair, was throwing himself and the chair to his right and swinging up a Llama .45 auto in Camellion's direction.

Victor Densor, the gunman who had opened the door, had instantly jerked himself backward in his chair when Dandy Phil shouted the warning. He was on the floor, struggling to pull a Walther P-38 from a right side shoulder holster.

Oscar Langrehr, the other man on the couch, had thrown himself to his right, against the arm of the bunk couch and was trying to pull a Star PD .45 autopistol from a left side pancake holster on his belt.

Instinct told the Death Merchant that Moffet was the most dangerous at the moment. Camellion ducked to his right and fired, Moffet's Llama .45 pistol going off in the same second. Camellion's 230 grain FMC slug slammed into Moffet's chest, into the center of his sternum, the contact of bullet with flesh shoving the hood back and he fell the rest of the way to the floor with the chair.

Moffet had fired at an upward angle. His .45 bullet missed the Death Merchant's left shoulder and skimmed in front of

Max Weems who triggered one of his Coonan Magnum pistols while the echoes of Moffet and Camellion's shots were still ringing; this time the firing was heard outside the office—Tensor had opened the door—all the way down to the main floor, although at the time the majority of the patrons weren't quite sure what they had heard.

But Jasper "Little Man" Powell was sure! He was positive. He pulled out of a sweaty China Sue, who sat up, blinked and said, "That sounded like shots."

"They was, you dumb broad!" Little Man said angrily, reaching for his shorts. "Get your clothes on and keep away from the door."

Galen Evinhouse, in the one-room apartment east of the north/south hall, had also heard the shots. He didn't shut off the TV. He got up, went to a suitcase, opened it, and took out a KG-99 assault pistol that resembled a cross between a submachine gun and a laser pistol. The weapon was actually a semi-automatic assault pistol with a magazine that held 36 9mm rounds. Evinhouse crept to the door and waited.

Downstairs, Cathy McManus leaned toward Tony Larocca, grasped the glass of her Bloody Mary a bit tighter and whispered, "They're in trouble. We had better do it."

"You're right," Larocca agreed. "We'll only have three minutes." He reached inside the shoulder bag on his lap, turned on the remote control device and pressed the button. Calmly then, he and Cathy pushed back their chairs, got to their feet and started across the large area packed with people.

Weem's flat-nosed bullet caught Cal Maple in the right side, six inches below the armpit. The powerful projectile broke a rib, tore through both lungs and made its exit out of the dying thug's left side, having cut through the hepatic veins and the aorta during the process. Maple would be dead in less than twenty seconds.

In an instant, Camellion, Weems and Tensor had backed from the office and were in the hall, Joe closing the door. Their only recourse now was flight.

"What about the back stairway," Tensor said, looking up and down the hall. "It's the shortest route to the car."

"No way," said Camellion who had already noticed that,

other than the door to Butler's office, there were four doors in the hall. "Butler's not dumb enough to have a lock on that door that can be blown apart with a slug. If we get trapped at the bottom of the stairs, we'd be boxed in."

"Then we go the front way," growled Weems, "and the sooner the better." He leaned to his left and put a .357 Magnum slug through the door just to let Butler and the three other men inside know they had better stay put.

"If Cathy and Tony didn't hear that shot, they're both deaf," Camellion said with a slight chuckle. Having pulled his second Black Widow, he started south down the hall, his eyes glancing every now and then at the door ahead on his left. He didn't know it but that door opened to the dead Huel Moffet's office-apartment.

With the Death Merchant watching the area to the front and Weems and Tensor, moving sideways, that to the rear, they soon came to the end of the hall (to the bottom of the perpendicular section of the L). There was little time for caution. Not only did they have to get out of the House of Pandemonium they had to flee the entire area.

Camellion stepped out and looked down the horizontal section of the hall. He was just in time to see the two hoods, who had stopped the three of them earlier, reach the top of the stairs that started upward between the kitchen and the dressing rooms. A third hood was with them, a big redheaded slob in herringbone denims and a flowered Tahitian sportshirt.

The Death Merchant was also in time to hear the big bang as the gunpowder he had removed from eleven shotgun shells exploded in Cathy's shoulder bag, the explosion igniting the plastic that was the smoke bomb and the six pint bottles filled with the nauseating stink mixture.

"We have company! Watch it!" Camellion warned Tensor and Weems.

He opened fire with both Black Widows, just as Roy Gomoll and Otis Anderson cut loose with slugs, Gomoll using a Heckler and Koch P9S auto, Anderson a Colt Detective Special.

Eugene John Itaska, the third gunsel, had a Colt Trooper .357 Magnum in his right hand, but he was behind the other two apes and was still trying to get into action.

Death plays favorites and so does Fate. When Camellion fired, he had automatically ducked to the right, this action saving his life. Gomoll's FMJ bullet burned through the air and came dangerously close to his left hip. Anderson's .38 hollow point came even closer. It burned through the material of his charcoal gray coat and ripped across his rib cage, so close to his skin that it left a faint burn mark on his blue-gray shirt.

Camellion didn't miss. The powerful bullet from the left Black Widow's number .308 brass cartridge case[1] ripped through Gomoll's coat and crashed into his stomach, the tremendous shock almost doubled the dying man over before the impact pitched him backward and started him on the journey that all men must make alone.

Otis Anderson was having the same kind of luck, bad. The Death Merchant's projectile caught him in the left side of his chest, bored all the way through his body and spun him halfway around. He let out a loud cry of fear and anger, but he had less chance to live than a Nazi war criminal in the middle of Tel Aviv. Uncertain of the route his slug had taken, Camellion shot again, and once more he pulled the trigger of the Black Widow on his left. The .45 hardball projectile from the right autoloader cut through the side of Anderson's bull neck, the slug tearing through both the right carotid artery and the larynx. With a stream of blood pouring from his mouth and his eyes rolling back in his sockets, Anderson dropped and John Itaska let out a scream. He had good reason to. The bullet from Camellion's left Black Widow had caught him in the groin, torn through his lower intestine and gone out into the air not far from his anus. Thinking that this could not be happening to him, he fell backward and tumbled all the way down the stairs, hardly hearing the shouts and screams of panic coming from the main floor of the House of Pandemonium. For once the place was literally living up to its name. There was only confusion, bedlam pandemonium. . . .

By now thick clouds of billowing black smoke were pouring from Cathy McManus' shoulderbag under the table, and

[1] There's nothing special about the loads. It's the ease with which these shot-shells function in the weapon that is special. The shells, however, are only a part of what gives the Black Widow "her" fatal sting.

spreading rapidly with the smoke was the disgusting odor of the stink bombs. By then, too, Cathy and Tony had left the club and were walking rapidly toward the van while other people around them raced for their cars.

"Down, Camellion!" yelled Tensor and fired both Ruger revolvers at the office door that had opened half a foot. Both 200-grain HP .44 projectiles tore through the thick wood, kicking it shut as far as the lock plate. Tensor saw the outside knob turn as one of the hoods inside closed the door the rest of the way.

Camellion instantly dropped to the rug. On the way down, he caught sight of four more hoods charging up the stairs, one of them, in the lead, carrying a deadly Heckler and Koch MP-5K submachine gun—*Damn! This just isn't my day!*

He rolled to his left toward the corner of the hall. During the second turn-over, when he was on his stomach, he fired both Black Widows at the first two hoods to reach the top of the stairs. Both men stopped as though they had smashed into an invisible wall of steel, then fell backward against the other two men who in turn lost their balance and fell to their knees.

Camellion didn't bother to fire at the two hoods still alive. They were tangled with the two other corpses and he couldn't see them clearly. Furthermore, his own position, out in the open, was becoming too precarious. He could be fired on too easily from any of the rooms in the north-south hall, and he knew that Tensor had not yelled a warning for the sheer pleasure of hearing his own voice.

Worse, time was running out. . . .

Hearing the roar of Tensor's .44 Rugers and Weems' two Coonan mag autopistols, the Death Merchant rolled quickly to the corner of the hall, wormed himself to the side of the east wall and saw that the door of the room south of Dandy Phil's office was half open and that Joe Tensor was putting .44 jacketed hollow point projectiles through the wood. Working in unison with Joe, Max Weems was tossing .357 Magnum slugs through the door of Butler's office and the door of the last room to his right, on the east side of the hall.

Camellion got to his feet, leaned around the corner and tossed off two quick shots down the east/west hall, then prepared to shoot off the lock of the door that opened to Huel Moffet's apartment.

Camellion got to his feet, leaned around the corner and tossed off two quick shots down the east/west hall, then prepared to shoot off the lock of the door that opened to Huel Moffet's apartment.

"Snap it up," yelled Camellion. "There are two more on the steps and they have a chatter-box."

Inside Butler's office, Dandy Phil and Vic Denser waited by the east wall, six feet to the right of the door. Oscar Langrehr waited in the southeast corner of the room.

Jasper "Little Man" Powell would never again have to wait for anything or anyone. He should have stayed put and waited. But, overanxious and impatient, he had opened the door at the wrong time—the wrong time for himself but the right time for the Cosmic Lord of Death who waits patiently by the side of every human being.

Two of Tensor's slugs had bored through the wood and slammed into Little Man's body, one going into his right shoulder and shattering the top of the humerus, the other crashing into his left lower chest. With a loud cry of pain and shock—and a loud scream of horror from China Sue—Little Man was slammed back against the doorframe. The .45 Colt autoloader slipped from his right hand and he fell to the carpeted floor, his head hitting with a dull thud.

Faster than a love-sick sailor on a three-hour pass, Tensor raced forward, jumped over the dying Little Man and charged low into the room while Max kept moving his eyes back and forth, from the door of Butler's office to the door of the last room to the east. In the ocean of life, Max Weems was a shark and he didn't intend to let an enemy fisherman even get close with a hook.

One almost did—Galen Evinhouse in the one-room apartment. Thirteen seconds earlier, one of Max's slugs had cut through the door at a very steep angle. Evinhouse, however, wasn't too concerned. Since he hadn't opened the door and since all the previous firing had obviously been directed at someone else, he assumed the bullet through his apartment door had been a stray. No one knew he was there—or did they? He'd make a test and find out. Ducking across the door, so that the knob was to his right, he reached out, put his right hand gently around the knob, opened the door and carefully pushed it out a few inches. Instantly, Max Weems opened fire, two .44 slugs tearing through the open space between door and wall. If Evinhouse had been in the usual position by the door, both slugs wold have zapped him in the midsection. Angrily, Evinhouse pulled the door shut and debated what course of action to take. Whatever was going on, he knew it was not the police who had come specifically for him; otherwise they would have called out to him with a bullhorn to surrender. What to do? He stared at the single window in the northside wall. . . .

China Sue, dressed only in a bikini and crouched down at the end of the table, was so terrified at seeing the terrible-faced Tensor that she didn't even have the presence of mind to cover her breasts with her arms. Horror and the worst kind of fear were in her eyes as she silently pleaded with Tensor not to kill her. Tensor hardly noticed. To him, China Sue was an enemy. She had been with Little Man; that alone was enough to seal her fate.

The .44 Ruger in Tensor's right hand roared. A moment later, he heard one of the Death Merchant's Black Widows go off. There was a kind of plop, and a hole, the size of a quarter, appeared in the center of China Sue's forehead, a micromoment before her head jerked back as if pulled by a steel cable. She sagged, her eyes closed, her mouth slack, as dead as she would ever become.

Tensor turned, darted out the door and raced after Weems who was backing toward the open door of the room into which Camellion had just charged. The last man to hurry into the room, Tensor closed the door, thinking that he was always in the wrong place at the wrong time. Or was it the right place at the wrong time? He saw that Weems was moving into the second room of what appeared to be a combination office and apartment and that the Death Merchant was approaching an opening in the east wall. A tall particle-board bookcase, with only three books in it, had been in front of the low, narrow opening, concealing it. Huel Moffet had not moved the bookcase back into position when Dandy Phil had called him on the intercom. Why bother? Moffet had thought at the time. All he had to do was lock the door to his apartment.

Tensor took a position to the left of the closed apartment door and began to reload his twin Ruger revolvers. In less than a minute, Weems returned to the office-living-room and glanced at Tensor. "The other two rooms are empty," Max said. "That means that the jerk who tried to fire on us is in the last room north of us. What the hell is Camellion doing in there?"

The Death Merchant saw that there was a blue five-drawer filing cabinet at each end of the short narrow space. *Ah ha! The secret files of Satan's Gentlemen. There must be a God above the clouds—maybe even beyond the orbit of Pluto!*

He was closest to the metal file in the south end when his eyes jumped to the labels on the front of each drawer. All were labelled *Memberships* except the bottom drawer. Camellion got down on one knee and stared at the label on the bottom drawer—*Green Mountain—W.C.*

Camellion had turned and was leaving the tiny room—*No time to look at the other file!*—when Weems moved close to him and pushed back the hat on his head. "Look, this is a worse mess than being in the middle of a Chinese tupperware party. By now those other two jokers on the steps are either waiting or have come up to the front hall. Any ideas?"

Shoving a full magazine into one of the Black Widows and pulling back the slide, sending a cartridge into the firing chamber, the Death Merchant glanced toward the south wall of the apartment, a sly look in his bright blue eyes.

"Max, how good are you with those Coonan jobs?" Camellion asked, pushing a magazine into the other Black Widow.

Weems looked insulted. "I could shoot the balls off a bumblebee if I had to," he said sourly. "But we're fighting cockroaches and I'm not Superman. What do you have in mind?"

"I'm gambling that our 'friends' have a lot of backbone, have come up the steps and are in the hall south of us," Camellion explained. "One would be waiting at the south-west corner. The other—and maybe two or three more by now—would be behind him."

"And Christmas comes on December 25th. So what?"

"These walls are ordinary plasterboard over two by fours.

85

Those .357 mag slugs of yours would tear right through them. Get the idea?''

Weems was skeptical. ''How do you know the walls are plasterboard? Oh! Yeah, the plans we got from the Feds.''

Tensor said, ''Suppose the jokers are in the other hall?''

''What about the mother in the last room on this side?'' Weems asked.

''I'll tell you how we'll do it,'' Camellion said. ''We'll need some luck . . .''

A Coonan .357 Magnum autopistol[2] eats up cartridges with a smoothness that is comforting to watch. Weems, using .357 Magnum rounds with super-expanding JHP bullets loaded to a low velocity of about 1,000 feet-per-second, began firing both semi-automatic pistols at the south wall, placing each bullet from three to five feet above the floor, spacing them out the full length of the room; toward the outside corner he fired four slugs.

Camellion had guessed correctly. Three hoods had crept up the stairs between the kitchen and the dressing rooms and were waiting in the first part of the hall. Roger Dimitroff, flattened against the wall, was by the southeast corner of the horizontal section of the hall. Behind the hulking Dimitroff were Emery Chumm and Nelson LaBrecht, both of whom carried Smith & Wesson revolvers.

Two of the big .357 mag slugs caught Dimitroff. One zipped into his right lower back, where the moon never shines, the second tearing in through his shoulder blades. Impact did the rest, the double force knocking him forward six feet before he dropped the H/K MP-5K SMG and fell flat on his face, his body twitching.

Weems had taken out Dimitroff so quickly that Chumm and LaBrecht were still trying to put their minds into proper gear when a .357 slug nailed Chumm in the right side of his neck, jerking him like a puppet on a long cord. He dropped his .41 S&W revolver and spun down with blood spurting from his neck.

For the time being, LaBrecht was lucky. All the projectiles

[2] Made by Bill and Dan Coonan. At first glance the Coonan .357 makes one think of the Colt M1905 autopistol. The Coonan is slightly larger.

had missed him, although three had come within a quarter of an inch of hitting him. By the time that Weems was putting the eleventh slug through the plasterboard, toward the east end of the wall, LaBrecht had rushed across the hall and was dashing down the stairs.

Weems quickly reloaded his two Coonan autopistols, raced into the next room and began firing at the north wall, placing all the projectiles from one weapon into the west end section of the wall. The crud in that last room east of the hall would surely have been waiting by the door, at least crouched by the west wall.

Wrong! Galen Evinhouse had crawled out the window in the north wall of the one-room apartment, had crept to his right on a small ledge and was lying flat on the roof of the first story.

Max Weems put in his last two magazines, pulled back the slides, then looked at Camellion and Tensor. "I'm ready."

"Yeah, time to go," Camellion said. A fully loaded Black Widow in one hand, he pulled open the apartment door with his other and looked out—up and down the smoky hall. By now, the smoke from the plastic smoke bomb in Cathy McManus' shoulder bag had reached the second floor and it mingled with the blue-gray smoke from the exploded gunpowder.

"Let's go," Camellion said. For only a moment did he hesitate. He pulled out his second Black Widow and put two .45 hardball slugs through Dandy Phil's office door. He could have saved his ammo. Butler, Danser and Langrehr were too professional to take unnecessary chances. They intended to remain where they were and wait. Sooner or later the police would arrive.

The Death Merchant raced south down the hall, came to the corner, turned and darted straight to the stairs. Their feet pounding the carpet, Weems and Tensor were right behind him. Camellion had chosen an easy escape route: down the stairs, through the kitchen and out the rear kitchen door.

His eyes scanning the area ahead, the Death Merchant ran down the stairs, keeping to the right, Weems and Tensor to the left. Lighting in this section of the night club was of the bright-white florescent variety. But Camellion and his men could no longer see the light fixtures overhead. All around them was a murkiness, a gray kind of opaqueness that undulated from the air pressure, as though a thick fog had drifted into the establishment. The homemade smoke bomb had done its work well.

Reaching the bottom of the stairs in the lower hall, the Death Merchant could barely see a dozen feet on all sides. Ahead, in the main part of the club, it appeared to be almost dark, the deep gloom due not only to the smoke, but to the subdued lighting that always prevailed within the main section of the House of Pandemonium. Even the dancing "flames" on the south and the east walls—on those sections that the Death Merchant would normally have seen—were obscured by the thick, drifting smoke. With the smoke was the odor from the six pint bottles that had been in Cathy's shoulder bag, a foul-smelling rancidness that made one gag.

"Christ! This stinks worse than outdoor crappers in the Soviet Union!" gasped Tensor who, moving behind Camellion, darted to the left as he and Camellion and Weems reached the end of the hall.

The sound of people shouting and coughing, of chairs being overturned, and of a human herd stampeding toward the front door and to the exits told Camellion and his two partners in mayhem there were still plenty of frightened, innocent people in the club. Good! The more confusion, the better.

Except in the parking lot. We have got to put a lot of distance between us and this high class clip joint!

Camellion and his two men left the hall, darted left and soon reached the first short swinging door off the kitchen. The Death Merchant pushed through the door, fully expecting the worst kind of trouble. None came. A Chinese cook took one look at him and dropped down behind a cutting table. Two black dishwashers yelled, "Don't shoot, don't shoot, man!" and fell flat to the floor.

"Stay down or we'll kill you!" Tensor shouted with a phony accent. "We represent the Eskimo Liberation Army! Remember that you damned trash!"

The three men raced across the kitchen to the outside door on the north wall. Several hundred feet more and they would be at the van. Possibly, depending on the situation outside, they might be able to make a get-go in the Mercury.

Camellion reached the door and holstered his two Black Widows. Weems and Tensor followed suit. To leave the club with weapons in hand would be the best way to draw attention to themselves.

"Act as frightened as everyone else," Camellion whispered and reached for the push-bar of the door.

Having had a large head start on the other patrons, Cathy McManus and Anthony Larocca had reached the van without any difficulty. As soon as Cathy explained to Frank Flavelton that Camellion and the other two were in trouble, the lanky, easy-moving Flavelton had backed out the van and had driven the very short distance to Morrison Street, parking just west of the parking lot entrance.

Larocca had then gotten behind the wheel and, with the engine turning over slowly, McManus and Flavelton had gone to the main section of the vehicle. Cathy had shut off the interior lights, pulled the shield over one of the portholes and had begun to watch the parking lot and the east side of the building.

Numerous cars pulled out, with engines roaring, and rushed past the van. Flavelton busied himself with activating a COEX radio frequency jammer whose megabyte "static" was emitted into the air via a wide-band antenna concealed in the roof and in the sides of the van. The COEX generator had only one purpose: to jam all police cruiser radios within a radius of 6.2 miles.

"Do you think they'll make it?" Flavelton said to Cathy who was intently watching the east side of the House of Pandemonium.

Cathy did not move her face from the window. "We all know the kind of man Richard Camellion is," she said coldly. "No matter where he sits, it's always at the head of the table. If he can get himself and the others out, he will. Hold on! I see them! All three. They've just come out of a door to the left of the garbage cans. From the kitchen I should think."

The Death Merchant and his two companions saw that the parking lot, while filled with confusion, mainly drivers cursing each other, was more orderly than they had expected.

There hadn't been any serious collisions. They saw, too, that the special van had moved out onto Morrison Street.

They walked rapidly, keeping six feet between themselves. There was no way of knowing who might be watching, and three men together, unaccompanied by women, could be suspicious.

They hurried around the east end of the garage and almost immediately saw that they were not going anywhere in the Mercury Cougar. Some driver, fleeing the parking lot, had slammed the left front end of his vehicle into the left rear fender of the Mercury, crumbling the fender inward so that it was wedged firmly against the tire.

"You have to be the world's biggest optimist," Tensor said drily to Camellion who was moving his left hand underneath the fender. "This damned car has had it."

"Yeah, we do seem to be accident-prone, don't we?" Weems said, smiling slightly.

The Death Merchant could feel that the fender was so entrenched in the tire that it was digging several inches into the rubber.

"I think I need a vacation in the middle of the Sahara," Camellion said calmly. He turned and started toward the van.

In single file, keeping well to their left, they hurried east, every now and then glancing back at oncoming cars moving at killing speed, rushing to leave the parking lot. Camellion and his two assistants in mass destruction could hear the sirens of police cars pulling into the front parking lot and could now see red lights revolving and flashing from the tops of the five cruisers. Three other police cars had already arrived and were parked toward the center of the east side lot. Four cops, ducking and dodging cars, were headed toward the front entrance of the night club. Three other policemen were headed toward the kitchen door.

Camellion, Weems and Tensor reached the special van without incident and got inside through the right side door, the Death Merchant telling Tony Larocca to "Get us out of here, and be careful how you do it. We wouldn't want a cop giving us a ticket, would we?"

"We've got trouble!" Cathy braced herself as Larocca drove the van into traffic, the driver behind him jamming on the brakes of an Audi sedan to keep from slamming into the right rear of the wildly painted vehicle. "You three were almost to the van when two cops and a black guy came out of a back door. The black dude fingered you. The cops nodded and started back to their cruiser. They'll be after us."

"How do you know he was fingering us?" asked Camellion.

"Well, he pointed at the three of you, and he and the cops were looking straight in your direction!"

"One of those brill-o-heads we saw in the kitchen!" Tensor snorted in disgust. "We should have scratched them and that gook."

The Death Merchant—by now toward the center of the van—looked at Frank Flavelton who was monitoring the COEX static generator on a small megohmmeter and an oscilloscope with a sweep speed of 10 nS/cm.

Flavelton didn't give Camellion a chance to speak. "The generator is working fine. The police back there can't radio in, nor can any dispatcher reach them, not as long as their cars are within our range."

Camellion didn't hesitate. He had planned meticulously for every possible emergency. There was nothing to do now but put plan B into operation.

"Tony, cut over to Fourth Street," Camellion ordered. "You'll be able to make a right turn on Howard. Howard will take you to the all-night car wash on the corner of Market and Van Ness."

Weems and Tensor were both skeptical. "Provided we can take out any police cars that follow us," Tensor said aggressively.

"We'll stop them," Camellion said, noticing that Weems had reached into a compartment underneath a short couch, had pulled out an AR-18 assault rifle and was attaching a noise suppressor to the barrel.

"Fire only at the cruisers, not at the police," Camellion said sharply. "You hear me, Max?"

"I'm not deaf." Weems grinned. "Don't worry. I won't snuff any of San Francisco's finest." He began to roll down the glass in the rear door. "I won't have to. I'm using armor-piercing slugs."

An expert road man, Larocca drove the souped-up van

around one car, then another, weaving in and out of traffic with an expertise finely honed by years of experience. He was almost to the end of Morrison Street when Camellion and Weems, looking out the rear window, heard the sirens and saw the flashing lights of two police cars a block behind them.

Camellion turned and called out to Larocca. "How far are we from Fourth?"

"A block and a half," Larocca said. He glanced again at the police vehicles; he could see them very clearly in the large outside-mounted mirror to his left. "What's the deal? Even in this traffic, the cops will be on us in another three minutes or so."

"Make a right at the end of this block," Camellion said. "You'll still be able to cut over southeast and reach Fourth. We'll try to shake them first with the Superslick. Speed up as soon as you make the turn. We'll catch them cold-footed."

"If the Superslick doesn't, I will," Weems said casually.

Approaching the turn, Larocca's foot pressed down on the gas pedal. He wanted the two police cars to speed up, or at least traverse the same turn as fast as possible.

The Death Merchant's right hand went to one of the levers on the right side of the rear door. The squeeze handle controlled thirty-two gallons of liquid, in a tank, nicknamed "Superslick," a chemical compound that, when mixed with ordinary oil, made the oil ten times as slick as soap sliding on the bottom of a full bathtub.

"Get set back there," Larocca called out. He then made the right turn onto Loomis Avenue with such a momentum that, for a split second, Camellion had the feeling that the wheels on the left side of the van had lifted from the pavement. They hadn't, the oversized off-road tires—Goodrich All-Terrain Radials—gripped the road with twice the force of the tires on the two police cars, whose drivers were beginning to close in on the fleeing van.

Now! Camellion's hand squeezed the handle of the lever, releasing Superslick that flowed through a one inch diameter pipe hidden underneath each side of the van.

The instant Larocca had successfully made the turn, he began to swing the van from left to right so that the two streams of Superslick would flow over most of the road. He then speeded up to 73 mph.

Camellion released the handle. No use to waste the precious fluid. The van had moved 150 feet from the corner.

The drivers of the two police cars closed in, the first cruiser tearing around the corner onto Loomis a hundred feet ahead of the second SFPD vehicle. The first car had gone only 25 feet when it ran into Superslick; the driver lost control of the vehicle as it began to slip and slide all over the pavement. In a panic, the driver tried to brake, his action only making the situation worse. Spinning to the left, the car kept on moving. It spun completely around, shot to the left, both the front and the rear wheels striking the curb with such force that the vehicle turned over while the second police vehicle began to spin to the right, its driver fighting the wheel and slowing down. The car spun to the right when the driver turned the steering wheel to the left. But the momentum of the vehicle was too great. The rear end rocketed to the right, the rear wheel hitting the curb with such force that the tire exploded with a *Bang* and was partially pulled from the wheel. The driver and his partner were thrown violently to the right, the driver's head and part of his upper torso going through the open window.

In the meanwhile, Larocca had turned onto Waverly Lane and was headed toward Howard. The danger now was not from the two police cars that had been stopped by Superslick, but from police vehicles that might be approaching from the opposite direction, the southeast. Logically, this was not very likely. Any police cars racing to the House of Pandemonium would take the route of least resistance. That route would be Market Street. Even if the van did meet any police on side streets, it was improbable that the cops would be suspicious of the van. The police at the night club had not been able to use their radios to broadcast a description of the van. By like token, the radios in other police cars would not function once the vehicles were within range of the COEX generator.

Once Larocca came to Howard Street, he slowed the van to within the legal speed limit and continued on to Market.

"The attendant at the car wash might remember the van," offered Cathy McManus coolly, "and if other people are around—let's face it! We can't dart all of them."

93

"We're not going to use the dart pistol on anyone," Camellion said firmly. "The attendant can't see the van once it's in the slot. The office is in front of the bays. As for other people, once the van is washed and we're gone, it isn't likely that they'll rush to a phone and tell the police they saw the van, if they hear a description on the news on late-night TV. By then, we'll be long gone; and there are a lot of black vans around."

"I was hoping it would rain about now," said Weems, "but even the thunder has stopped."

"We have to play it moment by moment after we get to the car wash," Camellion said. Again he thought of the file marked *Green Mountain—W.C.*

Their luck held. Three police cars raced by when the van, on Market Street, was only half a block from the car-wash on the corner of Market and Van Ness. Tony Larocca also had to wait while another police car shot by before he could turn left onto Van Ness. Even as Larocca was pulling the van into the rear area of Speedy Car-Wash (All Automatic Washing), Camellion—looking over the shoulder of Larocca—could see that four other vehicles were making use of the scrubbing bays. Three cars were in the process of being washed. The fourth, a pickup truck, had been dried and was pulling out onto Market.

"I'll pull into the nearest bay," Larocca said in an easy manner.

"That will be Number Four," Camellion said. He turned halfway around to Cathy who was adjusting her blond wig. "Cathy, you get out and pay the attendant. The police haven't connected a woman with the three men who got into the van."

Larocca pulled the van up to Number Four bay and stopped. Cathy got out and hurried to the booth that was glassed-in on its side and in front. Camellion, Larocca, and Weems watched anxiously through the open window of the right side door.

Presently, they saw her coming back to the van, and soon she was inside, a slight smile on her face. She explained as Larocca drove slowly forward into the Number 4 bay. "The attendant was cross because all he could get on his portable radio was static. I wonder why?"

94

Frank Flavelton said, "I'll turn off the generator once we're several miles from here. The longer it's on, the more confusion we'll create."

The instant the front wheels of the van touched the ground bar of the bay the numerous brushes began rotating and the liquid soap and the water began to flow.

In fourteen point six minutes, Larocca was turning the black van onto Market Street and the Death Merchant was taking a v.o.x. remote control detonator unit from his pocket. He pulled back the cover, turned on the switch, waited until the tiny light glowed red, then pressed the button. In the distance, far to the northeast, they could hear the blast. The Mercury Cougar was no more. The A-7 and the SR-22 had also been turned into instant junk. . . .

"That certainly shook the salt out of the police back there," Tensor said nastily, as though he might be carrying on a personal vendetta against the San Francisco police, "and I doubt if it made Dandy Phil any happier."

No one commented.

Now there was only a slim chance that the police would close in on the van or, for that matter, even connect it with the van used by the three gunmen who had created so much destruction at the House of Pandemonium.

"We're safe," Weems said confidently, then lit a cigarette and leaned back on one of the short, bright orange couches. "If the cops were wise to us, we'd know it by this time."

"You're forgetting one thing; we bungled the operation," the Death Merchant said in disgust. He surveyed Joe Tensor with cool appraisal. "We created a lot of confusion, put some guys to sleep forever and blew up a perfectly good car. That's all we did. We didn't succeed in black-bagging Philip Butler."

Tensor sighed. "I must admit our luck was all bad. If that deal back there had been in a graveyard, we'd have probably ended up with our pockets picked! Dandy Phil will sure be on his guard from now on."

"It's useless," Cathy McManus said. "Talking about what happened tonight is the same as discussing divorce. It's all about failure. . . ."

CHAPTER SEVEN

"The F.B.I. report tells us nothing," said Baxter Lincolnwell, giving his opinion and detesting the smell of embalming fluid that had drifted into the room through the air conditioning system. "If we accepted the report, we'd have to believe that Willis Colturvane was an upright citizen and is exactly what he's supposed to be—the owner of Big Green Mountain Outdoor Supply Company."

"The F.B.I. can only report the facts," said Weems who was sitting with his wooden chair tilted back on its rear legs, his feet, crossed at the ankles, resting on the rounded edge of a laminated table. "If Colturvane wasn't as crooked as a corkscrew, Dandy Phil wouldn't have a cabinet full of files on him."

"Max, that's pure assumption on your part." Joe Tensor pulled cellophane from a La Corona Whiff. "We can't be positive that *'Green Mountain—W.C.'* means Big Green Mountain Outdoor Supply company and Willis Colturvane." He glanced in the direction of the Death Merchant, who, seated at the radio table at the other end of the long, narrow room, was writing a report, using numbers from a TAC-COM[1] enciphering book. While Tensor disliked Richard Camellion on a personal basis, he admired him on a professional level. Camellion not only ignored failure, but went after an objective like a persistent, fanatical leech. Jesus! How he hung on!

Having completed his report, the Death Merchant placed the two sheets of paper on top of a Yaesu FT-901DM/ HF all-mode transceiver, looked at his wristwatch, then got up and walked toward Tensor and the other four persons in the

---

[1] Operated by Richard A March, one of the leading cryptologists in the U.S.

"safe" room hidden behind the embalming area of *Givens Funeral Home* (Air Conditioned Chapel—Low Cost & Better Service) that, in Company operational files, was listed as *Stringbean-10Y* and was one of the better funeral parlors in Daly City. A community of 75,000, Daly City was situated between the Pacific Ocean and the San Bruno Mountains, and was only a short distance from San Francisco.

Locally, Daly City was noted for two things: it's high proportion of Filipinos[2] and the disturbing fact that the deadly San Andreas Fault cut right through town.

Wearing black Garrison boots, slate-gray pants and a black silk turtleneck, the Death Merchant sat down in a contoured arm chair, his icy blue eyes raking the tiny, expectant group.

"We're going to proceed on the theory that Colturvane is somehow tied in with Dandy Phil and Satan's Gentlemen," he said quietly. "He could be a front man in any number of Dandy Phil's operations—drugs, gunrunning, what-have-you."

"He's been married three times," Catherine McManus offered in a crisp tone. "I don't suppose that proves anything for our purposes."

"It only proves that Colturvane probably considers tenderness a sign of weakness," Camellion said. "Like the majority of married men, Colturvane doesn't suspect that tenderness is really a sign of welcome."

"That's all very interesting," Joe Tensor said tensely, "but this is not a seminar in how to stay happily married. Who cares if that guy Colturvane has more women in his life than a gynecologist? I'd like to know what course of action we're going to take against him. It's been four days since we hit the House of Pandemonium. Since then, nothing!"

"You're going to have to develop patience," Cathy said not unkindly. "We made one false move. Let's not make another."

Tensor gave her a dirty look, but said nothing.

Max Weems shifted his body uncomfortably and tugged at one of the buttons of his maize-colored safari shirt. "We can

---

[2] There are over 115 Filipino clubs in San Francisco alone. The Filipinos are law-abiding. However, cock-fighting is one of their favorite sports which gives the police in the San Francisco Bay area a lot of trouble.

be certain of one thing. Whatever action we take, we can't expect much help from the F.B.I. The Bureau's Director has already complained to the Agency's DD/O[3] about our impersonating F.B.I. agents. I can't say I blame him. Ever since Dandy Phil told the police and the press how he was attacked by men posing as F.B.I. agents, the media, all over the country, has been making the most of it. The Bureau has been placed in a very bad light."

"Why not drop a sack over Colturvane?" suggested Deane Royall, the operator of Stringbean-10Y. He shrugged his narrow shoulders. "You failed with Dandy Phil. There's no reason you should flop with Colturvane, not if the operation is planned properly."

"I disagree with the entire concept," Lincolnwell said flatly. "Let's assume that Colturvane is connected in some way with Dandy Phil. Where's the evidence that Colturvane might have information we can use against the KGB in connection with the GA-1 microprocessor?"

"You're saying that we should develop a new lead?" Cathy said. She brushed a hand lightly across the top of her reddish hair, her expression forbidding. "It's true that we don't have any sensible method of determining if the KGB is tied in with Butler and the GA-1."

"We can't even make a move toward grabbing one of the Russians at the Soviet Consulate in San Francisco," complained Weems. "The Fox was adamant on that point." He removed his feet from the table and sat up straight. He then looked hopefully at the Death Merchant, as if wanting Camellion to say that Courtland Grojean's order didn't count."

"In this case, Mr. G. is right." Camellion's thin lips curved into the suggestion of a smile. "Think of how it would look to the world if a Russian diplomat were kidnapped from the Soviet Consulate in San Francisco? By the time Soviet disinformation specialists were finished, Uncle Sam would appear as a monster all over the world, especially in the Third World."

" 'Third World,' my ass!" grumbled Joe Tensor. "The 'Third World' is only millions of morons—too stupid to learn

[3] Deputy Director of Operations.

98

and too lazy to work—waiting for a free handout from the U.S. of A.!''

"The bottom line is that we don't dare grab any member of the Soviet Consulate in 'Frisco,'' Camellion said, acting as if he hadn't heard Tensor. "There's no point in even discussing such a route."

Deane Royall spoke up, his voice businesslike. "We can always console ourselves with the knowledge that the Russians are so successful at industrial espionage only because of the openness of U.S. society. For that matter, the openness of all Western nations."

"You're forgetting another reason," annexed Baxter Lincolnwell. "The Soviets have been playing the technology theft game for a long time. I don't have to remind any of you how they stole our atomic weapons know-how after World War II—first the A-Bomb, then the H-Bomb. They're masters at copy-catting. They copied the B-29 bomber and renamed it the TU-4. One of their first MiG engines was copied from a Rolls Royce. The list is endless."

Like vacuum cleaners! thought the Death Merchant. *The KGB sucks up everything in sight.*

Acquiring the information wasn't all that difficult either. About 30 to 35 percent of the technological data wanted by the Soviets could be obtained by open, legal means, by subscribing to periodicals such as Aviation Week, attending international conferences and by sending scientists to do research at American universities. The ridiculous Freedom of Information act was one of the more productive means used by the Russians. Merely by asking the right question, the Soviets could pull from the United States Government stacks and stacks of technical data not otherwise available to the public, much of it only recently declassified. *A law passed by liberals who should be shot for treason!*

But there was only so much technical data that the Soviets could obtain by legal means and methods. To obtain 70 percent of its technical information, the Soviet State Committee for Science and Technology depended on the KGB and on the military intelligence service, the GRU.

At the top of the list was microelectronics, computers, communications and advanced propulsion systems—all vital to the massive military buildup the Soviets had been engaged in for nearly two decades. Since the early 1960s the Russians had fielded some 200 new weapons systems. Soviet military manufacturing expanded 85 percent from 1965 to 1984, and the pace continues.

"What makes it so tough are the greedy Americans who willingly cooperate with the ivan sons of bitches," Tensor said fiercely. "Remember back in the late 1970s how the owner of Spawr Optical[4] went about trying to deal with the Soviets?"

"I believe Spawr made high-precision laser mirrors for U.S. projects," Cathy McManus said slowly.

"You got it, babe. What happened is that Spawr wanted to expand and he wasn't particular how he did it. What he did, he hired a West German representative and through him offered his laser mirrors to the Soviet Union. He sent his first shipments under falsified documentation, and naturally he didn't bother about asking for an export permit. He made several shipments that way, then maybe conscience got the better of him because he did make application for an export license, but was turned down. He tried another shipment and was caught."

Camellion shrugged. "The KGB and the GRU never become discouraged when they fail," he said. He then explained about a computer software company in a Virginia suburb of D.C. Software AG of North America had developed a highly sophisticated program for data base management named ADABAS. In 1979, a Belgian purchasing agent made contact with Software and attempted to buy the ADABAS program. Soon it became obvious to the officials of Software that the Belgian was a front man for the Soviet Union. Union. Software called th F.B.I. F.B.I. agents, posing as Software AG people, strung the Belgian along for several months. During his period, the Belgian tripled his offer and made repeated assurances that the company's proprietary interest would not be compromised, as the Soviets were not about to turn around and sell the program to Software's competitors. At length the Belgian became discouraged; yet that was not

---

[4] Corona, California.

the end of the matter. The Belgian went to another company—in the same building!—and asked them to buy the ADABAS program for him. This company, too, called the F.B.I. Finally, an F.B.I. agent, posing as a Software employee, told the Belgian he had stolen the program tape and offered it for sale. The Belgian took the bait. A phony tape was delivered, money exchanged hands, and the Belgian was promptly arrested.

"There's more," Camellion said. "In 1981, at two trade shows in Washington, D.C., Soviet diplomats tried to buy the ADABAS program from Software. When they were turned down flat, inquiries came in from the Hungarian embassy in the U.S. When the Hungarians were turned down, the Czechs tried, then the Poles."

"It figures!" Weems' lip curled. "The U.S. and Japan are the number one targets and the Soviets send their best intelligence people over here. We could kick out the whole kit and kaboodle of them like the French did in 1983, but that would only compound the problem. Now the French *Direction Generale de la Securite Exterieure*[5] had to start all over and sort the KGBs and the GRUs from genuine Soviet diplomats."

"The French didn't have much choice," Camellion said. "They still think it was the KGB who murdered Lieutenant Colonel Nut.[6]

"Well, that's the problem of the French; let them resolve it," Deane Royall said impatiently. "While we're at it, let's not forget to include the sheer stupidity of politicians in Washington who have helped the Soviets, beginning with that idiot Roosevelt who thought Joe Stalin would keep his word[7] —and that's not counting all the major U.S. firms that have

[5] The French equivalent of the CIA.

[6] Lt. Colonel Bernard Nut was the chief of the Direction General de la Securite Exterieure.

[7] In the immediate postwar period the Soviets transferred a large part of German industry to the Soviet Union—at least two-thirds of the German aircraft industry, the major part of the rocket production program, probably two-thirds of the electrical industry, several automobile plants, 500 large ships, and specialized plants to produce military equipment and weapons systems. The stripping of East Germany was supplemented by a U.S. program called OPERATION RAP. This program helped the Russians dismantle plants in the U.S. zone! By the end of 1946 about 95 percent of all dismantling in the U.S. zone was for the Soviet Union.

been only to anxious to do business with the USSR.[8] It's only proof of what Lenin said about us Americans: that we'd gladly buy the rope that Communism would hang us with!''

For a small moment, Royall glared at the group, his jaw set in the manner of a man who was well-satisfied with what he had just said. He then took a tentative sip of coffee from the brown mug in his hand.

Cathy frowned. ''Correct me if I'm wrong, but I was under the impression that the present administration is being extra tough with the USSR!''

''I mean those nitwits in the Carter administration,'' Royall said half-angrily. ''It was that moron Carter who gave the USSR the world's largest electromagnet. I forget the date[9]. I do remember it was Carter and his 'good ole boys' who committed that bit of stupidity. And it was Carter and his 'boy scouts' that gave the Russians—all in the name of 'peace'—a giant computer that the Soviets used for military research.[10]''

The Death Merchant cleared his throat, at the same time thinking that the Mercury, when it exploded at the House of Pandemonium, had not injured anyone.

''This is all very interesting,'' he said lazily, ''but it doesn't help with our present problem.''

Joe Tensor's huge brown eyes moved to Camellion. His voice sounded even more doubting. ''If you mean digging up a new lead, forget it. We don't have the time. Then again, if you mean dropping a sack over Willis Colturvane, that's a different matter.''

Weems jumped in. ''All we've accomplished so far is to stir up the San Francisco police and make the FBI hate our guts. If we fumble with Colturvane, we'll lose the entire ball game.''

[8] The reader is referred to *Technological Treason*, published by Research Publications, P.O. Box 39850, Phoenix, Arizona 85069.
[9] The world's largest electromagnet was delivered to the Soviet Union in June of 1977.
[10] President Carter's administration also arranged for the Soviets to have a giant $13-million computer for ''weather research.'' This giant computer, known as CYBER-76 and manufactured by Control Data Corp. of Minneapolis, was far more powerful than any other computer available to the Soviets at the time.

"A big goof on this one and we could get our heads blown off," Camellion said. "We're fighting under a dark star." He got up and started toward the Mr. Coffee machine across the room. "But Colturvane is all we have. We can either grab him at his home, at his place of business or on the street. Anyone care to comment?"

At the coffee machine, Camellion reached for a mug.

"Screw a 'dark star' and the sun and the moon and all the planets," Tensor said, looking accutely unhappy. "Colturvane and Dandy Phil will be expecting more trouble from us. I'm basing that on the assumption that Dandy Phil assumed we might have seen the Colturvane file in the hidden file room. For all we know, Butler and Colturvane might even suspect we will go after him—I mean after Colturvane."

"Now look who's doing a lot of assuming!" said Baxter Lincolnwell with a broad grin. Then, in a serious tone, "But I agree that we must consider every possibility. However, I'm convinced that strong-arming Colturvane in his home is not one of them."

The Death Merchant, walking back to his chair with a cup of coffee, was immediately interested. "And why not, Baxter?"

"You read the FBI report!" Lincolnwell seemed surprised; he didn't realize that Camellion was only playing the devil's advocate. "Willis Colturvane lives in a swanky section of San Bruno. A ritzy section that has its own private guards patroling the streets. Getting into the area—even close to his home—would be extremely difficult. Getting out with the target would be worse. No matter how well we planned it there would still exist a large margin of danger."

Intoned Cathy McManus, "Well, he goes to work. Why not grab him on his way to Big Green Mountain? There are any number of ways we could net him on the highway. I admit it would be somewhat difficult."

The Death Merchant settled back in his chair. "Negative, Cathy. Highways 82 and 280 are thick with traffic and well patrolled by the California State Police. The odds would be against us."

McManus' laugh was light and cheerful. "We wouldn't want to have a run-in with those valiant heroes from 'CHIPS,' would we?"

103

"What we need is a full CIA workup on Colturvane," Camellion went on. "But I'm afraid that would take too long. Frankly, I don't think we have the time."

"Why not?" Weems protested. "The KGB in San Francisco isn't going anywhere. Neither is Dandy Phil! And I'm sure that Colturvane isn't about to flee to Siberia!"

Deane Royall said quickly, "There are twenty-two street men in this area. They could put together a complete in-depth profile on Colutrvane within three days. Give the word and I'll set up the machinery to coordinate the effort."

"That's right, Max! They're not going anywhere," Camellion said. "But I've a hunch the KGB is going to make its move very soon. Soviet intelligence knows we're wise to what they're up to; at least they suspect we know, in which case they have to act accordingly. They won't pull back. That's not how the KGB operates, and they're desperate to get the GA-1 microprocessor." He looked at Royall, who was in his forties and well-muscled, although not a large man. His face was narrow, appearing sort of pinched-in, with harsh lines of ruthlessness etched around his mouth. "Very well, Duane. Get your boys to work. Joe is right. Dandy Phil and Colturvane could be expecting us to come at them again. If that's the case and they expect us to go after Colturvane, the Big Green Mountain location is the last place where they'd expect us to strike. And Deane, have your people find out all they can about the Green Mountain building, the kind of guards they have on duty, alarm systems, and especially a floor plan of the building."

"I'll get on it at once," Royall said. He went across the room, looked through a two-way glass in the wall between the embalming area and the secret "station," and, seeing that the outside was clear, pressed a button close to the outline of the door. Silently the door—fronted by a tall metal cabinet in the other room—swung open. In a moment, Royall was gone. He pressed another button in the wall, behind the cabinet. Cabinet and door swung shut.

Max Weems' eyes narrowed and he looked shrewdly at the Death Merchant. "Look, Camellion! We already know where Colturvane's Big Green Mountain business is located. It's part of the Majestic Mall on Bayshore Boulevard; it's between 'Frisco and Daly City. Bayshore is always clogged with traffic. Here's the good news. There's a highway patrol station only a mile south of Majestic.''

''I know where Big Green Mountain is located,'' Camellion said patiently, thinking about the U.S. Naval Air Station only a short distance away, just north of San Francisco Bay. ''But Colturvane's business is in a separate building, a building that sets off to one side. The showrooms are in front, the offices and storage, plus the mail-order center, in the rear. The parking lot is to the right, or to the north, whichever you prefer.''

''And Hitler took Moscow!'' scoffed Joe Tensor. ''I tell you, Camellion, if we try to net Colturvane at Big Green Mountain, we'll take one long slide and get nothing but a butt full of splinters!''

''I must agree with him,'' Baxter Lincolnwell said tightly to the Death Merchant. ''When you say that they wouldn't expect us to hit Green Mountain, you seem to forget we struck at the House of Pandemonium. There were hundreds of people there. It was certainly a place of business!''

''And that is precisely why Dandy Phil and Colturvane wouldn't expect us to pull the same stunt twice!'' Camellion smiled at Lincolnwell and Tensor. ''There's no telling what they might have waiting for us in and around Colturvane's house, and he's probably well-guarded on the highway, as well as in his office in Big Green Mountain. Yet—''

''If they're expecting us at all!'' McManus said mildly. ''We don't know for sure they are.''

''Good thinking,'' Camellion commended her. ''If they're not expecting an attack, so much the better. If they are, we'll be prepared.''

There's Alcatraz Island. It's deserted, and so is Hunters Point Naval Shipyard. . . . It's a daring scheme, but the odds would be on our side. . . .

''Weems' sigh was deliberately loud and meant to be a signal of disagreement. '' 'Prepared' you say! I'd like to know how! Didn't you hear me tell you that there's a CHIPS station only a mile south of the mall? And Bayshore is not only cluttered with traffic, it's an artery that can be easily blocked. Yet you rattle about being 'prepared!' ''

"We're tossing a spear into the dark," Camellion said and put down his cup. "The spear is intuition. Now all we have to do is go out and find the spear. That's logic. That's how we'll operate with the 'Colturvane Project,' with logic."

Weems, Tensor, and Lincolnwell stared at the Death Merchant, all three knowing that Camellion was actually going through with it, that he was going to try to net Colturvane at the man's place of business—right smack in the middle of Majestic Shopping Mall.

Incredible! Impossible!

"Well, it could work!" conceded Cathy McManus, her full red lips curling in a cynical smile. "Yes . . . it could work—and it had damn well better!"

Weems turned and glared at her. "This nuttiness must be contagious," he grumbled, then looked up at the ceiling.

"Look at it this way," Cathy joked. "When God created man, glasses had not been invented, but look where He put ears and noses. I'm sure Camellion's not going to take us on a suicide mission. That would be counterproductive." Carefully, she searched an amused Richard Camellion with sly eyes. "Suppose you give us the real lowdown . . . all those aces you have tucked away. . . ."

Tensor gave her a cold, disapproving look. "You'll be telling us next that asphalt means rectal trouble!"

A light glinted from the back of Camellion's eyes which, at times, appeared to be a slight luminescence.

"I can't give the details until I know the precise layout of the Big Green Mountain building. I can tell you that we'll need a whirlybird—sanitized of course—perhaps a fast cabin cruiser and—at this point I don't know how many cars. I haven't worked it out yet."

Shaking his head from side to side, Tensor got up and muttered, "I've got to have a stiff one over that bit of news." He strode over to a brown ballistic cloth six-pocket gear bag, reached down and pulled out a fifth of Christian Brothers Brandy and a can of chili powder.

Camellion was reminded of an accordion being stretched as Baxter Lincolnwell separated his lanky Henry Fonda frame from the chair, stood up, then looked from Cathy McManus to the Death Merchant. "I don't know how you intend to pull this off, but I do know we can't pose as law enforcement officers . . . and if innocent bystanders should be injured. . . ." He sighed and ambled over to the Mr. Coffee machine.

Cathy looked at Camellion, then reached for her cigarettes and small gold lighter. Camellion, glancing toward Lincolnwell, noticed the wooden crate resting on one end by the wall. Stencilled on the crate was *Sterling-Patchett 9 Millimeter Silenced Automatic Weapon*[11]. Camellion smiled at the word "silenced." *But they can call suppressed silenced if they want to. It's their country!*[12]

Tensor had filled a glass half-full and was carefully shaking chili powder into the brandy—only one of many reasons why he was called "The Strange One" (but never to his face).

Camellion turned to Cathy when she said, "You mentioned a helicopter. I assume we're going to use it to escape in. Where do we escape to and what do you intend to do about police choppers? I understand that the police in this area are very good at sky operations."

"Hell, there's all kind of chopper traffic in this area," Weems said, looking at Camellion. "Police, TV stations and what have you. If you want my opinion—"

The Death Merchant didn't, but he didn't get a chance to tell Max that he didn't. He didn't even get a chance to speak. A low but steady beeping began coming from the Yaesu FT-901DM/HF transceiver. The sound was a signal that the transceiver would begin receiving a message within 30 seconds. Even if no one had been in the room, the process would have been carried out automatically. The message would still have gone from "black box" to scrambler, from scrambler to decoder, and from decoder to teletype machine.

"I'll bet that's more bad news!" Tensor called after Camellion who had hurried to the transceiver, flipped the MR switch and was slipping on headphones. Impatient with the teletype, he wanted to hear the message before it reached the

---

[11] This is the official British silenced submachine gun, designed solely for special operations. The 9mm Sterling-Patchett is far quieter than its closest rival, the 9mm Heckler and Koch—quite a feat since the 9mm is a supersonic round, meaning it makes its own noise as it breaks the sound barrier. The S-P SMG also beats the Ingram M10 9mm and the old 9mm and .45 American "greaseguns" with suppressors.
[12] In Britain even automobile mufflers are called *"silencers."*

teletype, in the special telegraphy code that he and Courtland Grojean were using.

The others in the room hurried to the teletype that soon began clicking away.

"The Strange One" had been right. The news from Grojean couldn't have been worse—with the exception that Soviet missiles were headed toward the continental United States.

The first part of The Fox's message was the information that two members of the Soviet delegation of oceanography, posted to the United Nations, had arrived in San Francisco four days ago and were staying at the Soviet Consulate compound.

One Russian was named Viktor Chorf. The other man was Pyter Gorsetev. Neither the FBI nor the CIA had anything definite on either man; however, any Soviet or communist bloc official coming to the Soviet Consulate in San Francisco was suspect.

There was more to it than that in the case of Chorf and Gorsetev. The FBI and the CIA suspected that both men were agents of either the KGB or the GRU, mainly because only a week earlier, Company people had trailed Rostislav Krylivsky and Julia Uzhgorod, of the Soviet Embassy staff in Washington, D.C., to a hotel in New York City. Earlier, FBI agents had trailed Pyter Gorsetev to the same hotel. Obviously, Gorsetev had met with Krylivsky and the Russian woman. Why? No one had the answer. But now that Chorf and Gorsetev were in San Francisco, Courtland Grojean thought he had solved the riddle—the answer involved the second part of the message.

On the morning of that same day, Doctor Burl Martin had been kidnaped, presumably black-bagged by Soviet spooks or some of Satan's Gentlemen.

Dr. Martin had left his home in Santa Clara at 8:15, having been picked up by three security men of Kordic Micro-Electric Corporation. As usual, two expert Company streetmen had tailed the Kordic car in their own vehicle. Halfway to the Kordic plant, three cars had, for a time, hemmed in the CIA men who reported that the maneuver had been deliberate—and effective! They had lost sight of the Kordic car.

Doctor Burl Martin and his three guards had not arrived at the Kordic plant in Palo Alto.

At 10.20 hours (10:20 A.M.) the city police of Mountain View—a town between Santa Clara and Palo Alto—had found the Kordic car abandoned on a side street of that small city.

Dr. Martin and the three guards had vanished.

The car, an Audi sedan, did not contain any evidence of violence.

The teletype stopped clicking.

"That kind of news is all we needed," Cathy McManus said in a defeated voice and sank into an upholstered armchair. Her eyes went to the Death Merchant. "Your prediction was accurate. You said you felt the KGB would move fast."

"But not this fast!" Camellion's voice was low and as hard and as cold as his expression. "If we don't move three times faster now than those pig farmers, Dr. Martin will have to learn how to love living in Mama Russia."

"By now he's in the Soviet Consulate in 'Frisco," growled Weems who was dropping the paper tape from the teletype into an acid vat. He paused, as if catching himself in mid-thought. "Then again, maybe not!"

"Maybe not is more like it," Camellion said bitterly. "They could get him into the Consulate without any trouble, but getting him out would be almost impossible. You can't hide a live scientist in a hat box, and the Soviets know that any large crate that leaves the Consulate would be suspect. That means that Dr. Martin is stashed somewhere in this general area. Scratch off his three guards. They're dead and on their way to the bottom of the Pacific by now."

"The KGB is no doubt waiting to transfer him to a Soviet sub," offered Weems in an ugly voice, his handsome face twisting with anger. "Or they might take another route and try to fly him out to Cuba. It's useless to speculate. We know they'll put him on 'hold' until they think it's safe to make their move. As for where Martin is, we might as well be looking for a postage stamp in the middle of Brazil's Mato Grosso."

"Let's say it how it is," Tensor said with heavy sarcasm. "The pig farmers—as Camellion calls them—outsmarted us. Those KGB bastards are good at their job. You have to give them credit." He glanced in annoyance at Lincolnwell who, having returned to his chair with a cup of coffee, was loudly blowing his nose, sounding like a pregnant goose about to give birth to extra-large goslings.

"And all because of a tiny chip!" exclaimed Cathy McManus. "The Other Side must want it very badly to have resorted to such daring on a crowded highway. It makes sense. They couldn't steal the chip itself, so they decided to grab its inventor."

"Not a chip, my dear," Baxter Lincolnwell corrected her in a precise voice. "It's a microprocessor, and one that is revolutionary in its function. I realize you're not familiar with microelectronics, so let me put it to you another way. The GA-1 is so advanced that to compare it to other microprocessors now in use is the same as comparing the Wright brothers airplane to—say, the Concorde. Its uses are beyond limit, especially when applied to weapons and defense systems."

"We can be sure of something else," Weems said gravely, "if they succeed in getting Martin to the USSR, they'll force him to design a GA-1 for them, or make him wish he were triple dead."

"He'd be better off dead than a prisoner of the Russians," commented Cathy McManus, crushing out her cigarette.

Weems looked at the Death Merchant who had sat down in the chair by the radio table, the two sheets of the report, written earlier in the afternoon, in his hand.

"Camellion, the only lead we have is Willis Colturvane," Weems said. "When do we make our first move?"

"*When?* I'd like to know what our first move *is!*" Tensor said with cutting causticity.

Camellion's glare would have made a King Cobra shiver. In contrast, his voice was mild. "It's almost six. Flavelton and Larocca will be back shortly. Hopefully, they've done a good job in 'casing' the Green Mountain building. As soon as they and Deane return, I'll lay it out for the entire group."

"Over dinner," Cathy said. "I'm hungry."

Camellion nodded. "Over dinner!"

If those two Russians arrived in 'Frisco four days ago, why did Grojean wait so long to tell us. I want some answers from him!

The report of Dr. Martin's abduction had shaken the Death Merchant. Merely thinking about it drained him of energy. It hurt too much to laugh—

And I'm too old to cry.

CHAPTER EIGHT

From the roof of the Soviet Consulate building in San Francisco, one could see the wide Pacific. But it was how the Consulate was protected that concerned Colonel Pyter Laurenti Gorsetev who was a fanatic about security.

The entire six-story building was surrounded by a high ornamental iron fence that had been given an antique look. The fence was guarded by sound and vibration detectors of East German make. Pan and tilt cameras were placed at each corner of the building, conveying the images to a central control station on the second floor. The television cameras operated on infrared at night.

Windows on all floors were protected by very thin metal foil alarm strips. Every door inside the building contained a multiple-point dead-lock, except the four doors to the outside. They were protected by double-bolt "police" locks[1]. The doors to the "safe" rooms (three in number) and the door to the main Consulate office were opened by means of electronic pushbutton locks. Night and day two guards were at the main gate of the Consulate[2]. Two other guards "walked" the fence.

In spite of these precautions, Colonel Gorsetev felt that there was still a possibility that special operations personnel of the CIA might attempt to invade the building, in an effort to find Dr. Burl Martin.

However, on the third day after Dr. Martin had been

---

[1] The lock is in the center of the door. It contains parallel bars that make it impossible to "jimmy" the doorframe.
[2] The Soviet Consulate in San Francisco is located at 279 Green Street—phone (932) 922-6642.

abducted from his car, Gorsetev began to relax, much to the relief of his associates who had pointed out that American Intelligence would not be stupid enough to think that the *Kah Gay Beh* would take Dr. Martin to the Consulate, if for no other reason that it would be impossible to get him out, to transfer him to a point from which he could be smuggled from the United States. The rule of international law made the consulate "foreign territory." Beyond the Consulate grounds, the streets were USA. Gorsetev's aides also pointed out that, even if the CIA did think Martin was inside, the Americans wouldn't dare invade. The scandal—world-wide—would be too great. Such an attack would make the Americans appear barbaric.

In a relaxed, satisfied mood, Gorsetev took a sip of the red wine that Yuri Kunavin had poured. A delighted look sparkled in his gray eyes and he smiled at Kunavin. "An excellent wine. Surely it must be one of ours. From the Crimea perhaps?"

"No, Comrade. It's an American wine," replied Kunavin. "We bought it and other wines and liquor from what the Americans call a 'chain store'—and for less than three rubles a bottle."[3]

"The fools also know how to make microprocessors," smirked Viktor Chorf who turned his wide face to Kunavin. "As the Comrade Colonel has said, the wine is excellent." He chuckled. "But surely it didn't come from Station-Y?"

A head taller than the thickset Chorf, Kunavin looked down at Chorf, a hint of laughter rolling about in his long throat. "No, Comrade. The wine was not grown from the grapes at Station-Y."

"Make no mistake about it, the Americans are not fools." Gorsetev reprimanded his aide in a very mild way. "They are very intelligent. The weakness of the Americans lies in their childish naivete about power and world politics. It's a weakness inherent in their form of government. Democracies always cut their own throats with their 'freedoms.' You were

---

[3] $9.00-American.

not entirely wrong, Viktor. The Americans would rather be respected than feared. It is this that makes them fools."

"I was speaking partially in jest, Comrade Colonel," Chorf said quickly, some embarrassment in his small but heavily lidded brown eyes. "I respect the Americans for their inventiveness and would never underestimate their ability to resist what all of us know to be inevitable—the domination of the world by Communism." His hand tightening slightly on the glass of vodka, he sat down in a chair across from Colonel Gorsetev.

Yuri Kunavin, who held the rank of Captain in the KGB and was a *Boyevaya Gruppa* specialist[4], seated himself in a chair next to Chorf.

"Speaking of Station-Y"—Gorsetev looked directly at Kunavin—"you're certain that nothing can go wrong in southern California? If only they'd make up their minds in Moscova about the submarine!"

"Station-Y is in a desolated region, Comrade Colonel," explained Kunavin confidently. "The place is guarded by six members of the motorcycle syndicate and, as I told you days ago, I have four of my own agents with them. All four are illegals; there is no danger that they were ever suspected by American counterintelligence.

Gorsetev nodded. Almost word for word he could remember the report. The transfer of Dr. Martin from Station-Y would be made by helicopter to the coast. A fast cabincruiser would then take the scientist northwest through the Pacific and rendezvous with the submarine 150 English nautical miles from the American coast.

The problem was the submarine. Moscova had only three giant Typhoon submarines in area of the Pacific. Typhoons were the fastest submarines in the world, much faster than anything the Americans had. But a Typhoon was very noisy—a problem that Soviet designers had not been able to solve. And American ASDM[5] were the best in the world. Even though its Typhoon would be 150 miles from the western coast of the United States and in international waters, Moscova did not

[4] Special Operations—or combat.
[5] Anti-submarine detection methods.

want to risk the American Navy detecting the submarine and, worse, witnessing the transfer of the cargo. The Americans would be forced to "sit" and watch. Sub and cargo would submerge and Dr. Martin would be taken to the Soviet Union. But the cabincruiser would return to American shores. The men aboard the vessel would talk; they would tell everything they knew to the CIA, and the network, so carefully built by Colonel Gorsetev, would be destroyed. Other *otdels* would be compromised. The GA-1 microprocessor was important, but so was other research the Americans were doing. American biologists were spawning new life forms and speeding the evolutionary process from eons into a few years. They were custom-designing plants, animals and microbes, and were on the verge of a full-scale biological revolution. The Soviet Union had to have the secrets of that kind of biotechnology.

Kunavin added with assurance, "Even if it should take Moscova several weeks to decide what to do, Dr. Martin is safe. The CIA and the FBI can't possibly trace the property to any of the hooligans in the motorcycle gang. The place is owned by the wife of Willis Colturvane. You've read our reports about this greedy man—a highly respectable businessman in the daytime and the seller of stolen property at night—and a traitor to his country. He's scum. The point is that the FBI and the CIA can't connect him in any way with Philip Butler. Comrade Colonel, we have won. We have Dr. Martin. All that remains is getting him to the submarine."

Gorsetev's eyes narrowed. He disliked overconfidence, which had a tendency to put people off guard.

Viktor Chorf shifted his weight and recrossed his short, thick legs. "I think the Americans will do everything within their power to get Dr. Martin back. But there isn't anything they can do. First, they have to locate him, and we know that's impossible."

"I agree," Kunavin said. "The Americans are well aware of the possibilities of the GA-1. My God! Think of it! A device that small could be implanted in an infant's brain and the State could control the individual for life. Little wonder our scientists call mind-control 'human robotics!' "

For the first time, Chorf spoke in Russian. *"Ya neh doomayoo chto Bog v etom dele zameshen,"*[6] he said drily.

"Merely a figure of speech," Kunavin said with a harsh laugh.

Colonel Gorsetev's finely chiseled features twisted in amusement.

"God doesn't, but His 'representative' in Rome thinks he does! That damned Pope is giving us plenty of trouble, and the Poles—"

A loud buzzing from the safe room door interrupted him. Kunavin got up, went across the room and pressed a button on one side of the door. The electric lock clicked and the steel door swung open to reveal one of the women clerks from the Communications Center.

The woman handed Kunavin a folded sheet of paper. "For Comrade Colonel Gorsetev," she said pleasantly.

"Thank you." Kunavin stepped back and pushed the button. The door swung shut. He hurried over to an anxious Colonel Gorsetev, handed him the folded sheet, then sat down.

Kunavin and Chorf could tell from the expression on Gorsetev's face that the news was good.

Gorsetev looked up, smiled, and handed the sheet to Major Chorf.

"The submarine—a Typhoon—will be off the west coast in five days," he said to Kunavin. "We have the proper coordinates. There will be no problem in that area." The KGB spymaster was all smiles. "All that remains is to make sure that everything works smoothly between Station-Y and the transfer point on the coast. I personally will supervise the operation. The two of you will accompany me." He thought for a moment, staring at an uncomfortable Kunavin. "Tell me, Comrade Captain, is it possible to reinforce the station with more trash from that motorcycle gang?"

"Yes, sir. There are hundreds of the scum in this area," answered Kunavin. "The police can't keep track of all of them. Butler will want more money. But Comrade Colonel. . . ."

"Pay him!"

---

[6] "I don't think that God has anything to do with this."

"Why send more men to Station-Y when ten men are already there?" Clearly Kunavin was puzzled.

A sly look had crept into Gorsetev's eyes. "The helicopter is already at the station, isn't it?"

"Yes, but—"

"In case of trouble with the CIA, we can escape with Dr. Martin while those morons from the motorcycle syndicate are doing the fighting. We cannot be too cautious in such matters."

Major Chorf returned the message to Gorsetev, a concerned expression on his slightly freckled face. "Our leaving the Consulate will not be an easy task. The instant we set foot beyond the gates, American counterintelligence will pattern us."[7]

"Comrade Kunavin, doesn't a dry-cleaning truck come every Wednesday to the Consulate?" inquired Gorsetev, his eyes steady on the man.

"Yes, every Wednesday afternoon," replied Kunavin, sounding more perplexed than ever.

"Good! The day after tomorrow is Wednesday. That gives us more than enough time to discuss and perfect the plan I have in mind." Gorsetev stood up and held out the empty glass to Kunavin. "Now, Comrade, may I have some more of that delicious wine?"

---

[7] A method of trailing suspects, with one car leaving off and another one taking up the tail. Often a dozen or more vehicles are used.

CHAPTER NINE

While Richard Camellion realized that experience meant knowing a lot of things one *shouldn't* do, he also knew that it was impossible for a person to find time to do *anything*. If you wanted time, you had to *make* it. He and his Blood Bone Unit had made that time. They had worked harder than Roman slaves in preparing for the abduction of Willis William Coultervane.

Hot sun, a cloudless sky, and the humidity and tension where high as the Death Merchant and Catherine McManus walked toward the Big Green Mountain Outdoor Supply Company. The building, like the rest of the structures of Majestic Mall, resembled a gigantic, chalk-white flying saucer, or two mammoth dinner plates, one inverted over the other.

The other buildings of the complex—Sears, Pennys, Ebon's, etc.—looked like flying saucers piled on top of each other to form four short towers. As for the Big Green Mountain building, it was a two-story saucer with plenty of flat surface on the roof—*More than enough space for a helicopter.* . . .

"We should have Coultervane within the hour," Cathy said in a low voice that skidded with nervousness. "You know what will happen if we get to the roof with him and something goes wrong, like the chopper's not showing up? If that happens, we'll need a lot of strength for what we'll have to go through at the hands of the police!"

The Death Merchant smiled. "Real strength is the capacity to break a chocolate bar into five pieces with your bare hands—and then just eat one piece!"

Cathy glanced in slight surprise at Camellion. She considered him eccentric, to say the least, and resented her inability to pin him down. He didn't drink. He didn't smoke. She suspected that he was a bit of a hypochondriac. That didn't fit either. Persons concerned about their health were usually afraid of death.

There were other things about him—or rather the lack of things—that were puzzling. The others often made remarks about their personal lives—where they had been, what they had seen and done. Not Richard Camellion. Not a single word about his past, or his wants, or needs or desires. He might only have recently been born!

In planning any operation, he was utterly ruthless; yet she could sense that he possessed great sensitivity to the needs of people, particularly women.

Oh well—the hell with it. And with him. After this mission, if it succeeded, she would probably never see him again.

Cathy, at the moment, did not resemble Catherine McManus. Camellion, too, had lost his face. So had Weems and Tensor. It hadn't been necessary for the Death Merchant to play Hollywood makeup artist with Frank Flavelton, Anthony Larocca and Baxter Lincolnwell. They were with the Susy-Q. The only thing Camellion hadn't been able to disguise was Baxter's sniffing.

Decked out in an off-white pant suit, wearing dark glasses and a gray wig made of human hair, Cathy would have been recognized only by God (if God had been interested). To even the keenest eye, she was a woman in her middle or late sixties. Every wrinkle of her face told of past years, of age, perhaps of sorrow (the plastic putty and the invisible tape that pulled her cheeks back toward her ears were hot; the fake caps over her teeth were even more of an annoyance). Like the hands of the Death Merchant, hers were also "old," the skin shriveled and marked with liver spots.

Camellion, her "husband," appeared to be even older—and much shorter than his actual height of five feet eleven and a half. Shorter because he was stooped over, with a cane in his left hand, a shopping bag marked Sears on the sides in his right. His hair—what little there was around the "bald" hairpiece—was almost white, as was his thick but carefully trimmed mustache (both of human hair).

In the Death Merchant's shopping bag was an Ingram MAC-10 that contained a magazine filled with 16 nine-millimeter rounds. All he had to do was switch off the safety and start firing. There were two spare magazines for the M-10, each of 32 rounds. Worse, for anyone stopping one of the 9mm slugs, each bullet was a Hydra-Shok, or a bullet that had a deep, wide hollowpoint cavity formed with a post in the center of the cavity, the post forged in the same operation that formed the cavity itself. The center post was the heart of the Hydra-Shok design. It was post and cavity that could rip through human flesh[1] making a wound that was pure hideousness.

Of equal importance in the bag was a VOR omnirange VHF signaling transmitter that, no larger than a four-cell flashlight, operated on a wavelength of 2961.397 MHz. Powered by Vinex batteries, the small transmitter had an automatic relay—a precautionary measure. Should one set of batteries fail to function, the second set would take over.

There was another weapon in Camellion's shopping bag, one that resembled something right out of Buck Rogers. Actually, the special operations dart gun was almost identical in appearance to an auto timing C1-1040 strobe probe. Only the dart gun—marked without the name of a manufacturer— didn't have anything to do with timing light pulses in an automobile. Its function was either to kill or immobilize people, depending on the type of needle-like darts the shooter was using. Stored in the butt, the darts (capacity: 64), each half an inch long, were hollow, breaking once they entered the target. The darts that Camellion carried were filled with a solution derived from the pulp of the *Amanita pantherina,* a tan to brown mushroom that grew in the Pacific Northwest. The pure toxin would kill within seconds. Its watered-down derivative put a victim to sleep, instantly, for several hours. The aftereffects were not pleasant—vomiting, nausea, and the GI trots, for a week or more. Not pleasant, but such misery would pass. Death was forever.

Cathy's bag contained a MAC-10, spare magazines, and a VOR transmitter. But no dart gun.

Concealing the weapons and the transmitter in each shop-

---

[1] Test were made on *gelatin*, which has the texture and the toughness that resembles human tissue.

ping bag was a layer of genuine packages, each one purchased at a different store in Majestic Mall, each one with a receipt Scotch taped to its wrapping.

There were other weapons. In Cathy's large black pocketbook was a Walther PPK/S .380 pistol. The Death Merchant carried a Star PD in a right ankle holster, leather and piece concealed by his baggy pant leg.

There was only one chance in a thousand that the "old folks" would be stopped by police for some obscure reason before they were inside the Green Mountain building. In case they were, they could prove they were Mr. and Mrs. Jasper George Haggerware from Christopher, Illinois. Yes, sirree, Bob. . . . Come to California on a vacation they had. First one in twenty years or more. . . . Proof? Driver's license, social security card (carried by Camellion), and insurance (Mutual of Omaha and Prudential) and credit cards. Only two credit cards. Sodbusters in Christopher, Illinois, were not into credit cards.

Weems and Tensor, trailing a hundred feet behind Camellion and Cathy, also had expertly forged identification and had been given the Hollywood makeup touch by the Death Merchant.

As Camellion and Cathy drew close to the eighth door entrance of the Big Green Mountain Outdoor Supply Company building, he reflected on the difficulties that had developed in planning the operation. The United States Navy had refused to cooperate. There was no way it was going to give the spooks a helicopter from the Naval Air Station east of San Francisco, across the bay. Screw a CIA special operations deal.

A worried Courtland Grojean had pulled strings, and a chopper—first sanitized[2]—had been flown from March Air Force Base in California to the deserted shipyard that jutted out into San Francisco by from Hunters Point. It had landed in one of the empty drydocks, where the entire area was quickly covered with a huge canvas tarpaulin.

The CIA on-contract pilot—he introduced himself as "Jerry"—had brought other goodies in the civilian version of

_____

[2] All identifying marks removed; repainted; false civilian license numbers.

121

the Bell Kiowa eggbeater: two F10-93B surface-to-air-missile launchers and nine projectiles.

Another problem had been the huge shipyard with all its empty buildings, deserted docks and rusty old vessels. Tramps, dopeheads and other refuse of the human race had to be chased away and a security patrol set up around the drydock and the Dealey, an escort ship that had seen service in World War II. A relic with only ghosts of the past, the Dealey became Blood Bone Unit's headquarters in the shipyard.

A fishing boat was brought in from Los Angeles to the shipyard, its twin diesels carefully checked, its weak parts replaced.

By surreptitious means (such as breaking into the offices of a certain construction company and photographing blueprints of the Big Green Mountain building), the layout of the structure had been obtained.

There had been numerous other setbacks, each one small, but a big problem when put together. One by one these problems had been overcome. At the end of seven days, the necessary information and equipment had been obtained. Now, at 10:15 on a Thursday morning, Blood Bone Unit was ready to strike.

Reaching the entrance with Cathy, Camellion whispered, "Let's keep the world safe for democracy." He put his cane under his arm, opened the door marked PULL and stood to one side to permit Cathy to enter. He continued to hold the door for a young couple behind him and Cathy, the delay giving him a chance to turn his head and see that Weems and Tensor—Max thirty feet ahead of Joe—were walking casually toward the entrance.

Camellion followed the young couple through the door and joined Cathy. Together they walked slowly through the short, open foyer to the main section, their eyes moving back and forth rapidly behind their dark glasses. There were hundreds of people in the main display section their combined voices a steady, incongruent babble. On the floor, some items in display cases, was everything one would need for camping and living in the outdoors, or fishing and hunting. There were rods and reels, lures, tackle boxes, nets, aluminum boats, oars, rubber boots, tents (Camel Dome, Camel Geodesic and

Camel Alamo), sleeping bags, folding tables, folding cots, coolers, portable toilets, axes, hunting knives, air guns, crossbows and rifles; scopes for rifles, belts, car coats, sportman chests, steel security chests for long guns and hand weapons, binoculars, and clothes for men and women—from cheap hunting coats to $100.00 per pair desert cloth pants for men ($85.00 for women). There were leather boots of all sizes and shapes and brands, but only in black, brown and tan; walking shoes for both sexes, running shoes and various kinds of exercisers. Hammocks, terry cloth toweling hats to beat summer heat two ways. Lanterns. All kinds of pet supplies. And books on various aspects of life in the great outdoors. All of it a treasure house for people who loved to hunt and fish, camp out, just hike—or look for buried treasure. There was an entire rack of metal detectors.

The sales counters were to the west. North of the counters was the wide passage, decorated with potted palms, that led to the catalog mail order section (should a customer want his purchase sent to his home via UPS, freight or parcel post). Beyond the mail order section were the general offices. The original blueprints had called for the vast storage section to be behind the offices, but such an arrangement would have thrown the "saucer" out of shape and taken it out of proportion with the rest of the "saucers" of the mall. The problem was solved by "thickening" the "saucer," by building a second story and adding eight freight elevators.

Camellion had a good feeling about Willis Coultervane, mainly because he was convinced that the man was one of the gloves on the hand of Dandy Phil Butler. That most damning evidence against Coultervane was that, since the hit on the House of Pandemonium, Coultervane had surrounded himself with guards—four to be exact. The man was badly frightened. He had always eaten lunch in one of the mall's better restaurants. No longer. Now, one of the guards went to the Carriage House and brought Coultervane's lunch to his office.

Camellion's eyes surveyed the people around him and Cathy. There had to be floorwalkers. No use trying to decide who they were. Any decent security system involving floormen would have them disguised as shoppers.

Careful of their plastic shopping bags, Camellion and Cathy

edged through the crowd toward the wide corridor that would take them to the mail order section. From there it was only a few steps south to the general offices.

Getting to Willis Coultervane would not be easy. It would not be all that difficult either—in theory! When a customer returned an item to either the counter on the display floor or to the mail order section, he or she was given a blue slip on which was written the name of the item to be returned and the amount of the refund. The customer then had to go to the general offices and turn in the slip to Cash Refunds, after which he was paid in cash.

Coultervane's office was in "Executive Row," in the south central section of the general office complex. The freight elevators were to the west, beginning in the southwestern corner and extending to the central west portion of the first floor. Two flights of stairs went to the second floor which was the storage region. One set of steps was in the southwest corner of the first floor. The other stairs were farther north, between the sixth and the seventh freight elevators. On the second floor, two pair of steps led to the roof. One of the steps was in the center of the storage area, the second was in the northeast corner of the second floor.

The plan to kidnap Coultervane was not elaborate. All it required was precise timing, some smiles by Fate and good old-fashioned luck. The "old folks" would shuffle into the mail order section and pretend to look through one of the catalogs. The Strange One and Max Weems would saunter in behind them. Once Joe and Max were in the mail order section, Weems and Cathy would cover the workers in the general section of the catalog division while Camellion and Tensor dashed into the offices of Green Mountain to drop the net over Willis Coultervane.

The glue in the well-oiled machine? Suppose Coultervane was not in his plush office? Suppose he was in another office, in the toilet or—worse—in some other part of the building? Timing was important. Camellion and his people had to get their hands on Coultervane and get him to the roof before regular police or the store's security cops arrived and set up a SWAT operation. Once Coultervane was in tow, Camellion would signal "Jerry" on the VOR transmitter. It would take only 14 minutes for him to fly the Bell Kiowa to the roof of the Big Green Mountain building.

There was some concern on Cathy's part. Her concern was Jerry Harkloff. "I've never seen a helicopter pilot who wears bifocals! For God's sake! He's apt to fly us straight into the Pacific Ocean!"

Just the same, Jerry Harkloff was the pilot of the eggbeater and Blood Bone Unit was stuck with him.

Reaching the passageway, the Death Merchant and Catherine McManus headed slowly toward the mail order section.

By the time that Cathy and Camellion had reached the mail order division and were approaching one of the catalog tables, Max Weems was only forty feet from the mouth of the passage, on the display room side, and moving along unhurriedly as if he were going nowhere in particular and had until Christmas to get there. Five minutes earlier he had been spotted by two floorwalkers who had mistaken him for the shoplifter who, several weeks earlier, had managed to elude them and four of the uniformed mall police after he had been seen slipping a hunting knife into his pocket from a display table.

Pretending to be shoppers—father and son—Edgar Moran, the older man, and Stan Wright, the floorwalkers, intended to move through the people, come in behind Weems, grab him by both arms and take him into custody.

Weems, an expert with plays made in a crowd, sensed the two eager beavers coming in behind him, in spite of the people on either side and in back of him. At first, Weems had not been certain and considered the possibility that his sense of physical preservation might be working overtime. He soon found it was not. Each time he would pause, half turn and pretend to look at items on a display table, the two men would pull up short and pretend to be shoppers looking at items on a display counter.

Max wasn't carrying his two Coonan semiautomatics magnums; they were too large to be concealed in shoulder holsters. The bulges on each side would be too noticeable. He did have two S&W "super slim" M-439 9mm autopistols, one in a 4-D mini-holster on his belt, the second in a Jackass holster secured tightly to his right ankle. He didn't, however, want to use either weapon. The crowd was too thick. Gun fire could cause a human stampede that might interfere with the overall operation aimed at Coultervane. Besides, reasoned Max, Joe Tensor was moving behind him. The Strange One had surely spotted the two men and was assuming they were either detectives or floorwalkers.

Walking laggardly, Weems waited until Moran and Wright were directly behind him and were reaching out for his arms. Only then did Weems spin around and explode like a karate grenade that throws out shrapnel of blows and kicks.

Unaccustomed to such violence, Moran and Wright did not even have time to be surprised. Simultaneously, Weems delivered a *Chungdan Kwansu* middle finger spear strike and a free style short snap kick, his finger a bolt of lightning that struck Moran in the Adam's apple, and the tip of his right foot a stick of dynamite that exploded into Wright's testicles. At the same instant, Weems yelled "Pickpockets!"

Only seven bystanders had seen Max actually spin and take out Ed Moran and Stan Wright. But they weren't sure about what they had seen. They had heard the word "Pickpockets!" and assumed that the two men, now in agony and sinking to their knees, had attempted to dip into the pockets of the tall, nice-looking man in the tan suit.

Not that Weems was out of danger. Neither he nor the people gathering around Moran and Wright saw Fred Kintz, uniformed Majestic Mall cop. A 22-year-old hotdog who had failed to pass the extrance exam of the Daly City PD, Kintz had been only sixty-eight feet to the north, and right, of Weems when Max had turned and gone to work on Wright and Moran. Kintz didn't know what was going down. He did know that the two floorwalkers had not tried to pick the pockets of Weems. He knew because he and Stan Wright were good friends and often chased women together. Something wrong was going down and Kintz intended to find out what it was.

Foolishly, Kintz pulled his .357 Colt Trooper MK III revolver and, now more overanxious than ever, started to make his way toward Weems, shoving startled people to one side.

In the meanwhile, Weems had turned away and was almost in a run toward the entrance of the wide hall that connected the display floor to the mail order section.

The Strange One had been seventy feet behind Weems, and it was he who saw Fred Kintz moving as fast as he could trying to get to Max.

Joseph Edward Tensor made his decision. He didn't use the .44 AST Rugers that was in hidden leather on his ankle, nor did he have time to open the black attache case and take out the MAC-10 SMG. Instead, he moved his right hand underneath his coat, stepped up on the wide rim of a large pot filled with a decorative palm, pulled the H/K PSP pistol from its holster and, ignoring open-mouthed shoppers staring at him, snap-aimed at Kintz and squeezed the trigger. The shot sounded like the crack of a bull whip, the 9X19 Parabellum bullet striking Kintz low in the left side of the neck, the slug going in at a slightly downward angle so that it cut through the trachea. Kintz jerked, then fell, dying as he was went down.

Hearing the shot, Weems spun around, saw Tensor jumping from the rim of the pot to the floor and heard the frantic screams of several women who had seen Kintz executed. Men and women, up and down the large display floor, were turning and staring in first one direction, then another, uncertain of what they had heard. Yet the loud crack of the shot had made people direct their attention toward the sound of the shot. They only knew that something violent and unpleasant was happening, and they wondered about Tensor, who was running toward the entrance where Weems was waiting.

Their precious shopping bags at their feet, "Mr. and Mrs. Jasper George Haggerware" had also heard the shot which had sounded muffled in the distance and the acoustics of the passage. They noticed that other customers and some of the employees in the mail order section had also heard the muted shot but were uncertain what it was.

"Maybe it wasn't a shot," Cathy said in a low whisper as she casually turned one of the pages of a thick catalog with a bright green cover.

The Death Merchant glanced toward the mail order side of

the entrance to the connecting passage. "I wouldn't bet your virginity on it. I always think of Murphy's Law."

"You'd lose," Cathy said. "I'm not a virgin."

"In that case, we're in trouble!"

"What do we do?"

"We wait. Either way, we still have to escape."

Cathy was surprised. "We can't wait if Joe and Max are taken. Why should we—"

"I don't leave my people behind," Camellion whispered fiercely, cutting her off. "We don't walk away from Max or Joe. We wait and see what happens."

Several minutes later, Max Weems and Joe Tensor appeared in the end of the corridor, looked around the area, then, at a slight nod from the Death Merchant, walked briskly toward him and Cathy. By the time Joe and Max reached them, Camellion and Cathy were taking the top layer of packages from their shopping bags.

"We do it, but forget keeping the floor covered out here," Camellion said. "We hit the general offices together—that was a shot out there, was it not?" He pulled the VOR transmitter and the 21st century-looking automatic dart gun from his shopping bag as Cathy pulled out her VOR and a MAC-10 submachine gun.

Tensor placed his attache case on a catalog table and opened it.

"I had to terminate a store cop," he said mechanically. "It was either him or Max."

"He's right," said Weems who had his right pant leg pulled up and was taking a "super slim" M-439 pistol from the ankle holster.

Just about that time, other people in the immediate vicinity noticed the weapons and, afraid to yell and call attention to themselves, began to move back.

"Look, Momma, they got guns!" a little boy said.

It took less than a minute for the Death Merchant and his three people to shove magazines into Ingram MAC-10s, extra mags into waistbands, and take out handguns. Camellion had shoved his VOR transmitter into his left coat pocket and Cathy had handed her signal device to Tensor. The danger now was that someone would notify Willis Coultervane and that the target would escape before Blood Bone Unit could get to him.

Camellion and the other three ran toward the south, their hands filled with weapons, Cathy's large pocketbook dangling from straps over her left arm. By now, women were screaming and men were falling over each other in an effort to drop to the floor. Behind the 75-foot long counter, Green Mountain employees were frantically hiding behind desks and other places, afraid that the "terrorists" would begin spraying the area with hails of slugs—and how could two old people run so fast and with such agility?

Ahead of the Death Merchant loomed the large door that opened to the general offices. . . .

CHAPTER TEN

Always considerate toward people in his employ, Willis Coultervane—forty, almost fat and an exercise freak—was in his office with one of his bodyguards when Cecil Davis, the director of Big Green Mountain's security police, telephoned and reported that there had been a shooting on the display floor. The shooting appeared to be a "gangland thing," Davis said. The worst was that one of the store's uniformed policemen had been shot down and was dead. The State Police had been called and would arrive any moment.

Worried, Coultervane hung up the phone, leaned back in his chair and then explained what had happened to Albert Dufrenne, the bodyguard, finishing with, "Do you suppose it could be a phase of some decoy plan?"

"Relax," urged Dufrenne in an easy manner. A retired detective who had quit the San Francisco Police Department after twenty years service, Dufrenne smiled. "That shooting isn't part of any plan against you, Mr. Coultervane," he reassured the owner of Big Green Mountain. "A shooting only brings police. That's the last thing your enemies would want. Hell, it would be like telling you in advance they were on the way. Anyhow, the others are in the next room. You don't have anything to worry about."

Coultervane didn't reply. Nothing to worry about! He knew that Dufrenne would be singing a far different tune and that his confidence would vanish like smoke in a tornado if he knew all the facts, if he knew of Coultervane's secret association with Dandy Phil Butler and especially if he knew that Dandy Phil was working with Soviet KGB agents. Good God! If Dufrenne only knew!

For weeks, Coultervane had wished that he had never heard

of the GA-1 microprocessor. And he was involved! No, not directly. Nevertheless, he had permitted Dandy Phil to use the old winery near Sage in southern California. Phil had not said why he wanted to use the winery, but Coultervane suspected it had something to do with Doctor Burl Martin, the microelectronics genius reported missing by the press.

No . . . he was not involved directly. But if something went wrong, the Federal Government would certainly indict him as a co-conspirator. Uncle Sam would have good reason to. The winery was owned by Coultervane's wife, the deed and the taxes paid in her maiden name.

The telephone on the desk rang again. This time the caller was Mrs. Bertha Lambert, the manager of the mail order division. Her voice trembled so badly that Coultervane could hardly understand her as she told him that ''four people'' —terrorists—had just entered the general offices—''a-and one of the m-men said they were c-carrying machine g-guns.''

Coultervane, his face turning gray, dropped the phone, stared at Dufrenne and choked out, ''Four of them . . . four with machine guns . . . headed this way!''

Dufrenne came out of the chair as if propelled by springs. He pulled a .38 Colt Diamondback revolver from a shoulder holster, ran to the office door and locked it, after which he turned to Coultervane who had pulled open the middle drawer of his desk and was taking out a S & W M-39 pistol.

''Get in the exercise room,'' Dufrenne ordered in a harsh voice. ''The door to your office is the only way in. We'll kill them from the door to the exercise room. Move it, man!''

There were more screams from women and more wild scrambling to the floor as the Death Merchant and his force of three raced across the area toward the hallway between the general office space and Executive Row.

Most of the offices that comprised the Row were double rooms, with the offices of the secretaries being in front of the bosses' inner sanctums. Only Willis Coultervane had one giant room, with a toilet and shower on one side and a small exercise room on the other.

A major concern of the Death Merchant and the three persons with him was the means by which the police could reach Executive Row on the south side of the first floor—through the west door to the freight elevator section, the turn in the hall at the southwest end of the Row, the wide opening in the general office in the south wall and the fire door at the east end of the hall. Unless Camellion's information was wrong, this door was always locked.

Very conscious that time was running out, Camellion and his people rushed down the hall, moved east and stopped at the door of Coultervane's office.

At once, Camellion ordered Weems and McManus to watch the east, west and northern approaches—". . . and shoot to kill. Playtime is over. From now on it's only our survival that counts." He then turned to the Strange One whose large brown eyes were as calm as unpainted concrete.

"It's up to you and me to go in there and bag him," Camellion said. "We'll use the double-fire technique. One long burst by you and I'll go in."

"We'd better hurry it," snapped Tensor who had a MAC-10 in his right hand and a .44 Ruger in his left. "The police aren't going to take a lunch break before they come at us. Hear those sirens? An army is on its way."

The Death Merchant placed the dart gun and the MAC-10 on the floor and took off his coat, its removal exposing the .45 Star PD which he had taken from the ankle holster and placed in a mini-holster on his belt. He pulled the VOR omnirange transmitter from the coat, extended the antenna and pushed the ON button. At once the red light began to glow. Good. The signaling device was now broadcasting on a wavelength of 2961.397 megahertz. Camellion made one last check. The Strange One was ready. Six feet away, McManus was watching the approaches from the west, Weems the possible lines of fire from the east.

Camellion leaned the VOR transmitter against the wall, bracing it with his coat. *Jerry 'Four-Eyes' should be taking off about now!* He picked up the dart gun and switched it from single dart fire to full automatic. Next, he picked up the MAC-10 and turned to Tensor.

"We have to assume our information is correct," Camellion said. "The office is in front of us. To our left is the exercise room, the shower and toilet to the right."

"The door opens inward," Tensor said. "I don't have to tell you why that's to our disadvantage."

"You know what we have to do—play it as it goes down," replied Camellion, feeling tiny rivulets of sweat coursing down his cheeks. "Let's do it. Try the knob."

Standing to the right of the door, Tensor reached out with his right hand and tried to turn the knob. The door was locked.

Tensor stepped in front of the door and blew apart the lock with a three-round burst of 9mm slugs, the Hydra-Shok projectiles almost tearing the lock from its foundations. The impact of slugs on metal and wood only partially opened the door. Quickly, Tensor placed the hot muzzle of the small Ingram submachine gun against the highly varnished hardwood and gently pushed. The door slowly swung open as Tensor moved to the right and resumed his former position beside the wall of the hall.

"You in there!" Camellion shouted. "We don't want to kill you. We want you alive, Coultervane." The bluff: "We'll use grenades if we have to. You're either going with us or we're going to leave you a bloody corpse."

No reply.

"Make it an 'X' sweep, then I'll go in," Camellion whispered to Tensor. He darted around The Strange One and got down on one knee to the left of the doorway.

"Now!" Camellion said.

Joe Tensor leaned around the opening, looked past the inner side of the office door, saw that the door to the exercise room was open and fired, the short barrel of the MAC-10 spitting out three-round bursts, the deadly slugs ripping into the wooden framework of the door to the exercise room.

From his position to the left, Camellion could see the southwest corner of the office—the door to the toilet and shower. He could also see the small, portable bar and the business-type couch on the right side of the room. At once he detected that the position of the couch was off, one front end sticking out five or six inches more than the other end. Camellion smiled slightly—*Haste does make waste!*

He fired his MAC-10 simultaneously with Tensor, his own Hydra-Shok projectiles ripping into the back of the vinyl couch and tearing through the door of the toilet, the terrific impact of the expanding slugs tearing off pieces and bits of vinyl and wood.

Three of Camellion's 9mm slugs also tore into the chest of Albert Dufrenne. Turned into a corpse within a blink of an eye, Dufrenne slumped like a sack of wet sand, the .38 Colt Diamondback slipping from his dead fingers.

The Death Merchant tensed himself again—*Ironic! Most people are doing their best to live forever. I seem to always be going out of my way to get myself killed!*

The moment neared. Camellion relaxed his finger on the trigger of the MAC-10. Tensor also stopped firing.

The hell with it, Mr. Bones!

Hunched as low as possible, Camellion stormed into the office.

While not a coward, Willis Coultervane was terrified. His four bodyguards weren't any too happy either. Unused to dealing with fanatical terrorists, they had neither the experience nor the weaponry to deal with the situation. A crossfire was a proper tactic, at least in theory. Accordingly, Al Dufrenne had gotten behind the couch in the office.

Karl Brown, a light-skinned mulatto, was down on one knee to the left of the door between the office and the exercise room, a 9mm Hi-Power Browning auto in his hand. Standing behind and above him, Paul Wayne Vickers waited with an Astra .357 mag revolver. On the opposite side, Loren Heffermeier waited against the door that had been pushed to the wall, a S&W .44 mag in his left hand. Willis Coultervane, his S&W M-39 pistol in his hand, waited behind a massage table, feeling that it was only a matter of minutes before he was either blown to bits or became a prisoner of the madmen in the hallway.

First, one of the terrorists had called out for Coultervane to surrender or they would use grenades. That had been bad enough. Then they had raked the west side of the office and the door to the exercise room with machine gun fire, their method indicating that they knew the layout of the area.

"They must have killed Al," Vickers whispered.

"We don't know that," Loren Heffermeier said. "Can you see anything, Karl?"

"Nothing," mumbled Brown. Barely looking around the left side of the doorway, Brown could see the hall door of the office. No sooner had he spoken than he was startled by a man streaking into the office, a weapon in each hand.

"They're coming in!" Brown yelled. Those three words were the last he would ever speak . . .

The Death Merchant realized that he was taking a calculated risk—on the assumption that Coultervane and his four bodyguards were either in the office or the exercise room. That they were in the toilet or shower was not very likely. The area was too small.

Darting into the office, Camellion threw himself forward, spreading out his arms as he made a dive to the rug, his destination the west end of Coultervane's desk. He was halfway to the floor when Brown and Vickers fired and Heffermeier stepped to his left and transferred the S&W magnum revolver to his right hand.

Camellion fired almost concurrently with Brown and Vickers—the dart gun in his left hand, the MAC-10 in his right hand, the small SMG chattering, the electric dart gun silent.

Vickers' big flat-nosed .357 projectile came very close to whacking Camellion in the left side. It didn't—and close was not good enough. During that micro-moment, the huge hunk of metal cut across Camellion's back, only a tenth of an inch from his shirt, and kept right on going. It tore through the couch and thudded into the wall.

In contrast, Brown's 9mm hollow-point bullet buzzed six inches over the back of Camellion's head. It, too, found a home in the couch, coming to an abrupt halt when it struck a coiled spring in the padding.

The 9mm Hydra-Shok slugs from the snarling MAC-10 in Camellion's right hand were wasted. They slammed into the couch, raced across the room and chopped into the door of the toilet. Camellion wanted to keep anyone behind the couch or in the toilet down and out of action until The Strange One could move to the left side of the hall door and have a clear view of the west side of the office.

The darts, however, were not wasted. Working perfectly, the battery-powered dart gun spewed out 52 needlelike darts, the steel raining all over Paul Vickers and Karl Brown, but missing Loren Heffemeier who had not yet stepped into the doorway.

Vickers and Brown didn't know how lucky they were. They would live. In an instant, the derivative of the *Amanita pantherina* toxin in the hollow needles did its work in the bloodstream and switched off the consciousness of the two bodyguards—so quickly that they didn't have time to fire second rounds. Unconscious, they sagged to the floor, Vickers on his back, Brown face down.

Heffermeier, gasping in fear and astonishment, stared at Brown whose face and neck was peppered with what seemed to be some kind of translucent barbs.

Willis Coultervane began to tremble.

In the meanwhile, the Death Merchant had reached the floor, rolled over and crawled to the west side of the desk. He pulled the Star PD, switched off the safety and placed the compact autopistol on the floor. Out came the empty magazine of the MAC-10 and, from his waistband, in went a full 32-round magazine. Back went the cocking knob and a cartridge eased itself into the firing chamber.

He glanced toward the hallway door and saw The Strange One standing to the left of the entrance. Tensor nodded; so did Camellion who leaned around the front corner of the desk and triggered off a short MAC burst of slugs that sliced the air over the bodies of the unconscious Brown and Vickers.

"Last chance, Coultervane!" yelled Camellion, feeling foolish. *I don't even know if that fat-boy is in there!* "Either come out right now, or we toss in grenades!"

Camellion had reached one positive conclusion: Time was definitely up. Within the next few minutes, Blood Bone Unit would have to head west, move to the second floor and get to the roof. Jerry "Four-Eyes" could and would hover for four or five minutes. If they weren't there, he'd take off without them.

* * *

Thirty feet to the east, inside the exercise room, a nervous Loren Heffermeier waited by the door and whispered, "He's bluffing. I know he's bluffing."

Willis Coultervane stared in dismay at Heffermeier. The trouble with the bodyguard was that he didn't know who the "terrorists" really were. Neither did Coultervane who strongly suspected that the gunmen were CIA mercenaries capable of killing without batting an eye. And there wasn't time to argue with Heffermeier. Why bother? Judas Priest! It might be a nut who would fight to the last bullet. Yet Coultervane didn't want to shoot the man in the back. Everyone had his price and, sooner or later, everyone did business with everyone else. There was always the possibility that he could make a deal with the gunmen and they would release him. Then how would he explain to the police bullet holes in Heffermeier's back?

"Hey, Heffermeier! Look at this!" called out Coultervane in a soft voice.

Loren Heffermeier turned around and Coultervane's S&W M-39 autoloader roared, four times in quick succession, four 9mm hollow point projectiles that zipped into Heffermeier's chest and made him stagger back against the door before he dropped to the floor, a super-surprised look frozen on his face.

"I'm coming out," Coultervane shouted. "Don't shoot. For God's sake don't shoot."

"What were those shots?" Camellion demanded.

"The last man committed suicide!"

That son of a sad song probably shot him in the back!

"Come out with your hands empty and above your head— right now!"

Once the Death Merchant and Coultervane were in the hall with other members of Blood Bone Unit, Camellion told the store-owner the facts of life. "Cooperate and you might live to see next week. Try to run, try to get cute in any way, and we'll kill you. Let's move it."

With Camellion leading the way and Coultervane between him and Max Weems, the small group hurried west and soon were approaching the square turn in the north-south hall.

Coultervane and Weems walked with their backs turned to Camellion. McManus and Tensor composed the rear guard, their eyes darting to the closed doors of the executive offices and especially to the corner of the hall to the east and the entrances from the general office area.

Old pro that he was, Camellion knew that by now the police had arrived and had set up a watch-and-wait operation. Their first consideration would be the safety of the people in the offices—*Yeah, they'll try to 'talk' us out. They'll try to 'reason' with us.* At the end of the west side hall, the one that stretched from north to south, would be SWAT boys, all decked out in body-armor, with shotguns, Colt AR-15s and sniper rifles with scopes.

Camellion's eyes darted to the southwest, to the door that opened to the section containing the freight elevators. So close! Yet so far. . . .

And why haven't we heard the chopper?

Camellion stepped behind Willis Coultervane and shoved the barrel of the MAC-10 viciously into the small of the pudgy man's back. "Recite your little speech, sucker. One false word and we all die!"

Coultervane was only too anxious to do as he was told. Shouting as loud as he could, he told the police that he was a captive of a group of "PLO terrorists" who were going to hold him for ransom. "They said they don't want to harm anyone. They said that if you interfere in any way, they'll kill me and blow themselves up. They—"

"Make it convincing, damn you!" Camellion stabbed Coultervane in the back so hard with the muzzle that the man cried out in pain.

"They mean it!" shouted Coultervane. "Please don't interfere in any way—and they said to tell you to pull back your men on the second floor. PLEASE! These people are desperate."

The Death Merchant chuckled. "That should convince the boys in blue that this is worse than the outbreak of herpes!" He grabbed Coultervane by the back of the collar, pushed him out into the hall and looked to the north. At the end of the hall he could see a door closing. The ruse had worked. The police were moving back.

"Let's go," Camellion ordered. "We've got to move fast. It's a risk, but it's all we have."

As fast as was possible—and still maintaining security—the group moved. First through the door to the section of freight elevators, then up the steel stairs in the southwest corner to the second floor that comprised the storage area of Big Green Mountain. Here on this second floor was the real danger, one that could not be dealt with, for this large region was filled with thousands of crates, boxes and racks full of outdoor equipment. All this offered hundreds of places where police snipers could hide and kill Camellion and his three people within seconds.

Still in back of Willis Coultervane, holding onto the man's collar, the Death Merchant paused in the wide doorway.

"Tell them," he whispered to the store owner. "Your life depends on making it sound convincing. If we die, you go with us."

"POLICE! LISTEN TO ME!" Coultervane shouted fanatically, not faking. "THE TERRORISTS ARE WIRED WITH BLOCKS OF TNT UNDER THEIR CLOTHES. IF ONLY ONE OF THEM IS SHOT AND FALLS TO THE FLOOR, THE CIRCUIT WILL BE BROKEN AND THE TNT WILL EXPLODE. LET US PROCEED WITHOUT INTERFERENCE. T-THESE PEOPLE . . . T-THEY ARE PREPARED TO DIE!"

Only after Coultervane had shouted the warning three times did Camellion and the rest of his group proceed into the storage area and toward the stairs in the center of the second floor.

The silence was eerie, unnatural. Not a single worker was in sight, all having fled to safety.

Camellion and his group were at the bottom of the center stairs when they heard the *thubb-thubb-thubb-thubb* of a helicopter approaching from the northeast.

"Hot damn! There he is!" Weems said. "I'd feel silly up there, trying to flap my arms and fly!"

"It might not be Jerry," Cathy said in a low voice, her eyes darting warily from left to right. "It could be the police."

They were almost halfway up the stairs. Tensor said, "If it

is Jerry, he's late. It's been more than ten minutes since the transmitter was turned on.''

''Our people did a good job with the transmitter,'' commented Weems. ''Those Russian markings of manufacture will be the best evidence we left that we're the PLO.''

By now the sound of the helicopter indicated that the bird was very close, only several hundred feet away.

''It's the Bell Kiowa,'' Camellion said easily. ''I can tell from the sound of the rotor.''

''That's a lot of crap,'' Tensor said, sounding as if he wanted to start an argument. ''No one can tell what kind of chopper it is only by the sound of the rotor blades.''

Camellion smiled enigmatically and stepped in front of the metal door that opened on to the roof. Actually they were already on the roof, since they had moved through the opening and were now in the housing that was over the top of the stairs.

Camellion stepped to one side and crooked a finger at Willis Coultervane. ''Open the door, pal. If a cop out there has a nervous trigger finger, you can take the first bullet. Do it. Open the door.''

''After you do, don't even think of running,'' warned Cathy.

Coultervane paled, a trapped and desperate look spread over his face. He didn't protest, sensing that these people would just as soon kill him as kidnap him. He strongly suspected that in their eyes he was already dead. They had talked too freely in front of him to let him live. What he had heard about the transmitter and its Russian lettering was enough to silence him forever.

Coultervane pushed the door open, bright sunlight and a lot of helicopter noise poured in through the opening. The Death Merchant pushed Coultervane through the door, followed him and looked around the wide, windy opening. The roof was flat for most of its length, then it began to curve downward on all four sides. There were only ventilation pipes, protruding for several feet, a metal housing over the top of the stairs from which they had just emerged, long air-conditioning units and another housing over the top of the stairs in the northeast corner of the roof.

There was the helicopter. Jerry Harkloff had brought the snow-white Bell Kiowa seventy feet to the south of the air-conditioning units and was hovering the bird only a few feet above the asphalt roof. If any police were around, they were invisible!

It took only a few minutes for the Death Merchant and the rest of his group to climb aboard the whirlybird and for Harkloff to throttle up the Allison C18 turboshaft engine and lift off, the two bladed rotor revolving faster and faster, eating at the air, clawing into the wide spaces.

The saucer-shaped towers of Majestic Mall rapidly receded, becoming smaller and smaller, as did the cars in the parking lots, until they were only inch long toys. Bayshore Boulevard and its vehicles, moving on four lanes, became a narrow ribbon. Then it, too, was gone, as Harkloff expertly turned the chopper and, while continuing to climb, headed due north.

The interior of the chopper was cramped. To give the others more room, Cathy McManus went forward and sat down in the copilot's seat, every so often glancing fearfully at Harkloff who, every now and then, adjusted his glasses.

The noise of the rotors was tremendous, more so than usual, since the glass on the port and the starboard doors had been removed to enable the occupants to fire missiles from the two F10-93B launchers.

"There's not a police bird in sight," Weems yelled at the Death Merchant. "Hell, I bet we get to Alcatraz without any trouble whatsoever from the police." He looked expectantly at Camellion, but the Death Merchant only picked up one of the eighteen-inch long heat-seeking missiles and proceeded to load one of the shoulder-fired launcher tubes.

Weems could be right, and Camellion hoped he was. At the same time the Death Merchant was not one to permit overconfidence to interfere with common sense. There were too many possibilities, too many X-factors. Even if they got to Alcatraz Island without meeting any police helicopters, there was always the very real danger that something had gone wrong on the Coast Guard end. There were too many crooked policemen to expect flawless cooperation from the

San Francisco Police Department. The operation would have leaked to the press. Anyhow, the SFPD didn't patrol San Francisco Bay. That was the job of the U.S. Coast Guard whose cooperation had been a must. Accordingly, a high official from the Company had paid a visit to the commander of the U.S. Coast Guard in the San Francisco area. The officials had explained that the Coast Guard, in days to come, would get a request from the San Francisco police to stop and board a small blue and white fishing boat. The boat would be the Suzy-Q. The Coast Gurad would only pretend to obey the order. The official from the CIA explained to the startled commander that an operation, vital to the security of the United States, would be under way and that the Suzy-Q would be an important part of it. Therefore, under no circumstance would any U.S. Coast Guard patrol cutter interfere with the Suzy-Q. Later, the Coast Guard could tell the SFPD that it had looked for the vessel but missed it.

The official also reminded the coast Guard commander that to reveal any of the information carried a fine of $10,000 or a term of ten years in prison, or both.

One of the Death Merchant's prime worries was that police choppers might trail the Bell Kiowa to Alcatraz, witness the transfer from the eggbeater to the Suzy-Q, and then follow the boat to the deserted shipyard.

It was a risk the Blood Bone Unit would have to take.

Joe Tensor, as pragmatic as Camellion, began to load the other missile launcher.

Jerry Harkloff, now flying the white bird over John McLaren Park, was keeping the chopper at an altitude of only four hundred feet. The lower the craft, the less likely its chances of being spotted by police helicopters.

It was ironic that the deserted naval shipyard was only ten miles to the east, but to fly the bird straight to the shipyard was entirely too dangerous. Should police see the Bell Kiowa land, they would surround the entire area and the result would be catastrophic.

The chopper was three-fourths of the way to Alcatraz and over the northern section of San Francisco when Camellion and his people spotted the two police helicopters coming at

142

them. Both were Hughes Defenders, two-men deals that could cruise at 150 mph, against the Bell Kiowa's 120 mph.

There was a third helicopter, a Hughes TH-55 Osage, a red bird trimmed in yellow. It was flying at an altitude of a thousand feet and six hundred feet to port of the Bell Kiowa. It was not a police craft.

The police craft to starboard began closing in, but held its position when it was parallel to the Bell and only three hundred feet away. The second police craft remained at a steady hundred feet above the Bell and several hundred feet to port.

"This is sure enough to shuck your corn," Camellion said, picking up one of the loaded missile launchers and glanced at Weems who was looking at the little red Osage through a pair of binoculars.

Sitting flat on the floor toward the rear, Willis Coultervane looked petrified, fear freezing his face into a mask.

"Yeah, and it doesn't do much for the pea-hay either," yelled The Strange One who, on the port side, picked up the other launcher. "You take out the one on your side. I'll smear the other two. Max, can you make out what it says on the other side of that ship?"

"The letters say 'KTWK NEWS,' " Weems said. "It's a TV news chopper. That's all we need."

"Take all three out," Camellion yelled, "and don't take too long to aim. We don't want them buzzing off out of range."

The Death Merchant placed the launcher across his right shoulder, made sure the firing end was through the window, sighted through the optical box and squeezed the trigger.

Whooshhhhhhh! The eighteen-pound infrared terminal homing missile was on its way.

There was another *whooshhhhhh* from the port side and Tensor's missile streaked from its launcher.

The two police helicopters were doomed. At such short ranges it was only several seconds before the heat-seeking missiles found their targets and exploded, the two SFPD Air Patrol choppers vanishing in brief but bright flashes of fire.

Warren Dunaway, the pilot of the KTWK NEWS bird, was not a fool. The hell with the story. These terrorists were too well armed. The six o'clock news could get along without his "personal eyewitness" account.

Dunaway was pulling up and swinging the Osage away as The Strange One dropped another missile into the launcher, raised the tube-like device to his shoulder, aimed and pulled the trigger. Dunaway had gained only 2,400 feet distance when the WAr Hawk missile hit his craft and exploded. A big *BERRROOOMMMM!* A giant flash of red fire and thousands of pieces of metal and other debris began raining down on San Francisco.

By now, Jerry Harkloff and Cathy McManus could see the dim outline of Alcatraz Island in the distance. To their right and ten miles to the east of Alcatraz were the U.S. Naval Station, Treasure Island, and Yerba Buena island.

At full throttle the chopper flew over the Golden Gate Recreational Area beach. To the east was the long San Francisco-Oakland Bay Bridge. To the west was the Golden Gate Bridge. Ahead—Alcatraz, now deserted, although curious people were always coming to the island and rubber-necking at what was once the most notorious prison in the United States, the "Devil's Island" for super bad boys.

These snoops were still another problem for Blood Bone Unit. Or they could be. Most of them always came to the south side of the island, where the front of the prison faced. Seldom did anyone ever go to the northwest shore, off which the Suzy-Q was moored.

Within a very short time, Harkloff was taking the Bell Kiowa west of Alcatraz, at an altitude of only 165 feet. During those moments, the Death Merchant and the others caught sight of several small cabin cruisers moored south of the island and knots of people climbing the rocky incline toward the front of the prison buildings.

There was the Suzy-Q bobbing in the water. The boat was a vessel that had once belonged to Special Boat Squadron 4 and had been used by SEAL and UDT teams in 'Nam. The boat's design was actually an offshoot of commercial craft used to support offshore drilling platforms in the Gulf of Mexico. Fifty feet long, Suzy-Q had two shafts and was powered by General Motors diesels to a speed of 25 knots. Only her weapons were missing—a twin 50-cal. MG in a gun tub atop and behind the con, and the "piggyback," an 81mm mortar with a 50-cal. MG on top of the mortar. The gun tub had been removed and a mast with cargo booms had been added to the center foredeck.

Expertly, Harkloff descended over the stern, bringing the bird down until it was possible for Camellion and the others to leap from the port side of the chopper to the deck of the boat—including Harkloff. Technicians had equipped the Bell Kiowa with an automatic pilot. All Harkloff had to do was push buttons. After he pushed the last one he had 105 seconds to get out of the bird, more than enough time for him to leave the pilot's seat, go to the rear and jump to the deck of the Suzy-Q.

Bracing himself against the down wind from the rotor blades, Camellion waited, and so did the others on deck, including Baxter Lincolnwell and Tony Larocca. At length the last second clicked off and the automatic pilot took over the controls of the Bell Kiowa. The rotor began to rev up and the helicopter rose into the air. The bird would continue to rise until it was 700 feet above the water. It would then turn and fly due west until its fuel was exhausted, after which it would fall into the Pacific Ocean. Within moments, the Bell Kiowa was lost in the distance . . . a speck, then it was gone.

Joe Tensor and Max Weems hustled Willis Coultervane below deck and Roy Lee Orr, a contract employee, fed fuel to the two GM diesels and got the vessel under way. Wyatt Scronce, another "private contractor," was also in the wheelhouse.

Camellion turned to Baxter Lincolnwell. "How about it, Bax? Anything unusual happen out here while you were waiting for us?" Putting on amber-colored glasses, Camellion began scanning the sky.

Lincolnwell shook his head. "Everything's been quiet out here." He smiled laconically at Camellion. "We've been monitoring police calls. The entire San Francisco police department is in an uproar over the choppers you destroyed. There's been no mention of the PLO, only that 'terrorists' kidnaped Coultervane and used a helicopter to escape in. Congratulations. You and the others did a good job."

Camellion lowered the hand that he had been using for a sunshade. There wasn't a chopper in the sky.

"We still have more than forty miles to go," Camellion said. "If the police connect the chopper with this boat and the Coast Guard fouls up, we'll have had it."

"Yes," Lincolnwell said. "It's too bad that life's problems don't rear up when we're twenty and know everything. . . ."

CHAPTER ELEVEN

People who are rowing seldom rock the boat! Blood Bone Unit didn't have to row the Suzy-Q, and the boat had already been "rocked" by the series of events at the Big Green Mountain complex at Majestic Mall. If the police had spotted the Bell Kiowa discharging its cargo over the Suzy-Q and had notified the United States Coast Guard, it was now up to the Coast Guard *not* to find the small vessel.

The Coast Guard didn't. The Suzy-Q moved east, then turned south into San Francisco Bay with Roy Lee Orr at the wheel keeping the boat six miles from the 'Frisco shore to the west.

Without any trouble the Suzy-Q pulled finally into the deserted shipyard where it was quickly covered with a heavy tarpaulin. The ruse had worked. Blood Bone Unit had reached "home."

There was another reason why the Death Merchant and his people were elated: Willis Coultervane had revealed everything he knew. The Death Merchant had only had to point the .45 Star PD at the man and tell him he had the choice of answering any and all questions or dying, "inch by inch."

Coultervane had chosen to live.

Once Camellion and the others were inside the superstructure of the Dealey, Camellion used an AN/URC-101 SATCOM transceiver[1] to report to Grojean on the 229.9 MHz band, one

---

[1] Courtesy of Tom Kneitel, Editor of *Popular Communications*, 76 North Broadway, Hicksville, NY 11801.

of the bands used by the CIA at Camp Peary, Virginia[2]. So small it could be carried in a rack on a man's back—minus Black Box, decoder, and scrambler—the AN/URC-101[3], capable of both clear and secure voice as well as data transmissions, featured an internal low-noise synthesizer for operation with modems for data transmissions. To the Death Merchant, the set was a dream, the, 5 kHz spacing permitting more than 6,800 VHF channels in the 116-149.995 MHz AM and FM range, and 35,000 UHF channels in the 225-399.995 MHz Am and FM range. Another excellent feature was that the transceiver could be used anywhere in the world, since it had 20 watts of power for communication with various U.S. SATCOM satellites.

The Death Merchant kept the report simple and to the point. Although Willis Coultervane was deeply involved with Philip Butler, acting as a fence in Dandy Phil's hijacking operations, Coultervane was not directly embroiled with Butler in the KGB plot to steal the secret of the GA-1 microprocessor. Coultervane did not have any information of value. However, this didn't mean that the Death Merchant didn't have a lead. A short time before Doctor Burl Martin disappeared, Dandy Phil Butler had asked for Coultervane's permission to use the buildings of a winery in southern California. Located eleven miles northwest of Sage, or thirty six miles west of Palm Springs, the winery had been closed down since 1958. In 1974 the buildings and the surrounding 485 acres had been inherited by Coultervane's wife, Maxine.

Back came Grojean's reply, scrambler and decoder working in unison in milliseconds. "I see. And you feel that the KGB and Butler are holding Doctor Martin in the old winery."

"Affirmative," Camellion said. "The winery would be ideal. It's very isolated. They could hold him indefinitely out there. They won't. They'll want to get him out of the U.S. with all possible speed. The logical route would be a submarine."

"The KGB is not stupid. A submarine would be too obvious."

[2] Another "UHF aero band" at Camp Peary is 226.4 MHz.
[3] The set is manufactured by Motorola Government Electronics Division, Scottsdale, Arizona, and is for sale to civilians—but be prepared to write a large check. . . .

"But the most expedient," insisted the Death Merchant. "It's a long shot, like the winery. But it's all we have."

"You have worked out a plan of attack, with a minimum of time and a maximum of effort?"

"I will have by the time you do what's necessary to insure complete cooperation of the Navy people out here and the Coast Guard."

"Consider it done," Grojean said. "Your time out there is now fourteen hundred hours. You and your people can expect full Navy and Coast Guard cooperation no later than sixteen hundred hours."

The Death Merchant spoke coldly into the mouthpiece of the telephone-shaped mike and earpiece. "I want absolute authority to do whatever is necessary for the success of the operation. Designation 'Tar-Baby' will do."

"Complete authority you have. Keep me informed. One more thing, Tar-Baby: have you terminated Willis Coultervane?"

"Negative. He's talking his head off. McManus is taking it down on tape. He's giving all kinds of information about his and Butler's criminal activities. The Feds will be able to put Butler and several hundred Satan's Gentlemen away for a couple of thousand years—if I don't get to Butler first."

"Excellent. After Coultervane is drained of information, of data the FBI can use against Butler and his group, put him to sleep forever. We can't risk having a single word of this operation leaking out. The American people are too naive to absorb the reality of our secret war with the KGB. And keep to TRANSEC[4] and TEMPEST[5] at all times."

"Don't I always?" Camellion said drily. "Bye-bye, Mr. G."

The coordination was not all that difficult. All that was needed was the proper data which, within a few hours, was provided by Deane Royall, the Station Chief of Stringbean-10Y in Daly City.

In the Officers' Briefing Room in the superstructure of the

[4] Means "transmission security"
[5] Means "avoiding any compromising or inadvertant transmissions."

Dealey, the Death Merchant and his group poured over a detailed map of southern California. There wasn't any problem about reaching the general area around Sage. Blood Bone Unit would use helicopters from the U.S. Army base next to the U.S. Naval Air Station, both of which were across the bay from San Francisco.

"We sure as hell can't get very close with those choppers," said Randy Kooney, one of the contract employees. "They make a lot of racket. Shit, they'd be ready to blow us away before we even put down."

An ex-Marine, Kooney was muscular, had long dirty-blond hair and was wearing gray cowboy boots, blue jeans and an open-collared burgundy shirt. In a TWBLC[6] shoulder holster, he wore a 9mm SIG autopistol, and a dump pouch, containing two spare magazines, attached to one of the rig's securing straps.

. Max Weems offered, "We can get within five or six miles of the winery without those cruds hearing the choppers. There should be a way we could meet cars at a prearranged spot."

"Why don't we just land as close as possible, rush in and attack and get it over with?" suggested Roy Lee Orr. His skin was the color of coffee. He wiped his face with a bandana and placed the heel of his right hand on the butt of the holstered Beretta M-951.

"That's no good," Camellion said emphatically. "We try to hot-dog it and several of us could get iced."

"Or they might kill Doctor Martin, to keep us from getting him," said Deane Royall.

The Death Merchant fixed his eyes on Royall. "There must be Company people in Palm Springs?" *If for no other reason than to keep an eye on the "retired" mobsters living in the area.* "How about it?"

"Yes, there is a small station in Palm Springs," Royall replied hesitantly and adjusted his glasses, his expression that of a person who was emotionally uncomfortable. "We could land the choppers at the Palm Springs airport and proceed the rest of the way by car. It would be risky. There couldn't be

---

[6] The Wild Bunch Leather Company, P.O. Box 5216, Scottsdale, Arizona 85261.

any security. Who knows how word might leak to the targets at the deserted winery."

If the other men didn't notice Royall's slightly nervous manner, Camellion did, and Royall's body language—certain movements of his hands—confirmed that he was reluctant to tell more.

"Out with it, Royall. What are you holding back?" Camellion smiled. Royall drew back, his eyes narrowing in suspicion. For a moment the two men faced each other like strange bulldogs.

At length, Royall said, "We could use a small ranch outside of Valle Vista. The ranch. . . ." Again he paused.

"OK. The ranch is used by the Agency," Camellion finished. "Who gives a diddle damn? Get on with it."

"I could arrange to have cars from Palm Springs meet us at Rancho el Rosa. That's the best I could do," Royall said.

"How far from Valle Vista is the ranch?"

"Four miles to the south."

"Not bad," mused the Death Merchant, looking down at the map. "Valle Vista is only twelve miles north of Sage, or eight miles from the ranch to Sage."

"According to the map, there ain't even four hundred people in Sage," said Wyatt Scronce. "Man, that town must be the pits!"

"Yeah, and I'll bet half of them are bean-heads," Tony Larocca said unpleasantly.

"What the hell are bean-heads?" Randy Kooney frowned.

"Spics! Mexes!" Larocca snapped, "You haven't been around California long, have you?"

"Where I'm from is nobody's business," Kooney said. "Where you hail from isn't any of mine."

"Knock it off, both of you," Camellion lashed out. "Keep personalities out of it. I don't care if Sage is filled with Martians!"

The Strange One chuckled. "A lot of us are old souls," he said. "Incarnations of Atlanteans . . . paying now for past mistakes."

"Tell it to the KGB when you meet them," Camellion said. "You can give the pig farmers a lesson in ancient history before you scratch them."

Frank Flavelton was all business. "The winery is three and a half miles west of Sage. It's all open country, scrub-desert, tumbleweeds and everything that's worthless."

"But the ground is hard," Camellion reminded him. "We could land at Rancho el Rosa and then use vehicles of the jeep and the land-rover type. There's plenty of them in Palm Springs." He moved his finger along a blue line on the map. "What we could do . . . we could go south on Route 3. We go through Sage, then turn off onto the country road that leads to the winery. All we'd have to do is turn off the road half a mile or so from the winery and move in the rest of the way on foot. It would be a snap with night vision devices." He looked at the assembled faces around the table. "Any comments?"

"What about the cops?" Otto Vaughn, another "private contractor," was clearly concerned. "There's a deputy sheriff's station at Hemet. If someone hears the shooting and reports it—"

"Who's to hear it?" laughed Baxter Lincolnwell. "My dear fellow, the winery is out in the middle of nowhere. There isn't anyone around for miles."

"Yeah, you got a point," nodded Vaughn.

"What about the Indians on the Ramona Reservation, just east of Sage?" asked Randy Kooney, pulling a long cigar from his shirt pocket. "Hell, they're always snoopin' around lookin' for booze or something to steal."

"Forget the Indians and the police." Camellion's voice was firm. "For the most part we'll be using noise suppressors. If the cops or"—he smiled at Kooney, who wore his long hair in a pony tail—"the redskins get in the way, we'll blow 'em up. That's easy."

"Hold on, Camellion!" spoke up Jerry Harkloff roughly. "I was paid only—I said only—to fly you people off the Big Green Mountain building. My contact didn't say anything about risking my butt in a second shoot-out. If I go along I want ten grand, the same as these joes are getting."

"You're not going," Camellion said. "You will remain here until this mission is over. I don't have to tell you about Rule Three, do I?"

Harkloff shrugged. "Fair enough. The food's good and I don't have anything else to do for the next few days."

The Death Merchant's eyes moved to Roy Lee Orr, then onto Wyatt Scronce and the other two on-contract "throwaways."

"The four of you are getting ten grand each to go all the way, to hang in there until the operation is completed. If—"

"Or until we're dead!" Vaughn said with a cryptic smile.

"You got it," Camellion said. "If you have any complaints, now's the time to toss them on the table."

Orr and Scronce looked surprised. Scronce lit a cigarette. Kooney blew cigar smoke in Camellion's direction. "I'm in all the way. I don't mind killing people. I say, let's get the hell down to Sage and do it."

"I second the motion," grunted Orr.

"Me third," drawled Scronce.

All four were misfits, lovers of danger and adventure, men the average person would call freaks—"anti-social" types— *But men who are indispensable in this kind of operation.* . . .

Satisfied that he could count on the throwaway contract workers, the Death Merchant turned his attention to Deane Royall.

"Tell you what, get on the radio, contact the station in Palm Springs and tell them the Who, What and Why of what's going down. Tell them it's a Priority One and that the Palm Springs station will serve as a DSU[7]. Make it a P-One DSP[8]. Another thing: tell them to go out to a sporting goods store in Palm Springs and buy a good crossbow and a dozen arrows with steel heads."

"Shit, who said Robin Hood was dead!" With low chuckles rumbling around in his throat, Tensor, the Strange One, went over to his gear bag and pulled out a bottle of brandy, a beer mug, and a can of chili powder.

[7] Direct Support Unit.
[8] Defense Support Program.

CHAPTER TWELVE

The unhappiest man in the Bell Jet-Ranger was Philip Butler whose careful plans had crumpled into the dust. The kidnaping of Dr. Martin had gone off smoothly, without a single hitch. The payoff by the Russians of the one million dollars (in cash) was another matter.

Yuri Kunavin had come to Butler's office, in the House of Pandemonium, and had informed him that the money would not be paid until Dr. Martin was safely on board a cabin cruiser and on his way to a Soviet submarine.

"The money will be turned over to you on board the boat," Kunavin had informed him coldly.

Butler had been flabbergasted. "Why you son of a bitch! That means I have to go with you and your people—on the damned ship—to meet the sub!"

The trace of a smile on Kunavin's face had been a taunt. "Exactly. Another reason we want you with us is that we need you implicated completely, to the point where you couldn't talk to the authorities even if you wanted to. No one's forcing you to go. But if you refuse, you'll forfeit the million."

Losing his temper, Dandy Phil had threatened Kunavin with instant death, warning the Russian that all he had to do was press a button and half a dozen men would swarm into the office and "put a bullet in you before you have time to blink!"

Yuri Kunavin had not been impressed. "Shoot me," he said in a soft voice. "But think about what will happen to you after I'm dead. My government will see to it that the United States government is informed of the expert assistance you and your organization have given the KGB. The remainder of your life would be spent in a federal penitentiary. Or, the KGB would kill you. It's your choice. If you want the million, you will accompany us. That is final.''

Now, ten minutes after the Sikorsky-58 had lifted off from the winery grounds, Butler wished he had told the Russians to keep their damned million. Either way he was doomed. He and the four Russians had been driving in a rented Sikui motor home and were halfway to the winery when the news had come over the radio: Willis Coultervane had been kidnaped!

Speaking English, Colonel Gorsetev had accurately described the situation: ''It's now a race against time, but only in a manner of speaking. Time is on our side. Once we have Martin and are on our way to Jalma, we'll have the edge. They will raid the winery, but no one there knows anything about the route.''

''From what we know of Coultervane, he will tell everything he knows,'' Viktor Chorf had said. ''Fortunately, he really doesn't know anything. We must, however, assume he will tell the CIA that he's permitted Butler to use the winery. There is a possibility that the CIA will use helicopters to raid the winery before we even arrive. We cannot ignore that possibility, Comrade Colonel.''

''This is not the Soviet Union,'' Gorsetev had said in a severe tone. ''These stupid Americans blame the CIA for all their ills. The CIA will not want the local police involved. They will move quickly, but quietly and very surreptitiously. By the time they surround the winery, our people and the motorcycle trash will be gone and we'll be on our way to Jalma.''

That was another thing that irked Butler: the Russians spoke and acted as if he didn't exist! Way back in his mind, Butler wished he didn't. His world had crashed around him within the space of hours. So he'd get the one million dollars once he and the Russian agents were on the cabin cruiser. Fine, but what would he be coming back to? Willis was as crooked as two snakes making love, but he was a weakling. Hell, all they'd have to do is shove a gun in his face and he'd be confessing until the second ice age.

Never had Dandy Phil felt so alone and helpless. There was

only the darkness outside the helicopter and the soft glow of the green lighting within. Jalma was 190 miles to the northwest.

In the seat next to Butler, Dr. Martin sagged against the gang leader who roughly pushed him aside. The scientist was so heavily sedated that he was almost a zombie, unaware of where he was or what was happening to him.

Butler was instantly alert when the heavyset Russian with the manhole cover eyelids spoke in Russian. Damn them! raged Butler mentally. Why couldn't they speak American?

"Comrade Colonel, why not kill Butler when we land at Jalma?" suggested Viktor Chorf. "Why bother to take him with us on the boat? Four of our own 'illegals' will be handling the cabin cruiser, and they will be going with us on the submarine."

Colonel Gorsetev smiled. "We'll kill him on the boat. I want to see the expression on his face when he learns that we have taken him. . . . what's the expression? Ah, yes, 'taken him for one way ride.' "

Feeling more uncomfortable than ever and now slightly afraid, Butler glanced at his watch—9:55. In a few more hours it would be Friday.

Butler wondered if he would live to see Saturday. . . .

CHAPTER THIRTEEN

Perfect! Two Kaman Huskies SH-2 Navy helicopters had flown the Death Merchant and his small force to Rancho el Rosa, where three grim-faced CIA career men had been waiting with jeeps, each equipped with wide desert tires.

Then the drive to the winery, the three jeeps proceeding the last three miles with lights out. But infrared night vision devices were not needed. There was a full moon and the wilderness was brightly illuminated.

The CIA officers parked the jeeps within a clump of mesquite and Camellion and his nine men proceeded on foot for the last mile, the three drivers remaining with the vehicles. Every man, including the drivers, carried a Repco RPX transceiver which insured instant communication, a must. In addition to handguns carried in shoulder or hip holsters, each man had the best weapons one could use in a clandestine operation: Ingram MAC-10s with noise suppressors and two pouches filled with two magazines of .45 Hydra-Shok cartridges, forty rounds to a magazine. The Death Merchant also had a Barnett-Panzer crossbow of the paramilitary type.

Finally approaching the winery from the east, Camellion deployed the men so that the two-story stone house, the grape sheds and the vat building would be surrounded. Two men would move in from the west, three from the north, two from the south and three, Camellion, Randy Kooney and Joe Tensor, from the east, moving toward the front of the winery.

Lying flat in the sagebrush a hundred and fifty feet from the front of the house, Camellion very quickly saw that the crossbow wouldn't be needed. There were no guards posted. If there had been lookouts, they were now moving in and out of the house with the rest of the men, hurriedly loading camp-type mattresses and other items into half a dozen cars and three Volksie mini-buses parked in front of the house. What had troubled the Death Merchant more than anything else had been the sound of the helicopter that he and the others had heard, or thought they had heard, when they were four point seven miles east of the winery.

Camellion was now positive he had heard the chopper. The eggbeater had carried Doctor Martin away and the men who had been guarding the microelectronics expert were now hoping to get away before they were attacked by the authorities.

What was, *was*. What is, *is*. Kidnaping Willis Coultervane had been a gamble in more ways than one. Automatically the KGB had assumed that Coultervane had confessed about the winery and had gotten to Martin first. *Damn! And by less than an hour! But the ball game's still not over*.

"Those guys are in a hurry to get the hell out of there," Kooney whispered to Camellion and Tensor.

"They only think they're going," growled Tensor.

The Death Merchant had already pulled out his RPX walkie-talkie and was speaking into the mouthpiece. "The targets are pulling out. Move in as fast as possible and try to take as many of them alive as you can. Acknowledge."

One by one the other seven men said they understood.

"We'll crawl twenty meters closer and then open fire, first on the vehicles," whispered Camellion to Tensor and Kooney.

"How far is twenty meters?" asked Kooney.

"Almost seventy feet," Camellion told him and began to wriggle forward on the ground, the sweet smell of honeysuckle and mimosa drifting to his nostrils. "Take your time. Any loud noises will blow the whole deal."

It wasn't noise, however, that warned the four KGB agents and the seventeen Satan's Gentlemen who had been using the old house. It was the bright moonlight that enabled Bernie Coleman, carrying a dry ice cooler full of beer to one of the mini-buses, to detect the outline of Camellion who, at the time, was eight feet ahead of Kooney and the Strange One and only seventy-five feet from the closest mini-bus.

"They're here!" Coleman yelled a warning. He dropped the cooler, tried to pull a Colt .45 auto from his right hip pocket and duck behind a car. He failed. A three-round burst from the Death Merchant's MAC-10 ripped into his midsection, turned his stomach and liver into bloody mush and kicked him to the ground.

A dozen or so other men—some on the front porch, others moving to or from the cars and the buses—turned and raced for the safety of the house. But not Hugo McSpratan and Curtis ("Rubber Lips") Nenitz. They were close to one of the mini-buses. Diving back inside, the two gunmen pulled weapons, turned toward the east and prepared to open fire. They never got off the first shot. By then, Camellion, Tensor and Kooney had gotten to their feet and were charging ahead in a zig-zag pattern, the Death Merchant charging toward the house, his two partners taking time to rake the vehicles.

A long, raking blast of .45 Hydro-Shok slugs from Tensor's SMG stitched a line of jagged holes in the metal of the yellow mini-bus, some of them stabbing into McSpratan and Nenitz. McSpratan cried out in agony and shock and dropped the .38 Security Special revolver when a bullet caught him in the right side of the stomach. Another .45 projectile almost tore off his left arm at the elbow. A third bullet entered his throat just below the chin.

Rubber Lips Nenitz died even quicker. Two slugs erased his face, backed apart his brain and tore out the back of his skull, all in a single second. The S&W .38 Military revolver slipped from his hand and he fell back, a fountain of blood spurting from where his face and most of his head had been.

During that fifth of a minute, the Death Merchant had reached the front porch and was storming up the four long wooden steps, doing his best to watch not only the open door but the two dirty windows to his left and the three windows to his right. At the same time, Orr, Flavelton and Lincolnwell closed in on the house from the north while Larocca and Vaughn, from the west, rushed through the back door into the large kitchen, their MAC SMGs *phyyt-phyyt-phyyt*-ing out streams of high velocity death that knocked holes in pots and pans, made a mess of paper plates on a table and, ricocheting from an old-fashioned iron pump by the sink, made high screaming sounds. But the firing served its purpose: to keep the hoods disorganized in the front section of the house.

Coming from the south, Max Weems and Wyatt Scronce

159

jumped onto the front porch just as the Death Merchant was getting ready to charge through the door and Tensor and Kooney were rushing up the steps.

As he moved through the door, Camellion pulled one of the Black Widow autopistols from its ballistic nylon holster on his belt and prepared to kill or be killed. In a flash, as he swung around, he saw that the gunmen were in what had once been a large living room and that they were confused and in total disarray. The attack had come with too much speed, and the firing of the Death Merchant had been too intense for the enemy to set up any kind of real defense.

Moving with great speed, Camellion darted to his left, his right hand firm on the MAC-10 which he was using as a pistol—difficult because its silencer made the SMG very imbalanced—and his left hand around the snug butt of the Black Widow.

The Strange One and Randy Kooney were charging in behind Camellion, their hands filled with weapons.

As for Satan's Gentlemen, they tried their best to rally, for none of them were cowards (each man priding himself on his toughness and physical strength), yet brute strength was never the equal of submachine gun slugs.

The four KGB agents had also been taken off guard.

"Oobit yikh, oobit yikh veekh!" shouted Aleksei Antipin, so filled with rage and hatred that he had spoken in his native tongue. *"Kazhdova prokliatovo iz nikh!"* [1] Antipin ducked down, with the three other KGB agents, behind a dusty, ancient couch. Trained to be survivors, Antipin and his three comrades estimated that, as the fighting progressed, they might be able to reach the stairs and hide in rooms on the second floor.

"Don't fire at any of the damned Americans," whispered Georgi Astaskov. "We do not want to draw attention to ourselves."

The Death Merchant suddenly found himself in a sea of strange faces. He was right in the middle of the enemy. Tensor and Kooney found themselves in the same fix. Behind

[1] "Kill them! Kill every Goddamn one of them!"

160

Camellion and his two partners, Max Weems came charging through the front door, followed closely Wyatt Scronce.

Playing it cool—they wanted to live long enough to spend their tax-free ten thousand dollars—Tony Larocca and Otto Vaughn stepped from the south side door in the kitchen into a short hall that opened into the living room.

Allan Ohlau—all 243 pounds of him—flung himself at the Death Merchant, his big hands reaching out for the silencers of the Ingram MAC-10 SMG and Camellion's left hand, filled with the deadly Black Widow. He might as well have saved his time and energy. He hardly had time to be surprised at the speed with which Camellion let him have a short right spin kick, the bottom of the Death Merchant's booted foot halfburying itself in Ohlau's abdominal region.

Instant agony! Feeling as though red hot barbed wire was being dragged through his intestines, Ohlau was gurgling on bile and going down as Lennie Nuding and Joe John Numii started to rush the Death Merchant, Numii's right hand filled with a 9mm Super-Star pistol. At the same time, Ollie Wogers and Clyde Zion—low scum whose fathers could have been two of several hundred men—made a dive for the Strange One. Other members of Satan's Gentlemen rushed Max Weems, Randy Kooney and Wyatt Scronce.

Tensor had flung aside his MAC-10, which was almost empty, and was using one of his Ruger mag revolvers and—an earsyringe. He had, however, replaced the small, rubber bulb of the syringe with one that was much larger, and had it filled with DMSO, an instantaneous penetrating agent, and concentrated novocaine.

"Fools!" snarled Tensor at Zion and Wogers—the hell with Camellion and his "take as many alive as possible" crap, he thought.

Clyde Zion—so bearded he looked like the Apostle Paul—didn't even get off to a good start with his S&W .41 Military and Police revolver. Tensor pulled the trigger and the Ruger boomed, the large .44 flatnosed projectile exploding Zion's hairy face and, after splitting his brain, tearing out the back of his skull. The powerful bullet kept right on travelling, barely missing Billy Valerius and burying itself in the wall.

Ollie Wogers almost reached Tensor before he ran into the

Strange One's foot, the tip catching him squarely in his jingle-jangles. Wogers screamed like a woman being tortured with heated flatirons, the agony in his testicles so intense that it seemed to be trying to poke holes in the top of his head. His strength gone, a lump of despair in his throat, Wogers started to topple to the floor. He was on his knees when he received another TNT power kick from Tensor, a Shito-Ryu karate slam, a *Mae Geri Kekomi* (front thrust kick) to the side of the jaw.

Meanwhile, the Death Merchant was making short work of Numii and Nuding. Twisting to one side, Camellion managed to avoid the 9mm bullet Numii had flung at him from the Super-Star, the projectile breezing several inches to the left of his black nylon jumpsuit.

Joe John Numii was a dead man. The Death Merchant swung the MAC-10 and squeezed the trigger. *PHYYTTTTT-PHYYTTTTT*. The noise suppressor attached to the barrel of the Ingram M-10 whispered and small pieces of cloth jumped and fluttered from the six holes in Numii's sand-colored shirt. Stone dead, Numii wound to the floor, mouth and eyes wide open, blood gushing from his mouth.

Lennie Nuding was too slow. Like turtles, he and the gang members went after Weems, Kooney and Scronce.

"You're built upside down: your nose runs and your feet smell!" muttered Camellion as he slammed Nuding full in the face with the end of the silencer, feeling the maxilla and the zygomatic bones shatter under the hammer-like smack of the noise suppressor. Camellion was about to put a dent in Nuding's skull with the side of the silencer when big, bad Burton Young—he was built like a baby King Kong—grabbed Camellion's left wrist and twisted the Black Widow from his hand. The Safari Arms autopistol slipped from Camellion's hand. In the same motion, Young tossed a right uppercut, which Camellion managed to duck. He was about to slam Young in the throat with the muzzle of the silencer, but he didn't get the chance, nor did he have to. The Strange One had used his ear syringe to squirt DMSO and novocaine on the back of Young's neck. In less time than it takes a tornado to blow away a house made of straw, the mixture of DMSO and novocaine penetrated Young's skin and entered his blood stream. Instantly, the goof felt as if he were being turned to stone. Here, there, almost everywhere feeling fled, and he suddenly got the idea that he was looking out of eyes that, along with his head, no longer existed! The numbness reached his lower leg, then his ankles and quickly spread to his feet. Unable to maintain his balance, he toppled.

So did Nelson "Black Charlie" Widside and Max Wittenbach, the latter of whom had tried to blow away Randy Kooney with a double-barrelled shotgun. Just in time, Kooney kicked up and out with his left leg, his foot knocking the barrels upward as Wittenbach pulled both triggers. The weapon boomed, the double blast blowing two holes in the ceiling. Before Wittenbach could lower the now empty weapon, Kooney's SIG P-210 autopistol cracked twice, the two nine-millimeter slugs stabbing Wittenbach in the chest. He was kicked back against Tag Varner, who had tried to take out Max Weems with a series of karate chops, stabs and blows. Weems had grinned, spit in his face and ducked every attack. Worse for Varner, Weems had counterattacked and had just put Varner on a merry-go-round of pain with a *Yon Hon Nukite* four-finger spear thrust to the solar plexus. In agony, Varner now had only one hope: that Dale "The Hammer" Vasquiez, rushing in at Weems from the right, could save him. Called "The Hammer" because he preferred to fight with a small hammer in his right hand—the kind with a series of screwdrivers in the hollow handle—Vasquiez couldn't save Varner and didn't. Weems didn't waste any time. Always short-winded, he turned the Coonan mag pistol toward the wild-eyed Vasquiez and pulled the trigger. The big weapon roared, the .357 bullet stabbing Vasquiez's stomach, blowing through his spine and hitting Nelson "Black Charlie" Widside in the lower left side. Wyatt Scronce, about to blow away Black Charlie with one of his S&W .357 mag revolvers, was just as surprised as Black Charlie when the latter let out a short "OH-UHHH!" twisted his face in agony and fell. Scronce marvelled when he saw the Death Merchant take out Sid "The Sorrowful" Uffel and Billy Valerius with a series of fast kicks—a leaping left side thrust kick that caught Valerius on the jaw, then a lightning quick spin to a "Dragon-Whipping-its-Tail" kick that was aimed at Uffel's groin. But

163

the "tail" kick, falling short, only staggered Uffel. Snorting like an angry rhinoceros, Uffel rushed the Death Merchant who let the big dummy have a flying thunder kick squarely in the stomach, his foot almost giftwrapping Uffel's stomach and part of his liver around his backbone. Shock did the rest, and pain. The world went black and "The Sorrowful" started to sag.

Tony Larocca and Otto Vaughn were now against each wall at the end of the hall and peering into the large room. Roy Lee Orr had moved in through the front door while Baxter Lincolnwell and Frank Flavelton watched the ends of the wine sheds and the large building in which the fermentation vats were located. It was possible that some of the gang were in these three buildings.

Seeing that Camellion and the four others with him were wrapping up the supposedly bad dudes, Orr, Vaughn, and Larocca stood by and watched that free-for-all and the grotesque shadows the fighters made within the light of the three Coleman lanterns suspended from the ceiling.

Because of the dimness and the group of men in front of them, Vaughn and Larocca couldn't see the couch across the room, nor did they see Aleksei Antipin and the three other KGB agents crawl from behind the couch on their hands and knees and move toward the stairs in the northwest corner of the room.

Roy Lee Orr was more keen-eyed. He had hitched the Ingram MAC-10 to a ring on his wide leather belt and had unstrapped from his back his own personal weapon, a Weaver Arms Nighthawk semiautomatic carbine that resembled a submachine gun[2].

Huddled by one side of the doorway, Orr grinned malevolently. Yes, sir. That white boss Camellion he say to take as many alive as possible! And there are those four honkies creeping up the stairs, one after another, all in a row. How about that? Well, wait until the first two are almost to the top, then blow'em up. They'll fall back down on the last two white-faced cockroaches. Man, this is better than owning a whorehouse!

---

[2] Made by Bob Weaver of Escondido, California, the Nighthawk fires from a closed-bolt position and, with shoulder stock extended, has an overall length of 33½ inches. Sight radius is 21 inches. The magazine hods 25 9mm Parabellum rounds.

Watching the four KGB agents slink up the stairs, Orr raised the Nighthawk and let his eyes move through the open notch rear sight and travel on down through the front sight. He was getting set to fire when the Death Merchant spotted Emory Tallow, who had been slammed to the floor by Wyatt Scronce, reaching for the 9mm Super Star that had been dropped by the dead Joe John Numii.

"Friend, you need a throat operation, and I'm the hangman!" said Camellion who decided it was time to test a new knife that had been made by a friend of his on the east coast. Camellion shoved the Black Widow into his belt, pulled the Spartan[3] from its holster strapped across his chest and let sail the icepick-like knife, with the three-edged blade, at Tallow. He didn't miss. The blade of the Spartan buried itself in the lower left side of Tallow's neck, going in at a steep downward angle so that the steel handle protruded upward at a slant. The razor-sharp blade had sliced through a portion of Tallow's jugular vein and he was drowning in his own blood, choking to death in the crimson goo bubbling up in his throat. He fell on his face, his body twisting to and fro like an enormous worm.

Roy Lee Orr pulled the trigger of the Nighthawk, then again, and a third and fourth time and yelled, "HOLD IT UP THERE, YOU MAMMY WHACKERS!"

Only three steps from reaching the top of the stairs, Lev Boyko and Aleksei Antipin jerked, went limp and slid back down the stairs, stopping when they came to Vladimir Mitrofanova and Georgi Astaskov, both of whom realized they had been spotted. Neither Soviet agent was a fool. After all, imprisonment was better than death; and imprisonment they would get. Neither had diplomatic immunity, both being "illegals."

Placing their weapons on the steps, Mitrofanova and Astaskov raised their arms and stood up.

Seven of Satan's Gentlemen were alive, although only three were in reasonably good shape: Forest Throop, Tag Varner and Billy Valerius.

---

[3] Made for the Death Merchant by the famous knife-maker, E & T DeIntisis of Staten Island, New York.

165

Forced to sit on the floor surrounded by the Death Merchant and most of his men, the three hoods tried to tough it out. The two KGB agents sat quietly, expressionless. Astaskov and Mitrofanova realized they were trapped and that there wasn't anything they could do. Capture was part of the game. They had lost.

In response to Camellion's order to "start talking," Tag Varner glared up at him and snarled weakly, "Go to hell. We don't have to say a damn thing without our lawyers being present."

"Yeah. Give us our rights and take us in," said Throop angrily. "We have our rights under the Constitution."

Joe "The Strange One" Tensor grinned crookedly and turned to the Death Merchant. "These slobs sound like members of the ACLU, don't they?"

Added Max Weems, "I'll bet they're against the death penalty, too."

"Probably," said Camellion. "But I'm not." He pulled out one of his Black Widows, thumbed off the safety and looked from the two KGB agents to the three hoods.

"You lads might as well be good sports," he said in a pleasant voice. "One of you is going to talk. I don't care which one it is."

"Go to hell, you son of a bitch," Billy Valerius said with a smirk. "You don't scare us none with that damned gun. We know you ain't about to shoot!"

The Black Widow in Camellion's right hand roared. There was a thudding sound and a large piece of Valerius' skull, in the center of the forehead, went flying. Killed in an instant, Valerius fell back and lay still, his sightless eyes staring at the dirty ceiling.

"That's the trouble with being a good sport," Weems said in amusement. "You have to lose to prove that you are."

The Death Merchant's swift execution of Billy Valerius was more than a surprise for Tag Varner and Forest Throop. It was a catastrophic shock that killed all their confidence, reduced them to helpless cowards and forced them to admit that they were face to face with instant death.

Vladimir Mitrofanova and Georgi Astaskov were also severely shaken and afraid. This was not how the game was supposed to be played.

Camellion turned the muzzle of the Black Widow toward Tag Varner who made a noise like a perceptive turkey that senses it's the night before Thanksgiving.

"W-Wait! Wait!" cried Varner and threw up his hands. "All we can tell you is that the Russians c-called this dump 'Station-Y.' "

Camellion stared at Varner who had a boyish face fronting a shaven melon-shaped head. "Doctor Martin was here? He was held captive here?"

"We brought him here right after we grabbed him," Varner confessed fearfully. "The o-other men—"

"They were Russians!" cut in Forest Throop, his voice shaking.

"Other Russians came and flew him out in a helicopter, not more than an hour and a half ago," Varner said, twisting his hands. "We don't know where they was going with him. Honest to God we don't. Hell, ask them. They are two of the four Russians who were with us. You guys knocked off the other two."

Varner turned and glared at Astaskov and Mitrofanova. Both KGB agents ignored him and continued to stare straight ahead. They both gave a slight start when Camellion spoke to them in Russian.

"KGB—right? Which one of you wants to be stupid and die first?"

Georgi Astaskov, a major in the KGB and seven years the senior of Vladimir Mitrofanova, was convinced that he knew the American mentality. The CIA might shoot native American hooligans and thugs! Why not? Such trash was useless. But the CIA would not kill KGB officers. They would save them for interrogation.

Astaskov looked Camellion straight in the eye and smiled. "I have never heard of Doctor Martin. I—"

The Death Merchant promptly opened Astaskov's head with a .45 Black Widow projectile.

A corpse, Georgi Astaskov fell back and so did Captain Vladimir Mitrofanova—from fright.

"Give Joe Stalin my regards when you get to hell, pig

farmer," Camellion said in a quiet voice and turned the smoking muzzle of the Black Widow toward Mitrofanova, who was lanky, blue-green eyed and blond.

"*Nyet! NYET!* Don't shoot!" begged Mitrofanova. "I'll-I'll tell you what you want to know."

"Question number one," said Camellion. "Where have your pig farmer commrades taken Doctor Martin?"

The Strange One snarled, "They plan to get him out by submarine, don't they? We want to know the coordinates, where the sub will surface."

"Doctor M-Martin is on h-his way to one of our submarines." Perspiration poured from Mitrofanova's face and his voice betrayed his intense fear. "I-I don't know where the submarine will surface, nor the time of its arrival." He looked pleadingly at the Death Merchant. "American, you know how strict security is within your own intelligence apparatus. It is the same with us. Only Colonel Gorsetev and the others who left and took Doctor Martin with them know where the boat will rendezvous with the submarine. Kill me if you must, but I cannot tell you what I do not know."

Camellion and the others turned slightly when Baxter Lincolnwell came through the front door.

The Death Merchant returned his attention to Vladimir Mitrofanova. "You're telling us that Doctor Martin is going to be taken from the eggbeater and put on a vessel that will go out into the Pacific and meet the sub. Where will the chopper land and the good Comrades transfer to the vessel?"

"It was a Bell Jet-Ranger!" interjected Tag Varner, acting as if he were conveying vital information. "I know because the chopper was out in back of the house when we first got here with Martin. I was up close to it. It was a Bell Jet-Ranger."

Baxter Lincolnwell spoke up. "There aren't any targets in either the sheds or the vat building—as far as we can tell. Frank is still out there, just in case. We did find three empty fuel drums to the rear of the house. The inside of the drums smell fresh."

A worried look crossed Mitrofanova's face as he looked up at the Death Merchant. "I don't know where the helicopter will land. The landing and transfer point was on a Need-to-

Know basis. I was not among those who needed to know. That is the truth.''

"I think the son of a bitch is lying!" Weems tilted his head and turned a bit more to the Death Merchant. "I'll bet if you shot off one of his ears he'd come up with the name of the boat and could remember exactly where the chopper was going to make contact with it.''

Aware that Weems was working on the nerves of the KGB agent, Camellion went along with the act and pretended to consider Weems' suggestion. Vladimir Mitrofanova's eyes widened in alarm as he watched the Death Merchant raise the Black Widow.

"I tell you, I don't know where the helicopter is going to land,'' gasped the Russian, convinced that he was facing his own apocalypse. That he was telling the Americans what they wanted to know, giving them what information he possessed only increased his discomfort and decreased his self-respect, making him feel like a *inakomyslyashchiyesyi*.[4] "All I know is that the vessel is a large cabin cruiser and that the helicopter was filled with fuel before it took off from the rear yard. I swear on the blood of my mother that is all I know.''

"And the chopper?" Camellion looked closely at the Russian, watching every line in the man's face. "Was it a Bell Jet-Ranger? Don't lie, pig farmer!''

Interrupted Randy Kooney in disgust, "Who gives a fiddler's fuck what kind of chopper it was! What's the diff? They got away with Martin. That's all that matters—or should.''

Ignoring Kooney—who had ten feet of muscle and know-how and half an inch of brains—Camellion stared coldly at Vladimir Mitrofanova, who seemed confused and in agreement with Kooney.

"Y-Yes. The craft was a Bell machine. It was a Jet-Ranger,'' the Soviet intelligence officer said. Mentally he sighed in relief as he watched Camellion shove the Safari Arms Black Widow into a shoulder holster.

"This is enough to make me want to pee at the moon! Pterodactyl terds! We're at a dead-end!" Tensor complained angrily, looking around at the dead and the injured on the

---

[4] The closest translation would be the English word "heretic."

floor, all lying in twisted, grotesque positions, Allan Ohlau and Ollie Wogers moaning softly. Both men were in a bad way, bleeding internally.

"Well . . . where do we go from here?" asked Otto Vaughn, sounding like a little boy asking his father if he could go to the Saturday afternoon matinee.

"I'd like to know what we're going to do with these crumbs?" Tony Larocca motioned with his MAC-10 toward the injured men on the dirty floor and toward the three healthy thugs who stared up fearfully at the small band of commandos.

Lincolnwell finished blowing his nose, shoved the handkerchief into his pocket, sniffed loudly and looked at the Death Merchant who was shoving a full magazine into his MAC-10. "I say, Camellion. Joe's correct," Lincolnwell said in a practical way. "The helicopter has left with Doctor Martin and we don't know where it's going or where it will land. We don't know the name of the cabin cruiser or even what type it is. We don't know which direction it's going in or where the sub will surface and meet the boat. We *are* up a blind alley!"

He looked closely at the Death Merchant who didn't seem concerned, and Lincolnwell, sniffing, wondered why he wasn't. He knew that Camellion was not a man who took failure lightly.

"Wyatt, Tony, Randy, take our Russian friend out of here. He's coming with us. If he tries to run, shoot his knees off," Camellion said. He then nodded at Max Weems and the Strange One, both of whom had reloaded their MAC-10s and were pulling back the cocking knobs on top of the dandy little submachine guns.

"Terminate the rest," Camellion said cheerfully. "Should one word of this leak to the general public, the stink would give even more encouragement to the Soviet Union than those ignorant Catholic Bishops and their 'ban the missiles' policy that wants to leave this country defenseless."

"God, NO!" cried Tag VArner who guessed what "terminate" meant. He and Forest Throop became more panicky when they saw Camellion and the other men—two of them leading Mitrofanova by the arms—turn and head for the front door.

Only Tensor and Weems remained, their faces dark with ruthlessness and intensity of purpose.

Forest Throop blinked at the two men. "B-But you c-can't shoot us down in c-cold blood!" he blubbered.

"We'll make a deal," offered Varner, a small ray of hope still burning in his brain. The words flowed out of his mouth. "We'll tell you, tell you all we know about Dandy Phil. S-Sure! That's fair. We can give you enough on h-him to put him away for life. Okay? Okay?"

"We don't need any information on Butler," Weems said softly. "Willis Coultervane has talked his head off."

"But you don't understand," Varner said quickly. "Dandy Phil is with the Russians and Doctor Martin. He's with them in the chopper!"

Weems grinned. "That's nice. We'll kill him when we kill the Russians . . . saves a lot of time that way."

"And as far as killing you 'in cold blood,'" smirked Tensor, "would it help if we took you outside and warmed you up first?"

No sooner had the last word left Tensor's mouth than his finger gently touched the trigger of the MAC-10, the three-round burst slamming slugs into Varner's chest. Tensor's SMG continued to whisper projectiles through the noise suppressor while Weems fired, first blowing up Forest Throop, then raking the bodies on the floor with streams of slugs.

It took less than twenty seconds to turn the living room into a complete morgue, and when the firing stopped there were only bloody corpses, a blue haze and the smell of burnt cordite.

Pulling the empty magazine from his SMG, Weems said, "Say, did I ever tell you about the nearsighted zebra who fell in love with a pair of striped pajamas?"

Tensor was shoving a full magazine into his own MAC-10. "No, what happened?"

Weems let Tensor have a doty look. "What's the matter with you? That's the whole joke. There isn't anymore. . . ."

The group had moved over the desert as rapidly as possible and now were only five hundred feet from the three jeeps.

Glancing up at the big, bright moon and hating the satellite, Camellion said to Baxter Lincolnwell who was walking next to him, "Bax, as soon as we get back to the ranch, get on the 101 SATCOM radio and one of the Kamans and broadcast on the police bands. Mention something to the effect that 'three thousand kilos of the stuff was found on the premises'. You're fast on the uptake. Make it sound official. Word will leak out from some joker with a scanner that there was a big drug bust in this part of California. Sooner or later the press will connect the bust with the corpses we left back there."

"A good idea," agreed Lincolnwell. "Of course, it might be days or even weeks before the bodies are found."

Listening to the conversation, Roy Lee Orr said, "I could do it, Camellion." Then in pig Latin, "Iay ancay aysay itay ackbayardway ifay ouyay antway emay ootay!"

The Death Merchant chuckled. "I don't want you to say anything backward on the radio. We play it straight." He thought for a moment and added, "All at police the confuse wouldn't Latin pig."

"We all belong in a funny farm with double walls of rubber," growled Wyatt Scronce.

Walking behind Camellion and Lincolnwell, the Strange One wasn't amused. "We come out here to the middle of nowhere, shoot the saps, grab one commie creep and end up with no Doctor Martin, and we don't have one idea where to look for him—except the Goddamn Pacific Ocean! The Man on the east coast isn't going to laugh when we report one hundred percent failure!"

"Come on, Camellion, out with it!" urged Weems. "You must have something in mind. You're not going to take this lying down!"

"I'm not going to take it standing either!" Camellion was suddenly very serious, his voice low and implacable. "When we get to the choppers, we'll use the radio and contact the Commander of the Naval Air Station in San Francisco and the head honcho of the San Diego Navy base. We'll fly back to San Francisco and go to work."

"Go to work!" echoed Weems who sounded startled.

172

"Unless you mean we're going to depend on the SWS[5] buoys out there! Man, there's more than twenty thousand square miles of ocean in only several quadrants. We might as well look for a needle in Antarctica!"

"Max is right," intoned Tensor in a funereal voice. "Even if the buoys picked up a Soviet U-boat, how would we know it was the right sub? And even if we had a crystal ball and knew it was the correct baby, the transfer of Martin from boat to sub could be made and the sub long gone before we could even get there! We have to be practical. That means we don't have any leads—period!"

Camellion surprised everyone by saying, "But we do. We know that the Russians used a Bell Jet-Ranger, and we have a knowledge of Soviet psychology and KGB methods."

No one said anything.

The Death Merchant looked at his wrist watch—24.00 hours on the mark.

Exactly midnight!

We have until dawn. . . .

[5] Silent Warning System.

CHAPTER FOURTEEN

There are no miracles. There are only the results of unknown laws. Likewise, most problems can be solved by basic logic. Or as the Death Merchant explained: "Basic research is what I am doing when I don't know what I am doing."

Camellion didn't fool anyone. They all knew that he knew exactly what he was doing. They also knew there was one thing he couldn't control: Factor-X.

After the Death Merchant and his group returned to San Francisco and were in the main briefing room with Colonel Ralph Blair, the commander of the Naval Air Station, he explained that the Bell Jet-Ranger had lifted off from Rancho el Rosa with full fuel tanks.

"We know that the range of a Jet-Ranger, with no reserve tanks and a maximum load, is 490 kilometers, or 305 miles. The chopper that left the ranch carried six passengers. That's almost a maximum load."

"Mr. Camellion, please make your point," Colonel Blair said coolly. A dark-haired man of about forty (he kept the gray in his temples dyed), he had an intelligent face, a quick manner and was not at all happy having to take orders from—of all people—a civilian who was a goddamn "spook," especially a man who had called a special meeting at two fifteen in the morning! Blair had not be free to make the decision. The orders had come from D.C. at 19.00 hours the previous evening. He had to obey. Admiral William Travers, of the San Diego Navy base, and General Clint Jaggerson, the big boss of Edwards Air Force Base, had been given the same orders: *obey Richard Camellion.*

Accordingly, a telecommunications conference network was in effect—voice with triple scramble and computer shunt—

between the air station in San Francisco, the Navy base in San Diego, and Edwards AFB. An audio box with built-in speaker and mike was in the center of the long table in the briefing room. Identical boxes were in the offices of General Jaggerson and Admiral Travers.

Colonel Blair stared coldly at Camellion, who had come to the meeting with only Weems, Lincolnwell, Tensor, and Deane Royall. The rest of the men had remained on the rusty old Dealey in the deserted shipyard. Two CIA case officers and Cathy McManus would soon fly to Langley, Virginia, with Vladimir Mitrofanova, the only real prize that Blood Bone Unit had so far acquired. Willis Coultervane was not important, not any longer. His worries and cares of the day had vanished. So had he—into a steel drum at the bottom of San Francisco Bay.

Max Weems was not as polite as Colonel Blair had been.

"You're talking nonsense, Camellion. What you're really telling us is that Colonel Gorsetev and the Russians could have flown 305 miles in either direction—north or south. That's 610 miles. How can we build a search grid around 610 miles?"

"How can we be sure the Jet-Ranger didn't have spare tanks?" asked Deane Royall from the end of the conference table.

"The Jet-Ranger wouldn't need spare tanks to get to the coast," Camellion explained. "We also know that the Soviet agents are going to switch to a cabin cruiser. This leads me to believe that they are going to meet the sub pretty far out and can only do it with a boat. A small helicopter wouldn't have the fuel for the return trip."

Weems finished lighting a Pall Mall. "Let's say you're right. None of that tells us whether they flew north or south. Like I said, how do we set up a search area in a six hundred and ten mile square? The transfer from boat to sub wouldn't take ten minutes."

"There isn't any way we can know the answer," Blair said, his tone indicating that, as far as he was concerned, the matter was settled. "The only measure we can take is to send out patrol craft, both sea and air, and hope for the best." He turned his head toward the audio box. "What are your opinions,

General Jaggerson and Admiral Travers? Do you concur with what I have said? Over to you."

"I can spare four A-10 Close Support aircraft." General Jaggerson's deep voice came from the speaker in the box. "The A-10s are crammed with seek and search electronic gear. The craft are also heavily armed. But locating the Soviet submarine leads to another problem. Do we merely locate the submarine, or, if necessary, fire on it. We can't fire upon any vessel on the high seas, in international waters. We—"

The Death Merchant's voice was clear, loud and sharp. "General, if we find the Soviet submarine and it becomes necessary to fire, we will—and the hell with international law. You let me worry about that! Do you understand? Or must I repeat your instructions from the Pentagon?" I ask you: *do you understand?*"

General Jaggerson's "Affirmative" came out as a surprised, insulted growl.

Sounding mollified, Admiral Travers spoke up. "We'll use a dozen MK Three patrol boats from this end. They're of the Spectre class, are heavily armed and are very fast, almost thirty-five knots. I would also advise that we use Coast Guard cutters. However, my opinion is that locating the Soviet submarine will be a hit or miss proposition. The area is too large for any kind of effective search in so short a time. Over to you, gentlemen."

"We can narrow down the search area," the Death Merchant announced, turning his head toward the audio box but speaking to every man in the conference room. "The Jet-Ranger flew north. I repeat: the Jet-Ranger flew north."

He explained that in any field operation the KGB was always very cautious and that Colonel Gorsetev and the other Russians, holding Doctor Martin, would not have flown south because the beaches were entirely too crowded this time of the year. South of Los Angeles, the area was nothing but one long recreational beach, one mass of people from such coastal towns and cities as Redondo Beach, Newport Beach, Huntington Beach, San Clemente, Oceanside, Carlsbad, etc. Nor would the Russians risk landing the Jet-Ranger and changing to the cabin cruiser on the lower California peninsula—still

176

too many people, plus drug enforcement agents from both Mexico and the U.S.

The Strange One flatly disagreed. "The coast is just as crowded north of L.A. You've got Ventura, Santa Barbara, El Encanto Heights—a whole mess of beaches. Another thing, they could have flown 305 miles north."

Tensor got to his feet, picked up an eighteen inch steel ruler and a pencil and bent over the map. "Let's say they did fly north for three-0-five miles." He made a line with the pencil and the ruler. "Hell, that would place them off the shore of Monterey, between the 36 and 38 degrees longitude. Well, there are some deserted sections of beach along in that general area."

"The Russians didn't fly that far," Camellion said thoughtfully. He proceeded to say that while the Russians would want to land at a relatively deserted spot and get aboard the cabin cruiser in an area that was comparatively isolated— "They would want to cut down on air time, as much as possible. The KGB wouldn't risk interference from police helicopters. Keep in mind that they knew it was we who grabbed Coultervane. They knew we'd make him confess. All of you, pay attention."

With a pencil and ruler he made a straight line—"as the crow would flap his wings"—from Sage to Gaviota, the latter a small town a hundred or so miles northwest of Los Angeles.

"Right here is the closest deserted area. From Gaviota"—he moved the pencil straight west—"there is only deserted beach, not a single town. Oh sure, you'd find some beach bums, but generally speaking the area would be isolated. It's not fit for swimming or surfing. The waves are too big and there are too many rocks."

"Suppose you're wrong?" offered Max Weems.

"Right here is Point Conception," said Camellion, tapping the map with the pencil. "We move north along the coast and what have we got? Nothing but the little town of Jalma, then more deserted beach for another ten miles . . . nothing until we reach Arlight, past Point Arguello. If I were Colonel Gorsetev, I'd choose that general area. It would be ideal for his purposes."

He tossed down the pencil and looked around at the assembled faces, faces with expressions of doubt, of curiosity and, in the case of Lincolnwell and Colonel Blair, complete disagreement.

The Death Merchant didn't care what any of them thought. He had always listened to his instincts, to the Voice that whispered silently from the dark and unknown depths of his Unconscious. He intended to do so now. If he lost and the Russians won, the responsibility for failure would be his and his alone.

"Camellion, there is something you've apparently forgotten," Deane Royall said. "Why should the KGB need full tanks to fly to . . . say fly to Jalma or Arlight?" He paused as Lincolnwell loudly blew his nose, then said, "From Sage to that area is only about two hundred miles."

"I'll tell you what I think," said Camellion. "I think the KGB refueled the Jet-Ranger in the area I just showed you and then had it flown back to where it was rented, I'd say somewhere around San Francisco. No doubt the KGB from the Soviet Consulate in San Francisco made all the rental arrangements. You know how Soviet intelligence works. They never leave loose ends untied." His voice became more determined. "I'll tell you something else I think. The submarine won't surface too close to American sand. I estimate it will see daylight from one hundred to two hundred miles out. That's the grid search reference we'll use." He carefully made a circle on the map, the point of his pencil moving through the tiny towns of Jalma and Arlight, then west, out into the ocean. "We'll make the frame of reference a two hundred mile square and concentrate the planes and the vessels in that area."

"Mr. Camellion, even in so small an area, comparatively speaking, that's roughly forty thousand square miles," Colonel Blair said stiffly.

The Death Merchant smiled. "Which isn't quite as bad as a hundred thousand square miles." He spoke in a much louder voice. "General Jaggerson, those A-10s you mentioned. What is the effective search range for radar of each airplane?"

"I'm not sure offhand," replied Jaggerson. "I think about fifty miles. But Mr. Camellion, isn't it possible that the transfer has already been made. Doctor Martin might be on his way right now to the Soviet Union . . . a prisoner in one of their submarines!''

"He's got a valid point," said Tensor, as if talking to himself. "Shit! We might have already lost and don't know it.''

The Death Merchant replied to General Jaggerson: "Yes, that's possible, General. We have to work on the theory that Martin can still be grabbed from the Other Side. The KGB won't want high visibility. No bright sunlight for the pig farmers. At the same time, contact in the dark would be too risky. Too much chance for a slip-up. I'm betting the cabin cruiser will make contact with the U-boat at early dawn. If I'm correct, the Russians who escaped us in southern California are preparing to board the cabin cruiser right now.''

Admiral William Travers' voice came through the audio box. "Gentlemen, I suggest we coordinate our search plans. I agree with you, Mr. Camellion. It's a long shot, but it's all we seem to have.''

"Good, Admiral. Here is how we'll do it. Feel free to suggest technical details—you, too, General," Camellion said, one side of his mind thinking of what Courtland Grojean had said when Camellion had made his report, via the 101 SATCOME, after he had returned to San Francisco—". . . When this mess is over, win or lose, I hope you enjoy the climate in Burma, Camellion. . . .''

Damn Grojean. Damn Burma! But did it matter in the long run? After all, yesterday is but today's memory and tomorrow is today's dream.

And often that "dream" can be a nightmare!

CHAPTER FIFTEEN

The Trojan Meridian moved through the dark waters of the Pacific like some majestic animal. Sixty-two feet in length and powered by twin 185 Perkins diesels, the vessel was a very comfortable, all-weather, long-range yacht that could travel at a top speed of thirty-eight knots. The performance of the craft was outstanding. The sharp entry could cut through the water like a knife while the bow flare prevented plunging into head seas and kept the decks dry; and because of great lateral stability, the boat had less roll, both at dockside and underway. Named the Hero's Reward, the vessel was well worth the $1,210,000 the Russians had paid for her.

Always a worrier, Major Viktor Chorf was in the nine by fourteen feet, all-teak pilot house with Albert Fedorrekski, one of the KGB illegals who had lived as an American in the United States. For seven years, Fedorrekski had lived as "Fred Wilkerson" and had worked as an engineer at Quartz Products Corporation in Plainfield, New Jersey.

Mikhail Clenev, another KGB illegal, was on the jumbo sun deck, staring out into the darkness through a Vimmer infrared night vision scope. On the flying bridge was another illegal, Suren Toomputarov. He, too, was searching the blackness through an infrared vision device.

In the large master stateroom were Colonel Pyter Gorsetev, Captain Yuri Kunavin and two more illegals, Vasili Startsev and Gakin Pashail. Also present were Doctor Burl Martin, drugged into unconsciousness and lying on a settee, and Philip Butler, who felt completely out of place and more than slightly afraid. Relaxed on the settee, Gorsetev, dressed in white shorts and a white short-sleeved shirt, was drinking hot chocolate and secretly congratulating himself. The escape from the ranch had not even been close. There had been more than ample time to lift off and start the short flight to the point three kilometers from Jalma—and not one single bit of trouble from police authorities in helicopters. Why should there have been?

The landing of the Jet-Ranger had gone off as planned. Fifteen minutes later, everyone was on Hero's Reward and the yacht was headed out into the Pacific. The only people in sight had been in dune buggies several kilometers away.

The walkie-talkie next to Gorsetev buzzed. He picked it up on switched it on. "Da?"

The caller was Mikhail Clenev who reported that he had spotted a vessel several kilometers to port. "It's a large cabin cruiser and is headed southwest, away from us."

"It's not a problem," replied Gorsetev, speaking Russian. "But report any vessel you see. We can't be too cautious."

He switched off the walkie-talkie and, still speaking Russian, said to Vasili Startsev who, for the past hour, had been trying to set the correct time on his digital watch.

"Lieutenant Startsev, you have an American twenty-two caliber Ruger with you, do you not?"

"Yes sir. The weapon's in my bag."

"Take it out of your bag and get ready to kill this stupid American we have with us."

As Startsev slipped the watch back onto his right wrist, got up and went over to his bag, Colonel Gorsetev glanced at Gakin Pashail who was seated at the center table cleaning a Heckler & Koch P7 9mm pistol, and then smiled at Philip Butler who was sipping vodka mixed with lemon soda pop.

"About the money we owe you, Mr. Butler," began Gorsetev, enjoying Butler's discomfort. "I know you're anxious to be paid."

Although slightly drunk, Butler thought for a moment. He was walking through a mine field and knew it.

"Naturally I want the money. But how am I supposed to get back to San Francisco with a million dollars in cash? I know that Coultervane talked. Right now, the Feds probably have a warrant out for me!"

"We've solved that problem for you, Mr. Butler," Gorsetev said. "I can assure you that you'll never spend one day in an

American prison." Gorsetev noticed that Startsev had taken the Ruger target pistol from the bag and was cocking the weapon.

Butler also noticed and tried to appear nonchalant about it. He moved his eyes back to Colonel Gorsetev. "What the hell is this—gun cleaning time or what?"

Gorsetev smiled. "As I said, Mr. Butler, we have solved your complicated problem. You see, this boat is not going to return to shore. We're going to sink it. All of us are returning to the Soviet Union on the submarine—all except you. . . ."

Dandy Phil's mouth opened and stayed open. Then he snapped it shut, hatred flaring up in his eyes. It takes one to know one and he knew instantly that the KGB had pulled a double XX on him. . . .

Dandy Phil had few regrets. He had gambled all of his life and had won. This time he had lost. Hell, the damned Russians had stacked the deck from the very beginning.

"You Russian son of a bitch! I hope they blow you and that damned submarine out of the ocean!" Butler spat out. He knew he was as good as dead and would be very soon. Maybe it was just as well. Yeah, even better than living. Being dead was better than being a walking vegetable in prison for twenty years, or sitting on Death Row for five years!

"There's very little chance of the Americans finding us." Gorsetev moved his left hand slowly over his carefully combed hair, silent laughter in his gray eyes. "In another hour and a half we'll make contact with the submarine. But you won't be around. You're leaving now. Shoot him in the stomach, Lieutenant Startsev."

Startsev didn't. He couldn't. Dandy Phil threw the half-empty glass of vodka and lemon soda at him, then jumped up and tried to reach Colonel Gorsetev. He was halfway across the stateroom when Startsev, who had ducked the glass, shot him twice in the left side. One .22 long rifle hollow point hit Butler just above the belt, the second striking him in the hip, breaking the ilium bone.

Crying out loudly in pain and frustration, Butler flopped to the floor and began making "Uhhh-uhhh-uhhh" sounds, his fingers, claw-like, digging into the thick rug.

An angry Colonel Gorsetev, now standing, said angrily to Startsev and Pashail, "Get him out of here and throw him overboard. Let the sharks have a free meal."

CHAPTER SIXTEEN

By 15.00 hours the search was in progress, the Death Merchant and his force using four A-10 Close Support aircraft, two MK III patrol boats and five Sikorsky 3D Sea King helicopters. The two MK IIIs had been stationed at the U.S. Navy Supply Center north of the U.S. Naval Air Station, both of which were on the west side of San Francisco Bay—east of San Francisco proper.

Nine other MK IIIs were moving north from San Diego, but it was the consensus that these nine would not be effective. It would take them too long to reach the search area.

The method of seek and search was uncomplicated. The five Sea King choppers headed west. The two patrol boats moved west in a large zigzag pattern while the four A-10s, at a speed of 800 mph, crisscrossed the area. It was almost a certainty that if the cabin cruiser and the Soviet sub were found, it would be one of the A-10s that did the finding. There wasn't any method by which the pilots could recognize the cabin cruiser, until it was making contact with the sub. The big crack in the mirror was that by then—by the time vessel and sub were in contact—it might be too late to rescue Doctor Martin.

But not too late for Richard Camellion who, with his nine men, was riding in one of the Sea Kings—the command helicopter. The other four Sikorskys were filled with SEALS and USSAP[1] commandoes.

Without telling anyone, Camellion had made up his mind: either Blood Bone Unit would rescue Doctor Martin—*Or we'll have to kill him. That means killing any pig farmer who might be in the area and destroying the submarine!*

---

[1] United States Special Anti-Terrorist Personnel.

Hence the SEALS and the commandoes. If necessary, they would board the cabin cruiser and the submarine in an unheard-of action, that was technically piracy on the high seas.

Precipitate World War III? It was possible. It was not very probable. Other than being natural-born filth that polluted the human race, the Russians were cowards who fought only on their own terms, when they were ready, when the odds were on their side.

The Death Merchant had still another reason why he wanted the Soviet U-boat "dead," one he freely admitted to himself: he enjoyed killing communist trash. In particular, he enjoyed snuffing Americans who were traitors and worked for pig farmer freaks—*One way or another, I'm going to destroy that damned Soviet sub, if we find it . . . if I have the chance.*

At least their communications were first-rate, the best in the world. Using a new Collins tactical 150-watt 719D-15 HF transceiver[2], Camellion could communicate instantly with the two MK IIIs, the four aircraft and the other Sea Kings. Both the MK IIIs and all the aircraft were using the new 719D-15 HF transceiver that, easy to operate, had automatic microprocessor tuning, a built-in scrambler, and could be tuned from 2 to 29.999 MHz in 100-Hz steps. All the sets were locked to 18.416 MHz and set on open channel. The pilots of the A-10s, the Commanders of the two patrol boats and the pilots of the other four Sikorsky Sea Kings might as well have been sitting in Camellion's lap.

15.50 hours. The first faint streak of light was in the east, and so far all the reports from the four fast A-10s had been negative. The pilots of the A-10s had spotted numerous surface vessels, some moving west, but the pilots had no way of knowing which was the enemy vessel.

No sight of the Soviet submarine.

All decked out in combat gear, including ballistic helmet and combat goggles, Max Weems bent down and moved the bulky but light MMI weapon closer to his feet, at the same time announcing, "Something had better happen damn soon.

<hr>

[2] Ham operators who are interested in the 719D-15 HF transceiver can write to Collines Telecommications Products Division/Defense Electronics Operations/Rockwell International/Cedar Rapids, Iowa 52498.

In another ten minutes we're going to have a fullblown event called 'dawn.' ''

Everyone within the sound-muffled helicopter could hear his words, with the exception of the pilot who had on headphones, and possibly the copilot/gunner who was bent over the radar screen in the control compartment.

''I think we've lost the ball game,'' Tensor, the Strange One, said. ''Either they made the transfer during the night or—but I don't see how the planes could miss the U-boat if it's still on the surface. On the other hand, if they made the switch during the night, the U-boat has been long gone.''

''It's a large area, even the comparatively small part we're searching,'' Baxter Lincolnwell said thoughtfully, ''and there are numerous civilian ships down there. Radar can't tell the difference between friend and foe.''

''In this case radar seems to be like American education which maintains everyone is 'equal' in learning ability,'' Tensor said.

''Fuck a duck!'' exclaimed Wyatt Scronce. ''It was those damned crosstown buses and the lowering of standards to graduate apes that wrecked American education.'' He ignored the dangerous look that Roy Lee Orr gave him.

''Radar can tell the difference between a cabin cruiser and a submarine,'' Camellion said forcefully, ''and those pilots aren't blind.''

''You mean an *experienced* radar operation can tell the difference,'' corrected Lincolnwell, sniffing loudly. ''Whether or not the pilots of the A-10s can is a moot question at this point.''

''Well, I guess we're all pros, even if we don't find the sub,'' Randy Kooney said with a deep sigh.

''Yeah? How do you figure that?'' Tony Larocca cocked his head to one side in puzzlement.

''It's easy. Pros are people who get a job done even when they don't feel like doing it. And none of us want to be here—right?''

A moment later, Captain Edwin Rose, one of the A-10 pilots, reported to the Death Merchant that he had found the Soviet submarine and the cabin cruiser. Rose's excited words came in clearly over the telephone attached to the 719D-15

185

HF transceiver—"God! That sub is a big bastard! Four hundred feet long if it's an inch! It's got a raised part in the center of the hull, topside. It runs right into the sail!"

Feeling his heart pounding faster, Camellion switched the communications to the speaker box in the chopper, then spoke quickly into the mouthpiece of the telephone. "Rose, how high were you flying when you spotted the sub? And how do you know you saw the cabin cruiser?"

"The coordinate!" Tensor jumped in with both feet. "Ask him the location of the Russian bastard!"

Captain Rose's voice jumped from the speaker attached to the top of the fuselage. "There's a cabin cruiser—a big baby, I suppose it would be in the small yacht class—that's headed straight at the sub. The yacht is about nine klicks west of the sub. I was at twenty-six thousand when I detected the target on radar. I then went down to four thousand for a visual. The sub is there all right, sitting there like it owned the whole ocean. It's position is A-niner zebra-four, bravo at seventeen degrees, five minutes. Any orders, sir?"

"Slow your speed to 400 knots and fly west for sixty-four klicks; then turn around and come back at the same speed," Camellion said rapidly. "By then we should be on the scene. In theory, the Soviet skipper shouldn't be concerned. He's in international waters and we're always snooping in on Soviet vessels when we spot them. They do the same to us. There shouldn't be a problem. You got it all, Rose?"

"Affirmative."

Camellion spoke to the three other pilots of the A-10s. "You men stay clear of the sub. But stay high in the general vicinity. Patrol boat commanders, what's your position in reference to the U-boat?"

Reported Commander Charles Gray of the Sweet Willie: "We're still thirty-two kilometers from the position of the submarine."

"I'm twenty-one kilometers away from the sub," reported Commander Robert Cagey of the Silver Fish, the second MK III.

"The A-10s and the choppers can do what must be done," Camellion said. "Get there as soon as you can and keep the channel open."

Lieutenant Dewey Benjamin, the pilot of the command Sea King, said, sounding exhilarated, "We're sixty-four klicks from the Soviet boat. That's only forty miles and we're moving at a hundred and fifty-two knots per hour, and we've just picked up the sub on radar. We're practically there."

"Good. Drop down to a hundred and fifty feet," Camellion ordered. "Fly over the yacht first, then cross the sub. We'll see what kind of weapons they have, if any. You other pilots and gunners: hang off a thousand meters to port and be ready to fire when I give the word. Acknowledge."

At once came the "Affirmatives."

"We've got them cold," Tensor said and began checking his kill-equipment, paying close attention to his "Mean Mother One" which was fully loaded. "But Colonel Gorsetev isn't going to toss up any white flag from that yacht, and there isn't any way we can drop onto the deck of the ship without them smearing us all over the ocean."

Randy Kooney spoke up, his voice harsh and angry, "Listen, Camellion. I didn't sign on for any one-way suicide mission! Tensor's right. We can't get on that yacht or the sub without getting blown away—and you know it."

Max Weems looked at the Death Merchant who was casually checking his own Mean Mother. "We have to face one hard fact, Camellion: We've lost Doctor Martin. The Russians will kill him before they let us have him. How are we going to play it?"

A sly, calculating look crossed the Death Merchant's face. "I was thinking that every year it takes less time to fly around the world and more time to get to work."

"Oh shit," said Randy Kooney, twisting his mouth in annoyance.

"I said, how do we play this caper?" repeated Weems, his tone a demand.

Camellion's eyes glowed with a strange light and his low voice was chilling. "We're going to blow that yacht out of the water and send that Soviet U-boat to the bottom. The only regret I have is that we won't be able to send down divers to have a look inside that baby. It's about three thousand feet in this section of the Pacific."

*　　*　　*

187

The remainder of the sixteen minutes passed more quickly than a spinster's dream and very soon the command chopper and the other Sea Kings were approaching the Soviet Typhoon[3], flying over glass-like water, the waves moving from three to five knots, or Force-2 on the Beaufort scale—a "light breeze." Perfect weather for a slaughter. Pure dawn now, the sun visible in the east, all fire and radiant brightness.

The four other Sea Kings, maintaining their altitude, veered off. Lieutenant Benjamin began to drop the bird and started to go straight in toward the dark gray submarine.

"I say, look at the size of that thing!" exclaimed Lincolnwell with a kind of admiring awe. "It's not one of their Delta Class deals. By God! It must be one of their new Typhoons—and the yacht has pulled along side."

"It's a Typhoon," Camellion said, his voice dripping venom. To him, the submarine represented the worst form of horror and oppression the world had ever known—Soviet "freedom" that had murdered an estimated 40 million people since the days of Stalin, a "workers paradise" in which 18 million men, women and children were held in Gulags, a sinister hell on earth in which men, women and children died in droves from typhus, pleurisy and a hundred other illnesses, and were compelled by the lingering instinct of survival to eat rats, their own vomit and . . . even their fellow prisoners.

Throughout the length and breadth of the USSR, in thousands of camps, in prisons and on trains, was hidden a population larger than that of Canada[4], as large as Czechoslovakia or Yugoslavia, or of Belgium and Austria put together; and in each prison and in each work camp were the KGB sadists, the *parilka*, or "sweat room," and an utter lack of hope.

Even during World War II this slavery was going on—in Europe! Between a million and a million and a half Poles

---

[3] The Typhoon is the largest sub in the world and perhaps the noisiest. About 10,300 tons submerged, 9,400 surface. Overall length, 510 feet, beam 39.2 feet, draught 34 feet. The hull is titanium—lighter than steel but stronger. Nuclear-powered, the Typhoon has sixteen missile launch systems for the SS-N-8 missiles in tubes faired into the hull in front of the conning tower sail.

[4] In Death Merchant number 68, *Escape from Gulag Taria*—yet to be published—a full explanation of the Soviet slave system will be given—information printed for the first time anywhere.

were deported to the Soviet Union between 1939 and 1941. If these statistics were compared with the populations of England and the United States at the time, it means that the Red Army would have "liberated" the entire population of Greater London, Yorkshire, or Scotland. In the United States, KGB units—then the NKVD—would have stolen thirteen million people across the ocean and used them as slave labor—the entire population of greater New York, or the entire populations of North Dakota, New Hamshire and Arizona!

An extension of evil! thought the Death Merchant. *The submarine is but a minuscule extension of a greater evil, an evil that represents The Kingdom. . . .* [5]

By now the command Sea King was only five hundred yards east of the Soviet Typhoon and the Death Merchant and his men could see that the yacht, its bow facing south, had pulled up alongside the sub—the Skaldia-Volga—,the starboard side of Hero's Reward against the port side of the submarine. On the narrow forward deck of the U-boat, in front of the missile tubes housing, were the secured lines from the bow and the stern of the yacht.

The Death Merchant took the telephone from the 719D-15 HF transceiver and contacted Captain Rose. "Captain, how far are you from the pig farmer?"

"Uh—'pig farmer?' "

"The Soviet sub!"

"South—wait a second! About eleven klicks."

"Rose, come in fast and use your cannon to wreck the sail, the conning tower," Camellion ordered, noticing the slight gasps of surprise from Otto Vaughn and Frank Flavelton. "Then toss a missile or two to the rear of the stern, far enough away that the concussion wrecks the rudders and the screws. Do you think you can do it?"

"Watch me!"

"Luck—and out."

The Death Merchant barked orders at Lieutenant Barney Newheart, the copilot and the gunner of the command chopper. "Newheart, on our second go-over, when we come back

---

[5] There will be more about the mysterious Kingdom in future Death Merchant books.

from the west, rake the deck with your minigun. Blast the yacht, too. Acknowledge, please.''

"I understand, but sir . . . do you know—"

"I said DO IT. Or would you prefer a DD?"[6]

Lieutenant Benjamin's nervous voice popped out of the earpiece: "How far west do you want me to take the bird before I swing back over?"

"As little distance as possible, as short as can be done with a measure of safety. I leave that up to you."

"Good e-enough."

By now, the Sea King was practically on top of Hero's Reward and the Skaldia-Volga, and the Death Merchant & Co. saw—or rather sensed—that most of the enemy had moved from the yacht to the deck of the sub. There was a very brief spectacle of several dozen upturned faces staring at the low-flying Sea King whose five-bladed rotor was making a terrific *thub-thub-thub-thub*-ing sound. And there was Doctor Martin supported by a man wearing a white shirt and shorts and a second man whose gaudy shorts and shirt made him resemble a squat barbershop pole with arms and legs. The two Russians were half-walking, half-dragging the man between them to an open hatch in front of the missile housing.

The two pig farmers and Doctor Martin were only a dozen feet from the wide, square opening.

Then the sub was gone. There was only the calm Pacific Ocean, and the Sea King was moving west away from the U-boat, Lieutenant Benjamin starting to bank for another go-over when he was less than 300 feet west of the yacht and the sub.

"We don't know that the man is Doctor Martin?" offered Joe The Strange One Tensor, acting as if he were telling a joke.

"No, we don't," Camellion said drily, "anymore than we know there'll be an October 21, 1999. But who else would be so drugged that two pig farmers would have to help him?"

Tensor shurgged. "You have a point, you have a point. . . ."

The Sea King carried an XM27E1 six-barrel minigun in a pod below the nose of the eggbeater. Electrically controlled,

<hr />

[6] Dishonorable discharge.

the minigun could be fired by either the pilot or the copilot/gunner, the weapon geared for elevation, depression and traverse. Carrying 11,000 rounds of .30 claiber ammo, the rate of fire could be set at 2,000, 3,000, or 4,000 rounds per minute.

Play time! Lieutenant Newheart—his face glued to the instrument panel—opened fire the instant the big chopper had banked, turned and was headed east toward the sub. *BBERRR-RRRRRRRRRRRRRRRRRRR!* At the rate of 3,000 rpm, the minigun raked the forward deck of the Skaldia-Volga, a blitz of high powered projectiles, so much steel that it literally exploded the bodies of the terrified Russians racing for the open hatch. Heads, arms and legs, and pieces of heads, arms, and legs, separated from anatomized, totally torn torsos, flew upward and fell either to the narrow wooden-slat catwalk—which was also being ripped to pieces—or to the rounded sides of the submarine, to slide into the water, leaving long bloody smears behind them.

But Doctor Martin, Colonel Gorsetev and Major Chorf were safe. They had gone down the steps of the hatch only moments before the minigun had opened fire.

"We've lost Martin!" yelled Max Weems.

"Yeah, and all this mess because of a gismo you could put into a thimble."

Hundreds of .30 projectiles struck the Hero's Reward, the cloud burst of steel dissolving the pilot house, the forward deck, the upper jumbo sundeck, the fly bridge and the stern deck, scores of slugs also hitting the two 185 Perkins diesels and the fuel tanks. The Sea King was passing over the yacht—the minigun, now almost perpendicular, still firing—when the sleek pleasure craft exploded with a roar and a bright ball of fire, the instantaneous updraft pushing against the chopper. Fighting the cyclic and the collective throttle controls, Lieutenant Benjamin pulled in pitch[7] and kept right on going west, not wanting to be caught in any deadly blast from Captain Rose, who had swung to the north and, at five thousand feet from the submarine, was starting to make his kill-run.

---

[7] A term that means to make the helicopter rise.

If the minigun mounted on the Sea King was TNT, then the destructive power of the A-10 was an atom bomb!

Compared to the sleek fighters in the "F-series," the A-10 was an ugly bird. But trim has nothing to do with kill-power. Officially designated as the THUNDERBOLT III, the A-10 was nicknamed a "gun with wings"—and for good reason. While the Thunderbolt had wing pylons that could be filled with computer-controlled laser-guided missiles, or bombs, its main weapon was a GAU-8 gatling gun, the weapon taking up a prominent place in the fuselage, with the GAU-8 under the feet of the pilot (the ammo drum behind him) who sat in a titanium armored "bathtub" which also protected the essential parts of the flight control system. The seven barrels of the GAU-8 protruded through the nose of the airplane.

Pure death, the GAU gatling could fire—at a rate of either 2,100 or 4,200 RPM—three kinds of 30-millimeter rounds—HEI (high-energy incendiary), API (armor-piercing incendiary) and TP target practice).

Due to the rapidity of fire, any pilot had to have a very sensitive trigger finger, for a one second burst would put 70 rounds on target. At a range of 4,000 feet the first rounds would be impacting at the same second the trigger was being depressed. Therefore, in theory, a super-duper pilot could blow up scores of Soviet tanks with a single drum of ammo.

Tanks and other armored vehicles? The most deadly GAU-8 round was the API round with its subcaliber, high-density penetrator that was extremely effective against medium and heavy tanks—and, in some cases, submarines. . . .

The secret of the GAU API round was the penetrator that, made of depleted uranium, packed 14 times the kinetic energy of a current 20mm armor-piercing round. It was this special penetrator that made the A-10 Tunderbolt a kind of sub-killer.

Only a minute earlier, when the Sea King had attacked, Captain-Commander Boris Khristoforov had screamed, *"Chbavorniko! Chbavorniki! Chbavorniko!"* ("Dive! Dive! Dive!") from the main control center below the Sail, or conning tower. The Russian submariners were well-trained and very fast, and the Typhoon was a well-built boat. By the time Captain Rose was ready to fire, the hull of the Skaldia-Volga had disappeared beneath the water with only thirty-three feet of the forty-one foot high Sail showing.

Muttering loudly under his breath, a habit he had when under controlled stress, Captain Rose first shot off two DX4-Viper-Tongue missiles which streaked from the pylons, leaving a slight contrail behind them. A second later, he pressed the firing button of the GAU-8 gatling gun, the crashing *BERRRRRRRRRRRRRRRRRRR* shattering the already fragmented quiet of the early morning at the same time the two Viper-Tongues exploded. One V-T went off thirty feet to starboard of the stern of the sub, the second only ten feet behind the stern.

The ten second burst from the GAU-8 did what Rose intended it to do. The 700 armor-piercing incendiary rounds dissolved the top and most of the rear of the section of conning tower sail still above water and sent tons of twisted titanium plates shooting outward, port and starboard, to come down with a crash and splash into the sea.

Inside the enormous Typhoon, the Russians were calm, methodical and filled with a building and burning hatred for the Americans who had ruthlessly attacked their vessel.

Trying to ignore the various alarms and trying to duck water flowing down from the ceiling, Captain-Commander Khristoforov yelled into a mike, "Damage Control! Give me an immediate estimate of the damage."

First Officer Stanislas Ter-Sarkonov, a tall, sandy-haired man, was watching the "Christmas Tree" lighting up, every light red, every light a warning that water was entering the vessel. There was no danger that the sea could reach the nuclear reactor that furnished power for the vessel. All bulkheads to the nuclear reactor section had automatically closed.

"Comrade Captain, we must surface!" Ter-Sarkonov said, nervousness building in his voice. "If we submerge any farther we'll sink. I've already stopped the intake to the tanks; and we're only at nine meters."

"Give the order to surface," Khristoforov said tonelessly, "and set the self-destruct charges in all sections." Short, heavy and with a two day's growth of beard, he seemed drained of all energy.

Both First Officer Ter-Sarkonov and Second Officer Vitali Dmitrevich Bakholdin tried to speak at once. Bakholdin won.

"Sir, we can't destroy the vessel! What will Fleet Headquarters say?" He added for the benefit of the other officers, any of whom could be KGB or GRU,[8] "We must fight for the honor of our nation. We must—"

"Shut up, you idiot!" spit out Khristoforov. "Moscow can't hear you. What do you think Fleet Headquarters would think if we permitted the submarine to fall into the hands of the Americans? Who do you think is out there—the African or the Arab *chernozhopy!* We are going to fight. Break out the weapons and distribute them to the crew. The Americans don't want to sink us, they want to board us."

"But sir, you said set the charges!" a confused Vitali Bakholdin said. "When they go off—"

"We go down with the boat!" finished Khristoforov cynically. "We fight and will die because we're men and because we, as representatives of our nation, have been attacked in an act of piracy. Get to work!"

Ter-Sarkonov gave the order to the controllers to surface. Second Officer Vitali Bakholdin hurried off to open the arsenal and distribute weapons to the crew.

Captain Khristoforov turned and glared at Colonel Pyter Gorsetev and Major Viktor Chorf, both of whom were in one corner of the control compartment, flush against the wall. They had let Doctor Martin sink to the floor and he had rolled over on his back. With the two frightened KGB officers and Martin was Gakin Pashail, one of the illegals who had been aboard Hero's Reward. Pashail had managed to get inside the forward hatch behind Gorsetev, Chorf and Martin only seconds before the Sea King had opened fire with its deadly minigun.

"When I said fight, I also meant the three of you!" raged Captain Khristoforov, glaring at Colonel Gorsetev and the two other Soviet Intelligence officers. "If it weren't for you damned *sragavnyooksya*[9] we wouldn't be in this predicament."

Neither Gorsetev nor the other two men replied.

The damage reports came in as the submarine surfaced.

---

[8] It is common for KGB or GRU officers to be in the Soviet military, to keep an eye on the armed forces and to report any dissidents. No one ever knows who they are, except the "Home Office."

[9] "Assholes."

Three-fourths of the sail had been destroyed, blown off by whatever the Americans had used. The interior observation bridge, with its sky and attack periscopes, the radar station and the lookout compression compartment had been destroyed. The overhead bulkhead, between sail and control compartment, had been sprung and water would continue to pour in until the sub was above water.

Worse, concussion from one of the missiles had buckled inward a small section of the topside hull and had ruptured the pressure hull. That rupture was the mortal wound that would quickly kill the Skaldia-Volga, if she remained submerged. If she submerged to only a fraction below the surface, an estimated 378 liters of water per minute would pour into the boat. Captain Khristoforov had no choice. It was either surface or sink—and return to the Soviet Union on the surface! And the Americans were not going to permit that!

On Hero's Reward there was no trace. There was only the long, sinister form of the Skaldia-Volga that was under way and moving slowly in a southwest direction, the fully risen sun reflecting from her decks and the remaining twisted portion of the conning tower sail.

At only 4,000 feet the four Thunderbolt IIIs zoomed back and forth over the area. The command Sea King kept pace with the sub at a distance of 300 feet to port, even with the demolished conning tower. Two thousand feet behind the command chopper were the other Sea King gunships/transports.

The sub had not been on the surface for more than ten seconds when a gruff voice came out of the squawk box connected to the 719D-15 transceiver.

"Attention, Camellion. This is Major Clifton Ruff. Are we going to follow that submarine? Or did you bring us out here only to witness how a Thunderbolt can shoot the shit out of a commie vessel?"

Tony Larocca muttered under his breath, "I'll be damned if I'm going to get on that damned sub—no way."

Baxter Lincolnwell sniffed and pulled a handkerchief from his combat fatigues. "I think he intends to get inside the vessel!"

"That's even worse!" grumbled Larocca.

The Death Merchant's voice was as hard as the titanium of the "bathtubs" in the Thunderbolts. "Major Ruff. We are going to board the boat. By that I mean we're going inside the boat. Just keep listening in."

Another voice came from the box. "Camellion, this is Captain Roger Pugh of the SEAL force. I trust you are aware that the Soviet skipper has probably set destruct charges. He'd be an idiot to assume we wouldn't board his boat. Those charges are usually set from thirty to forty-five minutes. That gives the skipper plenty of time to destroy his log and code books."

"I'm aware of that destruct factor," Camellion replied to Captain Pugh. "Now please leave the air. I want to talk to Captain Rose."

"I'm here," Rose said.

"How much Gatling gun ammo do you have left?"

"More than enough to blow away the rest of the conning tower, if that's what you want."

Another voice came from the box-speaker and through the earpiece of the telephone. "This is Bradbury. What about me and Cavinens and Neuman? It might come as a surprise but we can shoot, too!"

"OK, Bradbury, be my guest," Camellion said. "I want you to blow one hell of a big hole in the end of the bow of that pig boat, on the topside, so that we can drop down into it."

"Why not the hatch in front of the missile compartment?" suggested Bradbury. "The missiles must be armed to detonate."

"That's right, but we don't want any radiation leaking from warheads. We're going to be inside that boat. Therefore, I repeat: blow a hole topside in the end of the bow, right above the superstructure."

Camellion thought for a moment. "Neuman? Your first name is Paul—right?"

"Affirmative," Neuman said leisurely. "What do you want me to do?"

"I want you to put a Viper-Tongue missile into what's left of the conning tower. The missile will tear away the remainder of the tower and give us a direct opening into the control compartment, unless the pig farmers are building subs different from what our intelligence reports. You got it straight, Neuman?"

"Affirmative," Neuman said. "I'll make my run first. Is that OK with you, Bradbury?"

"Go ahead. Blast the conning tower," Bradbury said. "Then I'll open up the end of the bow."

It took only three minutes for Neuman to bank, turn, roar in from the northeast and zero in on the conning tower with his laser-computer sights. Its two GE 9,000 pound thrust turbofans screaming, the Thunderbolt[10] streaked toward the doomed Soviet submarine. A nine foot long Viper-Tongue missile shot from a wing pylon when the airplane was only 3,000 feet from the target, a long, faint contrail of hazy vapor behind the slender red body. Instantly, Neuman pulled up sharply and took the Thunderbolt toward the wide blue while Lieutenant Dewy Benjamin pulled in pitch and jerked the command chopper away from the sub.

BLLLAMMMMMMMMMMM! The Viper-Tongue struck the jagged remains of the conning tower in the rear and exploded ten feet above the deck.

A large, rolling ball of bright fire, smoke and twisted, flying metal!

When the smoke cleared, and as thousands of pieces of metal and debris fell into the sea, the Death Merchant and his force saw that the conning tower had vanished and that in its place was a smoking cavity.

"Well now, ain't that a sight for sore eyes!" exclaimed Roy Lee Orr, looking and sounding astonished. "Man, we're right in the middle of a mini-war!"

"And he wants us to drop in the hull of that goddamn thing!" Wyatt Scronce said angrily, finger-jabbing the air in the direction of the Death Merchant. "Hell, to go inside that sub is plain suicide. I want to die at 100, shot by a jealous husband!"

"I have to agree with him," Randy Kooney said, looking at the Death Merchant. "What good is ten thousand bucks if you're dead and can't spend it?"

---

[10] The Thunderbolts are only a part of the Army Air Force team known as the Joint Air Attack Team—JAAT—that would be called upon to blunt an enemy's advance.

Tensor, across the aisle from Scronce and Kooney, glared at the two "private contractors." "How would you birds like your heads—one lump or three?"

"Hold it," Camellion said gently. "I'm not going to tell any of you how to fish or cut bait. You fellows do what you want. Personally, I'm going to drop down on the bow and invade the sub through the hole that Neuman makes. The little momma's boys and the cowards can sit up here and watch."

"Count me in. I've never seen the inside of an ocean-going pigpen!" Tensor said heartily. He nudged Max Weems good-naturedly in the ribs with his elbow. "And you can count in this screwball."

"Yeah, with my luck I can't get killed," Weems said with a mock sneer. "I'll live to be 80, broke, and eaten up with herpes!"

"Hey, here comes the other Thunderbolt!" announced Otto Vaughn. "That guy is really hell on wheels."

Chuckie Bradbury came in fast from the northwest, the Thunderbolt heading straight at the Skaldia-Volga which had stopped dead in the water. Suddenly he pulled back on the stick and took the warplane straight up. The Thunderbolt continued to gain altitude, so that one might have had the fleeting impression that Bradbury was attempting to defy gravity and shoot to the moon. At six thousand feet, Bradbury executed a perfect rollover, turned and began the descent—straight down at the bow of the submarine.

Bradbury had set the minigun to fire at 4,000 rounds per minute, and he opened fire at 3,000 feet, the terrible weapon roaring, the Thunderbolt screaming down at 500 MPH.

The firing lasted only thirteen seconds. Thirteen seconds was enough. During that thin slice of a minute the high explosive incendiary mix became alive in almost one thousand 30 millimeter shells that exploded all over the first ten feet of the bow. Even the triple-steel-tough titanium couldn't withstand such horrible punishment. Before such a hell-blast the hull dissolved with the rapidity of tissue paper caught in the fire of a blowtorch.

"Pull up! Pull up, damn you! PULL UP!" yelled Max

Weems, watching the Thunderbolt rocket down toward the submarine.

Bradbury did pull up—at an altitude of only 461 feet. When it seemed that the airplane would have to splatter itself all over the wrecked bow of the Skaldia-Volga, the nose lifted and the "gun with wings" shot up into the sky.

Bradbury's satisfied voice floated out of the squawk box in the command chopper: "How's that for an opening? Now it's your turn. All you have to do is go down there, drop in and shoot the bejesus out of those Russian sons."

"Uh huh, that's all we gotta do," Weems said, starting to put on a pair of thin leather gloves. "But what the hell, it's not half as dangerous as living in Brooklyn, or Miami!"

Staring at the gaping cavity in the bow of the sub—big enough to drive a truck through—the Death Merchant took the telephone from the 719D-15 transceiver and contacted Major Clifton Ruff, the commander of the USSAP force.

"Major Ruff, I'm changing plans. My group will attack from the conning tower opening. I want you and your men to enter through the opening that's just been made in the bow. Any questions?"

"Why the change in plans?" demanded Ruff. "We're trained for this kind of strike; you and your people are not. Another thing is that the center of the sub, around the control compartment, will be the best defended. And what about the self-destruct factor? I estimate five minutes getting in, fifteen minutes inside, and five minutes getting out. Even that's cutting it close."

The Death Merchant replied: "We're going in and down through the center because I have a hunch that Doctor Martin is still alive. If he is, he'll be toward the center of the boat. I agree with your estimate of the incursion into the boat."

"Then we're doing all this to get this precious Doctor Martin?" Ruff spoke in the affirmative.

"That's right. We know what he looks like. You don't. Anything else? We're wasting time."

"Happy burial," said Ruff. "Let's go in and get the job done."

* * *

199

The two Sea Kings, filled with USSAP commandoes, swung close to the bow of the sub which Randy Kooney had said reminded him of a wounded whale, with chunks of blubber torn from its back.

At only 125 feet, Lieutenant Benjamin swung the command helicopter over the hideous gap where the conning tower had proudly stood, and raked the hole with a blast of .30 projectiles from the minigun, the slugs creating such a howling of ricochets that the racket could be heard above the *thub-thub-thub* of the big rotor. As the Sea King passed over the sub, the Death Merchant and his men saw that the missile had not only blown away what had remained of the conning tower but had destroyed the main bulkhead and its foundations in the lower deck, exposing a large section of the control compartment below.

Benjamin swung the bird around and headed toward the stern, lowering the big eggbeater until its tricycle landing gear was only a few feet above the wooden slats of the catwalk running down the center of the rounded hull. Faster than chickens flocking around a nest of June bugs, the Death Merchant and his men jumped from both the port and the starboard openings of the Sea King whose nose was pointed southwest.

Not one man had objected. In fact, Tony Larocca and Randy Kooney had been the first to follow Camellion, whose psychological tactic had worked. *Fear of being called a coward is greater than the fear of death*—usually but not always.

Three hundred and sixteen feet to the south, another Sea King was discharging its cargo of khaki-clad commandoes, each man wearing a ballistic helmet, Kevlar K-15 body armor and Sherwood M-7 gas masks. Every commando carried a 9mm Beretta Commander pistol, M17B concussion grenades, tear gas canisters and a Heckler and Koch MK-5K nine millimeter submachine gun, each MK-5K with an extra-long magazine that held 60 rounds.

The Death Merchant and his group were similarly equipped, with the exception that each carried an Ingram MAC-10 SMG attached to his belt and an MM1—a "Mean Mother," a flat-black shotgun that was an update on the 25mm Manville riot gun of the 1930s. The Mean Mother contained twenty-four 12-gauge shotgun shells in a large drum that was spring wound. Complete with short metal-frame stock, pistol grip to the rear and another pistol grip in front behind the barrel, the Mean Mother weighed sixteen pounds.

Loading was simple but time-consuming. One first separated the drum and the rear pistol grip from the barrel and the foregrip; this was accomplished by unfastening the slide-lock assembly and permitting the drum to swivel apart for loading, which consisted of pushing shells into the twenty-four cyclinders and seating them with the heel of one's hand. The halves of the drum were then fitted together, swung back into the assembly and locked, after which one wound up the large, rotating drum. This was accomplished by cranking the drum counterclockwise until one felt it tighten and stop. All one had to do then was pull back the large cocking knob—in the rear—and go to work. When the trigger was pulled, the spent shell rotated away from the firing pin—clockwise—and a new shell came up into the battery, fully positioned, just as the trigger released the firing pin—the same kind of mechanism that operated when a double action revolver is fired.

Approaching the blasted-out opening, the Death Merchant looked around. The day was already heating up and there was the odor of oil, explosives and burnt metal and rubber. Far to the west was a plane, barely visible. To the north, far in the distance, was the peak of a sail of a pleasure craft. Due south, in the haze, he could see—or thought he could—the bow of one of the U.S. Navy's MK III patrol boats.

Camellion stared toward the bow and saw that the commandoes were already going down through the exploded section of the hull. He turned to his own men who were preparing lines and pulling up gas masks.

"Men, make sure the voicemitters in your gas masks are turned on," he said. "Otherwise, no one will be able to hear you when you talk. Now, let's do it."

"Crap," mumbled Wyatt Scronce.

Carrying the rolled-up rope ladder under his left arm, Camellion approached the edge of the hole whose sides were uneven, twisted and blackened—like a tin can exploded by a large firecracker. Camellion put down the rope ladder with its steel bar rungs, then moved closer to the edge but did not lean over or look down. One of his concerns at the moment was the reliability of Kooney, Scronce, Larocca and Orr in this kind of attack situation. Unless a man was highly trained and especially experienced—*Or half nuts like me and Joe and Max!*—stress could do strange things to him: Eye-hand coordination could be severely affected, as well as the ability to make decisions. Stress tended to make fighters hesitant and indecisive. There could be auditory exclusion, with peripheral sounds and sights blocked out. Add to these time-space distortions, with events appearing to happen more slowly and objects appearing closer than is the actual case.

Now is not the time to worry about it! Either they will hold up or they won't . . .

Camellion first tossed four concussion grenades into the hole and, as they roared off, one by one, followed them with three canisters of tear gas.

"Make those lines secure," Camellion ordered the men who had gathered around the sides of the opening and were looping tough nylon lines around twisted pieces of pipe and various other kinds of wreckage protruding upward.

The lines were for going down. The men would come up on the rope ladders carried by Camellion, Tensor and Weems, all three of whom secured one end of the ladders to wreckage, then tossed the rolled-up bundles into what amounted to a twisted shaft.

Into the huge fracture went another dozen tear gas grenades. Only then did the Death Merchant and his men—Mean Mothers slung on their shoulders by wide canvas straps—slide down the lines, the tough leather of their gloves protecting their hands. The clouds of gray gas thickened as they neared the main deck that, when the conning tower stood, had been the lower deck.

There were no ladders. There was only a metal stairway that moved up from the Main Control Compartment. Now the stairs lay crumpled, smashed by the heavy bulkhead door that had been blown downward by the exploding Viper-Tongue missile.

All around Camellion and his men, as they slid down, lay twisted pipes, wrecked ducts, valves and caved-in compartment walls. Some of the men slid down the lines, then paused on the lower deck to get their bearings and to wait until there was ample room for them to descend through the bulkhead opening.

The Death Merchant kept sliding until his feet approached the opening of the bulkhead. Only a few feet below was the fractured ceiling of the Main Control Compartment. Camellion swung to the left, released the nylon line, stood on the lower deck and looked down into the smoky, tear gas-filled compartment.

Tensor swung down beside the Death Merchant and whispered, his voice sounding hollow and mechanical through the voicemitter, "They will be waiting with everything they have. Hear that firing up front? The Ruskies aren't making it easy for the commandoes."

Camellion and Tensor looked down through the bulkhead opening and studied what they could see of the compartment. Most of the lines and the bottom of the three rope ladders extended down into the compartment, the last five feet of which were piled on the floor.

Weems said jokingly, "You know, we'll be damned lucky if we don't go to the bottom with this piece of Soviet junk. Wouldn't that be something to tell your grandchildren?"

"Max, Joe. We three will toss down grenades simultaneously," the Death Merchant said, his eyes narrowing calculatingly behind the facepiece of the gas mask. He slipped the Mean Mother from his shoulder. "After they explode, we three will drop down. The others can follow us."

Weems was already pulling a grenade from one of his canvas shoulder bags. "I keep thinking of what a Polack calls a 'maniac!' I suppose it doesn't matter."

He pulled the pin and flipped the grenade downward through the opening.

One! Two! Three! The concussion grenades—15 ounces of TNT in each—sounded like a hundred pounds of C-4 going off, the concussion especially severe within the confines of the control compartment, slamming through one's ears and stabbing at the center of the brain.

The sounds of more destruction came from below—the

tinkling of glass from meters and gauges, scores of loose objects being impacted against walls, floor and ceiling.

A moment later, Camellion, holding the Mean Mother in his left hand, grabbed the line with his right hand and slid down the ten feet to the floor of the Main Control Compartment of the Skaldia-Volga. The Strange One followed him down the line, then Weems.

Everywhere was haze, smoke, fumes and the stink of destroyed material. Camellion didn't bother to look for any definite targets. The instant he felt the floor under his feet, he went into a low crouch and, weaving back and forth, began triggering the Mean Mother shotgun—*BLAM! BLAM! BLAM! BLAM!*—spacing each round six feet apart and raking the area in front of him, moving the MM1 from left to right. The glass on the still flashing "Christmas tree" exploded. Shotgun pellets struck hand-wheels, switches, levers, meters. The gyro-compass board was shattered into hundreds of pieces. And then Tensor was firing—*BLAM! BLAM! BLAM!* Soon a third Mean Mother was exploding shells as Weems got into action, the roaring of the terrible weapons filling the compartment with walls of noise.

Camellion had studied a diagram of a Soviet submarine back in the main briefing room of the Naval Air Station in San Francisco. According to U.S. intelligence reports, all classes of Soviet submarines were built on the same general principle of compartment arrangement. In theory, this boat would be no different. There would be four major bulkheads, two forward, two aft. Forward in the Main Control Compartment would be an entrance that led to a corridor, off which would be the chart room, the rudder and hydroplane Check Room and the compressed air distribution center. What lay forward—officers quarters, mess, missiles, torpedo rooms, etc.—didn't matter. The Death Merchant and his group would not be going that far. They didn't have the time. Aft of the Main Control Compartment would be another entrance, beyond which would be the radar and sonar compartments, the radio room, the fire control center and the nuclear reactor watch room—and that was the maximum distance Camellion and Co. would travel.

The remainder of the small, makeshift commando force was coming down the lines when the Death Merchant shouted to Tensor and to Weems, "Joe, you and I will go sternward. Max, take the others and go forward. Not more than fifty feet. We don't have the time!"

Camellion and Tensor, now and then firing off 12-gauge shells in the direction of the stern bulkhead whose oval door was wide open, stumbled through rubble, going past what was left of the main periscope well and on past the two Controllers' chairs and the diving and the guidance yokes.

It was during a split second of lag time that two Russian sub officers leaned around the forward open bulkhead and fired off short blasts, Sergei Rebet using a Vitmormin machine pistol, Stanislas Ter-Sarkonov triggering a PPS43 submachine gun.

Five 9mm slugs from the Vitmorkin hit Baxter Lincolnwell squarely in the chest, two almost cutting in two the strap holding his bag of grenades. With a howl of pain and surprise, Lincolnwell found himself being knocked back by the terrific impact. Although no bullet had actually touched his flesh (every slug having been stopped by and buried in the Kevlar ballistic armored vest he was wearing under his fatigues), each projectile had punched into the material. In turn, the material—each deep indentation a sharp point against Lincolnwell's flesh—had hit him with a force that felt like hammer strikes.

Rebet and Ter-Sarkonov had made the fatal mistake of their lives. No sooner had they fired than they died from Mean Mother blasts fired by Weems, Kooney, Orr and Flavelton, hundreds of pellets shredding the two pig farmers like sausage coming out of a high speed meat grinder. They fell in a shower of blood, two floating clouds of blood mist amid thousands of pieces of fluttering cloth that had once been their clothes.

Weems kept firing slow calculated rounds at the bloody doorway to keep back any other Russians who might try to fire from the bulkhead.

"Use your MACS and handguns," Weems yelled. "These Mean Mothers are too bulky for close range. Get the brass out of your ass and the lead out of your feet! I'm almost out of shells!"

And so was the Death Merchant who, down on his left knee, was firing his own Mean Mother steadily at the stern end bulkhead as Tensor unclipped his MAC-10 from his belt and then reached over, unhooked Camellion's SMG from his belt and placed the little submachine pistol on the floor.

"The safety is still on," Tensor yelled and then pulled one of his Ruger .44 mag revolvers.

BANG! Camellion fired the Mean Mother's last shell. He tossed aside the empty weapon, picked up the MAC-10, and pulled one of his Safari Arms Black Widows while three Soviet submariners attempted to fire around the stern end doorway.

Tensor didn't wait until he saw a hand or arm or face. He fired the instant he saw several inches of the black barrel of a Soviet PPsh M-41 SMG and the dark snout of a Vitmorkin MP. The third pig farmer was playing it very cautiously. He had not yet tried to thrust his M61 "Skorpion" submachine gun around the side of the bulkhead. He had, however, thrust out his left leg, exposing three-fourths of his left foot.

Slaughter time for Soviet pigs! Like the Death Merchant, the Strange One considered a handgun only an extension of himself and was almost as good as Camellion at body-pointing[11] two weapons simultaneously. The .44 magnum projectile from the Ruger blew off Andrei Dzhirkvelov's left foot as a hail of .45 Hydro-Shok slugs from his MAC-10 struck the barrel of the PPsh SMG and several inches of the exposed Vitmorkin. The impact of the .45 slugs almost tore the weapons from the hands of Pavel Kiktev and Grigor Vasilyev. Dzhirkvelov didn't count. He had dropped his Skorpion, fallen forward on his face, and was promptly killed by the Death Merchant who, by then, was charging the door, a MAC-10 in his right hand, a Black Widow in his left.

Confused and afraid, Kiktev had time only to see a gasmasked face and a pair of blue eyes on fire. Then nothing. Oblivion! He died instantly, a Black Widow 230-grain harball

---

[11] Another name for *instinct shooting*. Either you have the talent or you don't. If you do, it can be improved by practice, practice and more practice. And if you don't have the talent, you'll never have it, in spite of all the books on "How To Shoot."

bullet shattered his skull and ripped apart his brain before he could even hear the sound of the shot.

Grigor Vasilyev was attempting to swing his Vitmorkin machine pistol back into position. He failed and was even deprived of the opportunity to see who was killing him. A three-round burst of .45 MAC-10 shots cut through his heart and almost pulled it out through the big hole they made in his back. Vasilyev did a quick three-step backward, spun and fell at the same time that Camellion finished off the magazine in the MAC-10 by raking both sides of the narrow passageway, the big bullets banging through plastic folding doors.

Very quickly, Camellion pulled back to the side of the wall and reached for a grenade while Tensor, to his right, raked the closed accordion-like doors with streams of .45 Ingram MAC-10 projectiles.

The Death Merchant jerked the pin, yelled "PULL IN!" at Tensor and, leaning to his right, rolled the grenade down the corridor.

BLAMMMMMMM! It seemed to Camellion and Tensor— the Strange One was shoving another magazine into the MAC-10—that the explosion shook even the seams of the Russian submarine. Camellion rolled another M17B down the corridor and then another while the echoes of the first and the second were still crashing up and down the length of the passage and reverberating against the inner sides of the Skaldia-Volga.

"Heh, heh, heh, heh!" giggled Tensor and cocked the MAC-10. He looked at Camellion who was also shoving a fresh magazine into his SMG.

"Those Russians are so stupid they think Peter Pan is something to put under the bed!" The Strange One said.

"Or study for six weeks to pass a urine test!" growled the Death Merchant. "What say? Should we do it?"

"We might as well. That's why we came down here. . . ."

Major Clifton Ruff and his USSAP commandoes attacked from the bow like iron men propelled by bolts of lightning. Methodically, they used concussion grenades, ignoring tear gas canisters because the Russians were also wearing gas masks. Grenades to make the Russians stay under cover. Then the commandoes charged the various compartments, their Heckler and Koch MK-5K SMGS roaring.

In only thirteen minutes the commandoes had passed the forward torpedo room and were in the main conference room of the tremendous Soviet submarine. Major Ruff called a halt.

"Our time is up," Ruff called out. "Everyone back out. Leave the boat with all possible speed!"

Stress, generated by violence and the subliminal fear of death, can do more than make a man freeze or distort his perception of the situation. Stress can also backfire and cause inexperienced fighters to fanatically attack the enemy, perhaps in an unconscious attempt to eradicate the source of their intense anxiety.[12]

This is what happened to Wyatt Scronce, Otto Vaughn, and Roy Lee Orr. Without waiting for the highly experienced Max Weems to toss grenades down the hallway, the three charged the bulkhead. Immediately, five Russians, all wearing gas masks and firing from the open doors of the chart room, the officers' wardroom and the compressed-air distribution center, raked Orr, Vaughn and Scronce with streams of machine pistol and submachine gun projectiles, hosing the three "throw-aways" vertically as well as horizontally. The 9mm and the 7.62mm slugs that were stopped by the Kevlar "armor," worn over backs, chests and part of the abdominal region, did not kill the three men. But the bullets that bored through the face plates of their gas masks, the sides of their necks and into their groins and legs did. Chopped apart as if attacked by axes, the three dead mercs fell in a spray of blood, their clothing hanging in tatters. Only by a quirk of Fate did slugs miss grenades in the shoulder bags of the three dead men.

The Soviet sailors and their officers were also at a disadvantage, in more ways than one. They were not trained to engage in hand-to-hand combat and in close fire-fights. Made overconfident by their brief success, the Russians left the security of their compartments and began to charge down the corridor that opened to the Main Control Center, the first two Ruskies skidding to a halt and choking in terror as Weems—to the right of the Russians, his back to the forward

---

[12] Sometimes in war this impulse is called "bravery" and medals are awarded!

208

wall of the Main Control Compartment—rolled in the first grenade.

The first two ivans and the other five behind them didn't have time to think another thought, good, bad or indifferent. The grenade exploded in their faces, the monstrous concussion killing all seven instantly. The first three, those closest to the explosion, were actually blown limb from limb, the explosion first ripping them apart, tossing arms and legs, heads and torsos, feet, parts of faces and internal organs against the walls and ceiling. The next three grenades only scattered the bloody mess and terrified scores of other Russians scattered throughout the various forward compartments.

Weems and the three men left alive with him then charged the corridor, their MAC-10s chattering short three-round bursts.

The Death Merchant attacked the radio room off to the right of the corridor while Tensor sent slugs through the folding door of the nuclear reactor watch room on the opposite side. After hosing down the door, Camellion turned, raced over to the Strange One and pulled back the thin folding doors of the reactor room as Tensor continued to fire short bursts through the opening as it widened.

Once the door was three-fourths open, Camellion spun sternward and raked every door in sight with the remainder of the .45 cartridges in the magazine of his Ingram submachine gun.

Tensor charged into the reactor watch room, Ingram MAC-10 in one hand, .44 Ruger revolver in the other. Two sailors were dead on the floor, riddled, and three others were crouched down by one end of a control panel having done their best to avoid the hail of steel death. Not one had a chance to get into action. A .44 magnum bullet from Tensor's Ruger went through one man's gas mask and exploded his head. The last six slugs of the MAC-10 finished off the other two pig farmers.

"It's clean," yelled Tensor, his voice having a slight ringing sound as it flowed through the voicemitter. "Get in here."

Faster than a wino reaching for a fifth of "Sweet Lucy," the Death Merchant was inside the watch room shoving a fresh magazine into his MAC-10. The Strange One also reloaded his Ingram SMG, then picked up one of the Soviet Vitmorkin machine pistols and examined the weapon that could be fired on full automatic or on semiautomatic.

"We're running out of time," Tensor said, noting with satisfaction that the Vitmorkin was fully loaded. He pushed the firing-set lever to automatic. "A few more compartments and that's it."

In agreement, Camellion nodded. "There are only two more compartments ahead before we reach the closed bulkhead, the large one to port and the smaller one to starboard. You take the starboard side. I'll go to port. Make sure your ear valves are in tight. We'll use six grenades first. They should make who's ever in those compartments shake, rattle and roll."

Camellion reached under his gas mask and checked the valve in his left, then right ear. Ordinary earplugs blocked out all noise, eliminated air circulation and created a stuffed-up feeling that made it impossible for one to hear orders. The Marlin-Vixdun silicone-rubber valves, worn by Camellion, Tensor and the rest of the force, including the commandoes, contained a highly sophisticated inner diaphragm that greatly reduced loud noises, yet made it possible to hear conversation.

"My valves are in place," Tensor said and reached for a grenade. "Let's get on with it and get the hell out of here. So far, we've been moving slower than the U.S. air mail!"

Camellion grinned. "Yeah, an inner sanctum crawl." He rolled the first grenade down the corridor.

There were six explosions in less than thirty-nine seconds, the terrific concussions within the narrow corridor ripping apart the folding doors and sending pieces flying inward. The echoes were still bouncing back and forth, rolling around like invisible marbles, when Camellion and Tensor charged, Camellion moving right, Tensor left.

Tensor was convinced that the average Russian was so stupid that he believed testicles were something found only on an octopus. He was wrong. While the Russians are backward when compared to the West, they have the same capacity for intelligence as any other people of the human race. Many Russians are extremely intelligent. Colonel Pyter Gorsetev was such a man. A realist, Gorsetev realized the submarine was doomed, that very shortly he and the other Russians would go to the bottom of this particular part of the Pacific Ocean. He didn't mind dying, and surrender was out of the question. He was positive of one thing: the Americans would not take Doctor Martin alive.

Gorsetev, Viktor Chorf and Gakin Pashail had carried Doctor Martin into the fire control center, the large compartment to port. With them were Captain Josef Khristoforov and Second Officer Vitali Dmitrevich. There they waited for the end.

Across the corridor, opposite the fire control center, was the small sonar compartment in which three NCOs of the sub's crew waited. The six concussions, in such close proximity, had left them dazed and mentally listless, as it did Colonel Gorsetev and the other men with him in the fire control center.

The Strange One, firing short bursts with his Ingram, charged the sonar compartment. The Death Merchant charged the fire control center, darting in at the end of the opening closest to him, his MAC-10 and his Black Widow firing as he expertly dove to the rear wall eight feet in front of him.

Captain Khristoforov and Vitali Dmitrevich, both armed with PPS43 submachine guns, were crouched to one side of the large well of the sonar drum, between the drum and the stern-end wall—to the right of Camellion who had sat up and was now facing the demolished doorway.

Gakin Pashail, his eyes wide and staring, was in front of Camellion, and to the left. He was behind a supply cabinet that he had pushed from the short outer wall facing the corridor.

Colonel Gorsetev and Viktor Chorf were down behind a desk that was directly to Camellion's left, the front of the desk not more than six feet from him. Doctor Martin, unconscious, was lying against the wall in back of the two KGB agents. He too had blood pouring from his nose and ears.

Mercy! Mercy! Mother Mercy! What do I do now?

It was the concussions from the grenades, which had deadened the reaction time of the Russians, and had saved Camellion's life. The sonar drum (or wave-sound amplifier) was four feet in diameter and five point six feet high. It was positioned in such a way that there were thirteen point two inches of space between it and the rear wall.

Captain Khristoforov and Vitali Dmitrevich had not seen Camellion rocket into the room. They had been too dazed and too busy staying down out of the way of flying slugs. They soon knew he was in the room from the sound of the shots he fired. He quit firing, however, in the middle of the compartment, just before he headed for the floor. So—where was he now?

Gorsetev, Chorf, and Pashail had remained down, knowing that curiosity, at the wrong time, often ends in eternal oblivion. Colonel Gorsetev was particularly experienced in close-in fire-fight situations. Not about to be the kind of dumb pig farmer who would search in a lumber yard for a draft board, Gorsetev patiently awaited developments and the proper opportunity, and he didn't intend to take undue risks.

Gorsetev got his chance a few moment later. The Death Merchant had made the dive to the floor, turned around and, looking from left to right, detected Khristoforov and Dmitrevich through the opening between one rounded side of the sonar drum and the rear wall. Khristoforov and Dmitrevich weren't quite sure what to do, but they got no chance to decide. Camellion's MAC-10 chattered merrily and a stream of .45 projectiles punched first into Dmitrevich, then into Khristoforov, killing both men so fast they never knew they were a split edge away from eternity.

During that blink of a moment, when Camellion had swung his head to the right and had triggered the MAC-10, he was aware that he was taking a calculated risk, that someone could be behind the desk whose knee-hole was covered in front. He had also detected a slight furtive movement in front of him to his left.

Even as the MAC-10 was spitting out its projectiles and killing Dmitrevich and Khristoforov, Camellion was triggering the Black Widow, chance-shooting at the movement by the side of the cabinet. The first .45 hardball tore upward and struck Gakin Pashail in the right leg, the dynamite impact breaking the femur bone close to the hip joint and knocking him to the right as his leg went out from under him. The Death Merchant's second hardball bullet skyrocketed upward, cut into Pashail's left rib cage, tore through his left lung and upper esophagus and went bye bye through the right side of his neck, leaving a bloody vapor trail behind it.

The instant Camellion stopped firing, he scooted around and turned so that his back was against the rounded sonar drum. He dropped the almost empty Black Widow on the floor, drew the second Black Widow and let his eyes, behind the face plate of the gas mask, jump to the front edge of the desk and to both ends.

At the same time, Colonel Pyter Gorsetev—snug behind the left four drawer section of the desk—motioned to Viktor Chorf—behind the right section of drawers—to rear up and fire.

Fearfully, Chorf did so—very quickly. But he never got off the first shot. He was trying to swing the PPS43 SMG barrel downward when the Death Merchant fired, the .45 projectile tearing through Chorf's mouth and almost pulling his head from his neck. Dropping the SMG on the desk, the dead Russian flopped down, blood gushing from the terrible wound.

Well, well. . . . It was "barberpole!" How about that!

Camellion's finger was still moving forward from the trigger of the Black Widow as he put down the MAC-10 and hurriedly crawled to the end of the desk, the end facing the rear wall. As silent as a creeping heart attack, he got between the end of the desk and the wall, sitting so that he could place both feet on the metal.

Colonel Pyter Gorsetev felt that the wind would never blow again and that Time had disappeared. They were all dead and he was alone. Briefly, he toyed with the idea of turning around and putting a 7.62mm projectile into Doctor Martin. Damn it! He couldn't. The sound of the shot would expose his position, not only to the American already in the room but to the one in the corridor. Or had the second American, the one in the corridor, been killed?

Should he crawl behind the desk to the rear wall and risk the possibility that the other man hid between the wall and the desk?

Or could he be in front of the desk?

Again, he might have crawled behind the sonar drum!

In a desperate quandry of indecision, Gorsetev debated whether he should crawl around by the side of the desk on his end. But what could he accomplish if the American in the room was waiting behind the sonar drum? Or suppose the American in the corridor came in?

Wait. Gorsetev, feeling his heart pounding, decided to wait.

Gorsetev need not have concerned himself about the "other American." The Strange One was out in the corridor, right up to the edge of the opening of the fire control center. He had to assume that Camellion was alive and well and playing it safe, or wounded and playing it safe. At least still alive.

Tensor didn't dare call out. Camellion couldn't answer without risking his position. Cursing in pig Latin under his breath and thinking of the seconds racing into the past, the Strange One waited.

The Death Merchant couldn't afford to wait. On full alert, he reached into a pocket of his battle fatigues, thumbed five .45 cartridges from a spare Black Widow magazine and braced himself with his back against the wall and with both feet placed flat against the end of the desk. Simultaneously, he threw the cartridges toward the front of the compartment and pushed outward with his feet, using all the strength he could muster in his powerful legs.

The desk moved a foot and a half away from him.

The cartridges fell, several hitting the cabinet that had protected Gakin Pashail, the other three clattering to the floor.

The intense strain was too much for Colonel Pyter Laurenti Gorsetev. In desperation, he jumped up and fired a long burst of PPS43 SMG slugs at the other end of the desk, the fourteen 7.62mm steel-cored lead projectiles stabbing into the wall a foot above Camellion's head. In the meanwhile, Camellion had moved around to the inner corner and was leaning out behind the desk and moving the Black Widow upward.

During that second of lag time, the Death Merchant placed two .45 projectiles in Colonel Gorsetev's chest. The impact was kicking the dying KGB officer backward when Camellion's third bullet hit him in the chin and blew away a partion of the mandible bone. The big hunk of metal went through his throat, broke several vertebrae and tore out the back of his neck. A total coldcut, blood flooding his wrecked gas mask, Gorsetev dropped, his head hanging at an odd angle.

"Jose! Are you out there?" Camellion called out.

"I'm here."

"It's safe. Come on in. Doctor Martin's in here."

Tensor moved into the compartment, on his way in motioning to Randy Kooney and Max Weems, both of whom were running down the corridor toward him.

Doctor Burl Martin was dead. Camellion could not find the least trace of a pulse—and if any person recognized a corpse it was Richard J. Camellion. The microelectronics scientist had not been shot. There wasn't a mark on his body. Furthermore, the flesh of his hand and his cheeks was still slightly warm.

"Concussion must have killed him." The Death Merchant stood up and moved back a few paces from the corpse. "The pig farmers kept him drugged for days. In his weakened condition, his nervous system couldn't take the repeated auditory shocks."

"Or he might have had a heart attack," offered Randy Kooney.

"Or died of the Canary Islands crud!" Max Weems said angrily. "Dead is dead, and unless we move damned fast we'll join Martin and all the rest of them."

By the time the Death Merchant and his five men had crawled up the ladders and had pulled up Baxter Lincolnwell on a line, the commandoes had left the dying submarine and were in one of the Navy's MK III patrol boats moving away from the sub.

The Death Merchant was the last to leave the stern deck of the Skaldia-Volga. He was moving up the metal catwalk that had been placed in position from the deck of the patrol boat when there were loud rumblings inside the submarine, from

215

bow to stern, the hull shaking so violently that Camellion almost lost his balance. Only with difficulty did he manage to move the rest of the way on the catwalk, and then he practically fell to the deck of the MK III. The sailors didn't bother to pull in the catwalk. There wasn't time. The vessel began pulling away from the long Typhoon Class submarine.

From the stern deck of the patrol boat, Camellion, his group of five, Major Ruff and some of his men watched the Skaldia-Volga sink. Because the explosive charges had blown large holes in the bottom hull, the sub did not sink in any conventional manner, with either the stern or the bow going down first. The entire vessel simply disappeared, sinking straight down from bow to stern. When the sub was gone there was only an oil slick and some innocent-looking floating debris.

Frank Flavelton took a deep sigh, his voice was twittery and jumpy. "Well, as Liz Taylor and Shelly Winters have said so often, 'It's all behind us.' "

"It's going to be a problem with that nuclear reactor," Major Ruff said stiffly. "But radioactivity leaking out into the water—eventually, anyhow—is not our problem."

"We did our job," Camellion said coldly. "The KGB didn't get to keep Doctor Martin and we put a big dent in the Soviet apparatus that concerns itself with the products turned out in Silicon Valley."

Joe Tensor finished lighting a La Corona whiff, clucks and clicks and other odd noises rolling and tumbling about in his throat. "And we had a fine time doing it. We creamed those Russian pieces of filth. Yes, sir! Death is fascinating!"

Major Ruff gave The Strange One a disapproving look and turned away.

Tony Larocca nudged Max Weems, a curious expression on his face.

"By the way, Max. Remember what you said about a Polack? What *does* a Polack call a 'maniac?' "

Weems grinned. "Another polack in a whore house with a credit card!"

Larocca and the other men guffawed, all except the Death Merchant. He was thinking about a nation in faraway Asia, a nation that called itself *Pyidaungsu Socialist Thammada Myanma Nainggnan*—

Burma!